The Women
on the Wall

Books by Wallace Stegner
Available in Bison Book Editions

All the Little Live Things
Beyond the Hundredth Meridian: John Wesley Powell
and the Second Opening of the West
The Big Rock Candy Mountain
Joe Hill
Mormon Country
Recapitulation
Second Growth
The Sound of Mountain Water
The Spectator Bird
Wolf Willow
The Women on the Wall

The Women on the Wall

by Wallace Stegner

University of Nebraska Press • Lincoln & London

First Bison Book printing: 1981

Most recent printing indicated by first digit below:
3   4   5   6   7   8   9   10

Library of Congress Cataloging in Publication Data

Stegner, Wallace Earle, 1909–
The women on the wall.

Originally published in 1950 by Houghton Mifflin, Boston.
I. Title.
PS3537.T316W6   1981   813'.52   80–22461
ISBN 0–8032–4111–9
ISBN 0–8032–9110–8 (pbk.)

Reprinted by arrangement with the author

Acknowledgments

THANKS ARE DUE to the *Atlantic Monthly* for permission to reprint "The Berry Patch," "Saw Gang," "Goin' to Town," "Two Rivers," and "The Chink"; to *Harper's Magazine* for "Beyond the Glass Mountain," "The Women on the Wall," "The Volcano," and "Butcher Bird"; to *Mademoiselle* for "The View From the Balcony" and "In the Twilight"; to the *Virginia Quarterly Review* for "Bugle Song," "Hostage," and "Chip Off the Old Block"; to *Cosmopolitan* for "The Double Corner" and "The Sweetness of the Twisted Apples"; to the *Southwest Review* for "The Colt"; and to the *Rocky Mountain Review* for "Balance His, Swing Yours."

"Bugle Song," "Goin' to Town," "Two Rivers," "Butcher Bird," "The Colt," and "Chip Off the Old Block" are incorporated into the novel *The Big Rock Candy Mountain*, but since they were first written and first published as short stories, and since all of them have appeared in anthologies elsewhere as stories, it has seemed legitimate to include them here. For the rest, "Goin' to Town," "In the Twilight," "Chip Off the Old Block," "The Women on the Wall," and "Beyond the Glass Mountain" have been included in one or another volume of the *Best Short Stories*. "Two Rivers" in 1942 and "Beyond the Glass Mountain" in 1948 won second prize in the O. Henry Memorial Award volume.

Contents

The Women
on the Wall

Beyond the
Glass Mountain

SOMEONE had left a funny paper in the booth, and while he waited with his ear intent on the regular buzzing rings, Mark let his eye follow the pictured squares. I know somebody that likes your new hat, Emmy, Kayo's balloon said, and Emmy's pleased balloon said, Well, for thirty-nine-fifty they ought to, who is he? and Kayo's balloon said It's Beefy McGuire, he'd like it for his birdsnest collection, and on the fourth ring the line clicked and Mel's inquiring voice said, "Hello?"

The voice was as familiar as yesterday, a voice whose wire-filtered flatness Mark had heard over telephones ten thousand times. The rising hairs prickled on the back of his neck; he felt as he might have felt if a door had opened and the face of someone long dead had looked casually out.

And he noted instantly, in refutation of his fears, that

the voice was sober. He found himself leaning forward, grinning into the mouthpiece.

"Hello, you poop-out," he said. "This is Canby."

The old password came naturally, as if he were back seventeen years. In their college crowd everybody had called everybody else Canby, for no reason except that someone, probably Mel, had begun it and everyone else had followed suit. There had been a real Canby, a sort of goof. Now he was a CPA in Denver, and the usurpers of his name were scattered from coast to coast.

"Well, Canby!" the filtered voice said heartily. "How's the boy?"

There was a pause. Then Mel's voice, more distorted now, beginning to be his clowning voice, said suspiciously, "What was that name again?"

"Canby," Mark said. "Cornelius C. Canby." He raised his head, grinning and waiting for the real recognition.

"Cornelius C. Canby?" Mel's thickening, burbling voice said. "I didn't get the name."

"It's a hell of a note," Mark said. "Your old friend Canby was here, and you didn't even get the name."

Mel's voice was thick as glue now, like something mired down, except that on occasional syllables it fluttered upward like a mud-heavy bird. It was a maudlin, wandering, caressing voice, very convincing to strangers and drunks, and it always made any drunk his instant pal. "*Canby?*" it said. "D'you say *Canby?* Cornelius Canby? Well my God. Wonnersnevercease. *Canby,* after all these years! Come on over here and shake my hand. Where are you? Hire a car. Wait a minute, I'll come and get you myself."

"Don't bother," Mark said. "I can walk over in five minutes." He grinned again into the mouthpiece. "Are you at home or out at some bar?"

"Just down at the corner pub having little drink," Mel

said. "But I'll be home in minute, home quick as you are.
Not far away." There was another pause. "What was
z'name?"

Mark was beginning to feel a shade uncomfortable.
The clowning was routine, but there was a point where it
should have stopped. It left things uncertain. "You
stinker," he said, "this is Aker. Remember me?"

The drunken voice was an amazed buzz in the earpiece.
Out of the buzz words formed. "You mean Belly Aker, the
basketball player, erstwhile holder of the Big Ten scoring
record?"

"The same."

"Not Mark Aker, the eminent penicillinologist?"

"It is he."

"Well my God," Mel said. "I remember you. Seen your
name in the Alumni Magazine."

The words degenerated into a buzz, then became articu-
late again. "You old spore-picker. How's boy?" Then in
a moment the earphone bellowed, "What the hell you
standing around there for?"

"Hold it," Mark said. "I'm on my way."

He hung up and stepped out of the booth self-
consciously, looking around to see if anyone had been
close enough to hear the nonsense he had been talking. As
he walked through the drugstore and out into the street
he found himself explaining as if to some critical stranger.
Just to listen to Cottam, you'd think he was a maudlin sot,
but that's just a manner he wears. He put it on for the
same reason some people put on dark glasses . . .

He found himself at the corner of College and Dubuque
Streets in Iowa City, at a little past ten on a Sunday
morning in May, and as he stopped on the corner to let a
car pass, the utter and passionate familiarity of everything smote him like a wind. Mel's voice on the wire had

prepared him for nostalgia. Now the past moved up on
him in a wave; it was as if he had never left here, or had
just awakened from a long confused dream and found the
solid and reassuring edge of reality again.

The brick street ran warm and empty down across the
powerhouse bridge and up the other side, curving under
big elms and hickories. On the crown of the hill across
the river the Quadrangle's squat ivied towers barely
topped the trees, and over on the other hill to the right
the stone lace of the hospital tower rose above the massive
rectangularity of the medical buildings. The lawns below
Old Capitol were almost deserted, and the locusts were
shrilling in the streetside trees.

Odd compulsions moved him. He found himself reciting
the names of all the main university buildings. Crossing
the river, he ran his hand along the cool cement rail as if
establishing a contact, and halfway across he looked back
to see how the union and the reserve library strung out
along the riverbank, and the footbridge arched across to
the experimental theater. The banks of the river had been
landscaped since his time, but otherwise he saw no change.
The highway traffic west poured across the Iowa Avenue
bridge, and the law commons clung to the limestone bluffs.
Mark looked curiously at the few students he met, wondering if they felt as he felt the charm and warmth that
lay in the brick streets and the sleepy river and the sun-
warmed brick and stone of the university. Probably no
one appreciated things like that until they were gone and
lost and irretrievable.

On his left as he stepped off the bridge he saw the little
eating shack where he and Mel had had long johns and
coffee practically every morning for four years. The mere
look of its outside, patched with coke signs and Baby
Ruth signs and Chesterfield signs, filled his nostrils with

the peculiar and unique odors of the place: coffee and smoke and slightly rancid fat, oily-sweet doughnuts and baked paint and the reek of the bug-spray they used on the cockroaches, and under all the watery, tarry, wet-mud smells of the river.

The metal rasping of the seventeen-year-locusts rose loud as a crescendo in a symphonic poem as he climbed the hill, and it struck him as amusing that he too should return here at the end of exactly seventeen years. He couldn't quite imagine where those years had gone; it did not seem that either he or the town had changed a particle. The tennis courts he passed reflected hundreds of re-membered mornings like this, and in the field house beyond them were whole lifetimes of recollection.

He would have liked to go in under the big round roof just to soak himself in the sensations he remembered: smell of lockers opened on stale gym clothes and stiff sweated socks; steam and thumping radiators and liquid soap smell; sweat and medicated foot baths and the chlo-rine smell and the jiggly reflecting chemical blue of the pool; splat of naked feet on concrete, pink of bare flesh, lean bellies and tiptoe bunching calves, the bulging triceps of the gymnastics team working out on the horses. Most of all, the barnlike cold of the basketball floor, and the tiny brittle feeling of coming out before a game to warm up in front of that crowd-faced emptiness, and the clubbing roar of crowd-sound as you drove in for a set-up. It was the same roar whether you made it or missed it.

All of it was still there — unimaginably varied smells and sounds and sights that together made up the way he had once lived, the thing he had once been, perhaps the thing he still was. He was in all of it, and Mel with him. It came to him like a pang that never since the days when he and Mel used to fool around after lunch in the Quad

cafeteria, throwing rolled-up paper napkins at water
tumblers, had he had a completely relaxed and comfortable
ability to enjoy himself. They had made games out of
everything; whole Sunday mornings they had spent
throwing curves with pot covers in Mel's mother's kitchen.
In those Damon-and-Pythias days there had been a sharp
and tingling sense of identity and one intense and constant
comradeship, and those were the best days of his life.
Passing the field house he passed himself and Mel as they
had used to be, and the feeling that he had not merely
lived it but was somehow contained in it was as pervasive as
the mild spring morning, as insistent as the skirring of the
locusts. It was like sky-writing on the big warm sky.

The light over the whole hill was pure, pale, of an ex-
aggerated clarity, as if all the good days of his youth had
been distilled down into this one day, and the whole
coltish ascendant time when he was eighteen, nineteen,
twenty, had been handed back to him briefly, intact and
precious. That was the time when there had been more
hours in the day, and every hour precious enough so that
it could be fooled away. By the time a man got into the
high thirties the hours became more frantic and less
precious, more needed and more carefully hoarded and
more fully used, but less loved and less enjoyed.

Then he was pushing the doorbell button, bracing himself obscurely for something — for joy? for recognition?
for a renewed flood of this potent and unexpected nostalgia? — and the door opened. Mel stood there in his
shirt sleeves, a little mussy as usual, still deceptively
round-armed and round-faced, with his beaked nose and
his tender child's mouth.

He was either drunk or playing drunk. He smirked, and
his eyes blinked in owlish amazement. "Let me shake
your hand!" he said, and hauled Mark inside.

Tamsen got up off the couch where she had been sitting with a highball in her hand. As she came forward, smiling, transferring the glass to her left hand, Mark noted how she adjusted her face for greeting. She was probably prettier than she had ever been, her hair in a long bob with sun-bleached streaks in it, her face smoothly tanned, her eyes candid, her smile white and frank. Presumably the two of them had been drinking together, but where Mel was frowsy and blinking, with red-streaked eyeballs, she was smooth and sober and impeccable.

"Of all the unexpected people!" she said, and gave him a firm hand. She left him in no doubt who was in command in this familiar house, who had established dominance.

Mel's hand pulled him around. "Canby, you old snake in the grass, where you been? I've tried to call you up every night for ten years."

"You did," Mark said. "Twice. Once in New Haven and once in New York. Both times at two in the morning."

Tamsen laughed. "Old Melly," she said, almost as if affectionately. "Every time he gets tight he wants to call somebody up. The further away they are, the more he wants to call."

Mel was standing spraddling, a little flickering smile on his mouth. One hand was on Mark's shoulder. With the other he captured Mark's right hand again and shook it slowly. His breath was heavy with whiskey, and Mark felt dismayed and half sick. He had been so sure at first that the thickening voice had been put on as part of the old clowning act. Now he was bothered precisely as he had been bothered by those telephone calls. Even while he laughed at the ponderous solemnity, the incoherent, bumbling, repetitive nonsense, the marvelously accurate imitation of a soggy drunk, Mark backed away, because he couldn't be quite sure that the act was conscious any

more. The act had become the man, and he went around
living and acting out a grotesque parody of himself; or if
it hadn't become the man, then it had been put on de-
fensively so much that communication was no longer possible. Nothing had come of those telephone calls except
a mumble of doubletalk and affectionate profanity, and
yet Mark felt that there had been in each instance a need,
a loneliness, a reaching out. He felt that there was the
same thing now, if Mel would let it show. The old comradeship was there; this drunken parody was embarrassment as much as anything, the defense of a thin-skinned
organism.

"Been peeking down those microscopes," Mel said
solemnly, pumping Mark's hand. "You biological old pot-
licker. D'you invent penicillin?"

"I'm a modest man," Mark said. "Two or three other
people helped."

He got his hand free, and as his eyes crossed Mel's
there was almost communication between them, a flash
of perfectly sober understanding and warmth. Mel's delicate, bruised-looking lips pursed, but then the look slipped
and was gone, and he was pawing for Mark's hand again,
saying, "Canby, you old Rhodes Scholar, slip me the grip."

Tamsen was amused. "You should charge him. Remember when he paid a barfly a dollar an hour to shake
his hand down at Frank's?"

"Kept me poor," Mel said, with a sweet imbecilic grin.
"Lose all your friends, got to buy more." He smiled into
Mark's face, hanging to hand and shoulder, and Mark
looked deep behind that idiot alcoholic smile trying to
compel expression of what he knew was there: the recognition and the pain. Mel beamed at him.

Tamsen too was staring, tipping her head sideways. "I
can't get over how much you've changed," she said. "You
used to be such a string bean."

"Cheer up," Mark said. "I'm still a string bean at heart."

"No fooling," Mel said. He plucked the cloth of Mark's sleeve, sniffed his fingers. "Where'd you get that jacket?"

"Montreal," Mark said, and immediately felt an obscure guilty shame, as if he had been betrayed into boasting, rubbing in the fact that he had gone up and out in the world and Mel had been marooned behind. "I was up there a couple weeks ago at a genetics conference," he said lamely, in extenuation.

For an instant he was furious at Mel, so furious he shook. In college it had been Mel who had everything — money enough, and clothes, and a car, and a home where starveling students could come like grateful sidling dogs off the street. And he had been brought up well, he had good parents, his home was full of music and books and a certain sense of social grace and personal responsibility. Mel had taught the whole unlicked lot of them something, how to win and how to lose, how to live with people and like them and forgive them. He had never owned a dime's worth of anything that he wasn't glad to share. Now the shoe was on the other foot. Now Mark had gone higher and farther than any of them had ever aimed, and it embarrassed and enraged him to know that he could give lessons to Mel. And it was unjust that having shared everything for four years in college, they couldn't share this trouble that Mel was in now.

Tamsen's level blue eyes were inspecting him, and it struck him that here at least was something they had never shared. He had always known more about Tamsen than Mel had. When he stood up as Mel's best man he could have told the bridegroom the names of four people who had slept with the bride. He wished now that he had; he had wished it a hundred times. And catching Tamsen's eyes, twinkling with a little spark of malice, he knew she understood precisely what he was thinking. She had always been shrewd, and she had been all her life one of the world's most accomplished and convincing liars. When she went after Mel she had fooled even the people who knew her best, made them believe she was infatuated. . . .

"I tell you for sure," she said, "if you'd been as good looking then as you are now I'd never have let old Melly take me in to church."

"Maybe there's still time," Mark said.

Mel's tugging hand hauled him around. "You've *changed*, you know that, you damn Yale professor?"

"So have you," Mark said, but his attempt to hold Mel's eye was unsuccessful, and he added, "I stay in nights, now. Once I got free of your influence I steadied right down."

"That's fact," Mel said. "Terrible influence. Half stiff ten-thirty Sunday morning. Blame that boy of mine. Got his old man out playing baseball with a hangover before breakfast. You ever meet that boy?"

"Never did."

"Where is he, Tam?"

"He's around," Tamsen said. "How about me getting you two a drink?"

Mark let her go. It was a way of getting Mel alone. It seemed to him that some of the drunken pose fell away from Mel as soon as his wife left the room. He looked into the streaked eyes and shook his head and grinned. "How are things going anyway?"

The eyes were round and innocent. "Things going wonderful. I run the business now, since my dad died. My dad was a good business man, you know that, Canby?"

"I know that," Mark said. "It wasn't business I was thinking about." With a quick estimate that he might have only two minutes more before Tamsen returned, he opened his mouth to say what he had come to say, and found that his tongue wouldn't go around it. In that instant it was clear that you did not come in on an old friend and say, "I hear your wife's been playing around with a golf pro. I could have warned you about her that way. Probably I should have. But I hear you found out all right, and were all set to get a divorce. Bailey told me that much, a year ago. Then I heard that instead of getting a divorce you went down to St. Louis, you and Tamsen and the boy, and stayed six months, and came back home and no more said about any divorce. Get rid of her. She'll cheat on you all her life, and break you in the process. If she's pulled some lie out of the bag and convinced you that you were mistaken, don't believe it, she could lie her way out of hell. For the love of God, get that divorce, for the sake of the boy and for your own sake. She'll suck you dry like an old orange skin. You're already so far gone I could cry — soggy with alcohol and with that comedy-routine front on all the time. Come and stay with me, I'll line you up with Alcoholics Anonymous if you want. Give me a chance to pay some of what I owe you."

You simply did not say things like that. Even thinking about them made them sound self-righteous and prying. Instead, you looked uneasily at your oldest and closest friend, trying to surprise in his eyes the things you knew were there, pain and shame and bitterness and defeat. But there was too thick an insulating layer between. Seventeen years were too many. Mel was like the elk in Jim Bridger's Yellowstone story. He grazed on the other side of the glass mountain, clear and undistorted, looking only a hundred yards away. The hunter's gun went off, and the elk didn't even raise his head, didn't even hear the report. He just went on grazing, with blankness like a membrane over his eyeballs and an unpierceable transparent wall between him and the world.

Mel's lips twitched. He lurched forward, looking puzzled

and solicitous. "Whazza name?" he said, besotted and polite, and turned his ear sideward like a deaf man.

Mark pushed him away angrily just as Tamsen came in with glasses. Mel took two and handed one to Mark with a crooked grin. "Here, rinse your mouth," he said.

Tamsen raised her glass. "Here's to the local boy who made good." They clicked glasses elaborately all around. Irritated, baffled, frustrated, gnawed by that odd obscure shame, Mark drank with them to himself.

"I was thinking about you the other day," Tamsen was saying. "We were down watching the spring canoe race and two kids went over the falls by the power plant just the way you and Mel did once."

"I hope they didn't swallow as much water as I did," Mark said.

"Yeah, but this the other day was an accident," Mel said. "You, you pot-licker, you put us over there just to duck me."

"I was along," Mark said. "I went over too. Remember?"

Tamsen shook her head. "You were a pair," she said. "I guess I'd forgotten what a pair you were."

They sat nursing their drinks, the door open upon the street and the locust noise, and groped carefully backward for the things to remember and laugh about, gleaning the safe nostalgic past. But it was not the canoes over waterfalls, the times Jay Straup tried to climb Old Capitol steps in his old Model T, the picnics on Signal Hill when all the farmer kids used to creep up and spy on the college kids necking, that Mark wanted to remember. People who recalled such things and shook their heads over them bored him. He kept looking at Mel in search of that spark of understanding, and he kept wanting to say —

Remember the times we used to go out on dates and come in late in your old Ford, and stop down along one of the river joints for a pork tenderloin and a ginger beer, two or three o'clock in the morning, only a truck driver or two on the stools? How good sandwiches tasted at that hour, and how late the moon would be over the bluffs when we came out yawning and started up to your house? Remember the mornings we woke up in this house, this very house seventeen or eighteen or twenty years ago, and found the sun scrambled in the bedclothes, and had a shower and breakfast and went out onto the sidewalk, not for anything especially, but just to be outdoors, and walked under those trees out there up to the corner and back again, loafing, alive to the fingertips, talking about anything, nothing, girls, games, profundities? Remember? It isn't what we did, but what we were, that I remember, and I know that what we were is still here, if we'd peel off the defenses and the gag-lines and the doubletalk routines and the Montreal jackets.

The porch thudded with feet and a chubby boy of twelve came in with a bat in his hand. He stood forward gravely when Mel introduced him, shook hands with polite indifference, coasted into the kitchen and came back gnawing on a cookie.

"Canby, my friend," Mel said to him, "you'll be as fat as your old man."

The child was a curious blend of his parents, with Tamsen's deceptively clear eyes and Mel's twisting delicate mouth. He looked at his father over the cookie, grinning.

"Stay away from pappy," Tamsen said. "Pappy started out to cure a hangover and behold he's swizzled again."

A grunt that sounded almost like an angry outburst escaped Mel. He lunged for the boy. "Come here!" he said, as the boy eluded him. "Come here and I'll knock your two heads together."

Still grinning, the boy banged out onto the porch. "How about another drink for the two old grads?" Tamsen said.

"Why not?" Mel said, but Mark rose.

"I've got to catch a train at twelve-thirty."

"You don't have to go," Mel said. "You just came, Canby."

Mark put out his hand to Tamsen. "Good-bye," he said. "If you ever come east don't forget me."

He was trying to decide whether the look in her clear eyes had been triumphant, or whether there had actually been any look at all, as he and Mel went out the sidewalk and down to the corner. They did not speak on the way down, but on the corner, under the warm shade, their voices almost lost in the incessant shrilling of the locusts, they shook hands again. Mark knew there was no use in trying to say any of what it had been in his mind to say. But even so he gripped Mel's hand and held his eyes.

"I wish you the best, you bum," he said, and his throat tightened up as it sometimes tightened at an emotional crisis in a play. "If you're not so stiff you can't listen straight, listen to this. I wish you the best, and if there's ever a time I can . . ."

He stopped. Mel was looking at him without any of the sodden fuzziness that had marked him for the past hour. His eyes were pained, intent, sad. On his delicate bruised lips there was a flicker of derision.

The Berry Patch

THAT DAY the sun came down in a vertical fall of heat, but the wind came under it, flat out of the gap beyond Mansfield, and cooled a sweating forehead as fast as the sun could heat it. In the washed ruts of the trail there were no tracks.

"Lord," Perley Hill said. "It's a day for seeing things, right enough."

He jerked off his tie and unbuttoned his shirt, rolled up his sleeves and set his right arm gingerly on the hot door, and as Alma steered the Plymouth up the long slope of Stannard he looked back across the valley to where the asbestos mine on Belvidere blew up its perpetual white plume, and on down south across the hills folding back in layers of blue to Mansfield and Elmore and the shark-fin spine of Camel's Hump. Just across the valley the lake was like a mirror leaned on edge against the hills, with the

white houses of the village propped against its lower edge
to keep it from sliding down into the river valley.

"It's pretty on a clear day," Alma said, without looking.

Perley continued to look down. "Things show up," he
said. "There's Donald Swain's place."

" 'Twon't be his much longer," Alma said.

Perley glanced at her. She was watching the road with
rigid concentration. "Having trouble?" he said.

"I thought I told you. He's in hospital in St. Johnsbury.
Stomach trouble or something. With Henry and George
in the navy, Allen can't run it alone. Donald's had him
put it up for sale."

"I guess you did tell me," he said. "I forgot."

"Already sold half his cows," Alma said.

They passed an abandoned farm, with a long meadow
that flowed downhill between tight walls of spruce.
"Looks like a feller could've made that pay," Perley said.
"How long's it been since Gardner left here?"

"I remember coming up here to pick apples when I was
about fifteen," Alma said. "Must be ten-twelve years since
anybody's worked this place."

Perley drummed on the door, grinning a little to himself at the way Alma never took her eyes off the road
when she talked. She faced it as if it were a touchy bull-
critter. "Kind of proud of yourself since you learned to
drive, ain't you?" he said. "Be putting Sam Boyce out of
business, taxiing people around."

She took her foot off the accelerator. "Why, you can
drive," she said. "I didn't mean —— "

"Go ahead," Perley said. "Any OPA agents around, you
can do the explaining about the pleasure driving."

" 'Tisn't pleasure driving," Alma said. "Berrying's all
right to do."

Perley watched the roadside, the chokecherry bushes
getting heavy with green clusters already, the daisies and

paintbrush just going out, but still lush in the shaded places, the fireweed and green goldenrod flowing back into every little bay in the brush.

Just as Alma shifted and crawled out onto a level before an abandoned schoolhouse, a partridge swarmed out of a beech, and Perley bent to look upward. "See them two little ones hugging the branch?" he said. "They'd sit there and never move till you knocked them off with a stick."

Alma pulled off the road into the long grass. An old skid road wormed up the hill through heavy timber, and the air was rich with the faint, warm, moist smell of woods after rain. Perley stretched till his muscles cracked, yawned, stepped out to look across the broken stone wall that disappeared into deep brush.

"Makes a feller just want to lay down in the cool," he said. "If I lay down will you braid my hair full of daisies?"

The berry pails in her hands, Alma looked at him seriously. "Well, if you'd rather just lay down," she said. "We don't have to —— "

"I guess I can stay up a mite longer," Perley said.

"But if you'd rather," she said, and looked at him as if she didn't quite know what he'd like to do, but was willing to agree to anything he said. She'd been that way ever since he came home. If he yawned, she wondered if he didn't want to go to bed. If he sat down, she brought a pillow or a magazine as if he might be going to stay there all day.

He reached in and got the big granite kettle and set it over her head like a helmet, and then fended her off with one hand while he got the blanket, the lunch box, the Mason jar of water. "Think the army had wrapped me up in cellophane too pretty to touch," he said.

"Well," she said, "I just wanted to be sure." She looked at his face and added, "You big lummox."

He nested the pails, hooked his arm through the basket,

slung the blanket across his shoulder, picked up the water
jar. "If I just had me a wife would do for me," he said,
"I'd lay down and get my strength back. With the wife I
got, I s'pose I got to work."

"Here," Alma said mildly. "Give me some of them
things. You'll get so toggled up I'll have to cut you out
with the pliers."

All the way up the skid road under the deep shade their
feet made trails in the wet grass. Perley jerked his head
at them. "Nobody been in since yesterday anyway," he
said.

"Wa'n't any tracks on the road."

"Thought somebody might've walked," Perley said.
"Haven't, though."

"Be nice if we had the patch all to our lonesomes," she
said.

They came out of the woods into a meadow. A house
that had once stood at the edge was a ruined foundation
overgrown with fireweed, and the hurricane of 1938 had
scooped a path two hundred yards long and fifty wide
out of the maples behind. Root tables lay up on edge,
trunks were crisscrossed, flat, leaning, dead and half-dead.
Perley went over and looked into the tangle. "Plenty
raspberries," he said.

"I've got my face fixed for blueberries," Alma said. "We
can get some of those too, though. They're about gone
down below."

Perley was already inspecting the ruined cellar. "Ha!"
he said. "Gooseberries, too. A mess of 'em."

"It's blueberries I'm interested in," she said.

"Well, I'll find you some blueberries then." He tight-
roped the foundation and jumped clear of the gooseberry
bushes. Fifty feet down the meadow he went into a point

with lifted foot, the pails dangling in one hand. "Hey!" he
said. "Hey!"

When she got to his side he was standing among knee-
high bushes, and all down the falling meadow, which
opened on the west into a clear view of the valley, the
village, the lake, the hills beyond hills and the final peaks,
the dwarf bushes were so laden that the berries gleamed
through the covering leaves like clusters of tiny flowers.

"Thunderation," Perley said. "I never saw a patch like
that in fifteen years."

Before she could say anything he had stripped off the
army shirt and the white undershirt and hung them on a
bush, and was raking the berries into a pail with his spread
fingers.

By the time two buckets were full the wind had shifted
so that the trees cut it off, and it was hot in the meadow.
They went back into the shade by the old foundation and
ate lunch and drank from the spring. Then they lay down
on the blanket and looked up at the sky. The wind came
in whiffs along the edge of the blowdown, and the sweet
smell of the raspberry patch drifted across them. Away
down along the view that this house had had once, the
lake looked more than ever like a mirror tipped against
the hills. Below the village Donald Swain's white house
and round red barn were strung on a white thread of road.

Perley rolled over on his side and looked at his wife. "I
guess I never asked you," he said, "how you were getting
along."

"I get along all right."

"You don't want me to sell any cows?"

"You know you wouldn't want to do that. You were
just getting the herd built up."

"A herd's no good if you can't get help."

"People are good about helping," she said.

"What'll you do when there ain't any more people around? Seems like half the place has gone down country or into the army already."

"It's been going since the Civil War," Alma said, "and still there always seems to be somebody around to neighbor with."

He rolled onto his back again and plucked a spear of grass. "We should be haying," he said, "right now."

"Sunday," she said.

"Sunday or no Sunday. There's still those two top meadows. Those city kids you got can't get all that hay in."

"All they need is somebody to keep 'em from raring back in the breeching," Alma said. "I'll be behind with a pitchfork if I have to."

"I can see you."

She did not stir from her comfortable sprawl, but her voice went up crisply. "You thought we ought to sell when you got called up," she said. "Well, you've been gone going on a year, and hasn't anything gone wrong, has there? Got seven new calves, an't you? Milk checks have got bigger, an't they? Learned to drive the tractor and the car, didn't I? Got ten run of wood coming from DeSerres for the loan of the team, an't we, and saved the price of feed all that time last winter."

"Allen Swain can't make it go," Perley said.

"His farm don't lay as good as ours, and he's got a mortgage," she said. "Mortgage," the way she said it, sounded like an incurable disease. She half rose on her elbow to look at him. "And I an't Allen Swain, either."

"So you want to be a farmer."

"I am," she said.

Perley picked another stem of grass and grinned up

into the tops of the maples. They had been growing densely before the hurricane, and the going down of trees on every side had left them standing tall and spindly. The wind went through their leaves high up, a good stiff wind that bent and threshed their tops, but only a creeping breath disturbed the grass below. It was like lying deep down in a soft, warm, sweet-smelling nest.

"Laying here, you wouldn't think anything could ever touch you," he said. "Wind could blow up there like all get-out, and you'd never feel it." Alma's hand fell across his chest, and he captured it. "Unless you stuck your head out," he said.

For a while he lay feeling the pulse in her wrist.

"Smell them raspberries?" he said once, and squirmed his shoulders more comfortable against the ground. "There ain't anything smells sweeter, even flowers." Alma said nothing.

"Funny about a berry patch," he said. "Nobody ever plowed it, or planted it, or cultivated it, or fertilized it, or limed it, but there it is. You couldn't grub it out if you tried. More you plow it up, the more berries there is next year. Burn it over, it's up again before anything else. Blow everything down, that's just what it likes."

He filled his lungs with the ripe berry odor and let the breath bubble out between his lips. "Don't seem as if you'd ever have to move," he said. "Just lay here and reach up and pick a mouthful and then lay some more and let the wind blow over way up there and you never even feel it."

"It's nice," Alma said. "I didn't hardly think the blueberries would be ripe yet, it's been so rainy."

"Makes you think the world's all right," Perley said, "the way they come along every year, rain or shine."

Alma stirred. "We better get busy," she said. "Some gooseberries, too, if you'd like some."

"Might use a pie," he said. He sat up and stretched for the pails. There were only the granite kettle and the two-quart milk pail left. "You lay still," he said. "I'll get some."

" 'Tisn't as if I needed a rest," she said. "Here I've been just having fun all day."

"Well, take the kettle then. It's easier to pick into." He picked up the milk pail.

"Perley," Alma said.

"Uh?"

"This is what you want to do, isn't it? I mean, you wouldn't rather go see somebody?"

He watched her steadily. "Why?"

"Well, it's only two more days. I just ——— "

"I already saw everybody I want to see," he said. "I was saving the last couple days."

"Well, all right," she said, and went into the blowdown with the kettle.

He picked very fast, wanting to surprise her with how many he had, and when after a half-hour he worked back toward the side where she was picking he had the pail filled and overflowing, mounded an inch above the brim. He liked the smell of his hand when he scratched his nose free of a tickling cobweb. For a moment he stood, turning his face upward to watch the unfelt upper-air wind thresh through the tops of the maples, and then he came up softly behind Alma where she bent far in against a root table to reach a loaded vine. He bent in after her and kissed the back of her neck.

"How're you doing?" she said, and worked her way out. Her shirt was unbuttoned halfway down, her throat was brown even in the hollow above where her collarbones joined, and her eyes sought his with that anxiety to know that he was content, that he was doing what he wanted to do, which she had shown all the time of his furlough. "I got quite a mess," she said, and showed the berries in her pail. "How about you?"

"All I want," Perley said. He was watching the sun dapple the brown skin of her throat as the wind bent the thin tops of the maples. "I wouldn't want any more," he said.

The Women on the Wall

THE CORNER window of the study overlooked a lawn, and beyond that a sunken lane between high pines, and beyond the lane a point of land with the old beach club buildings at one end and a stone wall around its tip. Beyond the point, through the cypresses and eucalyptuses, Mr. Palmer could see the Pacific, misty blue, belted between shore and horizon with a band of brown kelp.

Writing every morning in his study, making over his old notebooks into a coherent account of his years on the Galapagos, Mr. Palmer could glance up from his careful longhand and catch occasional glimpses, as a traveler might glance out of the window of a moving train. And in spite of the rather special atmosphere of the point, caused by the fact that until the past year it had been a club, there was something homey and neighborly and pleasant about the place that Mr. Palmer liked. There were children, for one thing, and dogs drifting up and down, and the occasional skirr of an automobile starting in the quiet, the diminishing sound of tires on asphalt, the distant racket of a boy being a machine-gun with his mouth.

Mr. Palmer had been away from the States a long time; he found the noises on the point familiar and nostalgic and reassuring in this time of war, and felt as if he had come home. Though California differed considerably from his old home in Ohio, he fell naturally and gratefully into its procession of morning and afternoon, its neighborhood routines, the pleasant breathing of its tides. When anything outside broke in upon his writing, it was generally a commonplace and familiar thing; Mr Palmer looked up and took pleasure in the interruption.

One thing he could be sure of seeing, every morning but Sunday. The section was outside the city limits, and mail was delivered to a battery of mailboxes where the sunken lane joined the street. The mail arrived at about eleven; about ten-thirty the women from the beach club apartments began to gather on the stone wall. Below the wall was the beach, where the tides leaned in all the way from Iwo and Okinawa. Above it was the row of boxes where as regularly as the tide the mail carrier came in a gray car and deposited postmarked flotsam from half a world away.

Sometimes Mr. Palmer used to pause in his writing and speculate on what these women thought of when they looked out across the gumdrop-blue water and the brown kelp and remembered that across this uninterrupted ocean their husbands fought and perhaps bled and possibly died, that in those far islands it was already tomorrow, that the green water breaking against the white foot of the beach might hold in suspension minute quantities of the blood shed into it thousands of miles away, that the Japan current, swinging in a great circle up under the Aleutians

and back down the American coast, might as easily bear
the mingled blood or the floating relics of a loved one lost
as it could bear the glass balls of Japanese net-floats that
it sometimes washed ashore.

Watching the women, with their dogs and children,
waiting patiently on the stone wall for that most urgent of
all the gods, that Mercury in the gray uniform, Mr. Palmer
thought a good deal about Penelope on the rocky isle of
Ithaca above the wine-dark sea. He got a little senti-
mental about these women. Sometimes he was almost
frightened by the air of patient, withdrawn seriousness
they wore as they waited, and the unsmiling alacrity with
which they rose and crowded around the mailman when
he came. And when the mail was late, and one or two of
them sat out on the wall until eleven-thirty, twelve, sometimes twelve-thirty, Mr. Palmer could hardly bear it at all.

Waiting, Mr. Palmer reflected, must cause a person to
remove to a separate and private world. Like sleep or in-
sanity, waiting must have the faculty of making the real
unreal and remote. It seemed to Mr. Palmer pathetic and
somehow thrilling that these women should have followed
their men to the very brink of the West, and should re-
main here now with their eyes still westward, patiently
and faithfully suspending their own normal lives until the
return of their husbands. Without knowing any of the
women, Mr. Palmer respected and admired them. They
did not invite his pity. Penelope was as competent for
her waiting as Ulysses was for his wars and wiles.

Mr. Palmer had been working in his new house hardly
a week before he found himself putting on his jacket about
eleven and going out to join the women.

He knew them all by sight just from looking out the window. The red-haired woman with the little boy was

sitting on the wall nearest him. Next was the thin girl who always wore a bathing suit and went barefooted. Next was the dark-haired one, five or six months pregnant. And next to her was the florid, quick, wrenlike woman with the little girl of about five. Their faces all turned as Mr. Palmer came up.

"Good morning," he said.

The red-haired woman's plain, serious, freckled face acknowledged him, and she murmured good morning. The girl in the bathing suit had turned to look off over the ocean, and Mr. Palmer felt that she had not made any reply. The pregnant girl and the woman with the little girl both nodded.

The old man put his hands on his knees, rounded his mouth and eyes, and bent to look at the little boy hanging to the red-haired woman's hand. "Well!" he said. "Hi, young fella!"

The child stared at him, crowding against his mother's legs. The mother said nothing, and rather than push first acquaintance too far, Mr. Palmer walked on along the wall. As he glanced at the thin girl, he met her eyes, so full of cold hostility that for a moment he was shocked. He had intended to sit down in the middle of the wall, but her look sent him on further, to sit between the pregnant girl and the wrenlike woman.

"These beautiful mornings!" Mr. Palmer said, sitting down with a sigh.

The wrenlike woman nodded, the pregnant one regarded him with quiet ox-eyes.

"This is quite a ritual, waiting for the mail," Mr. Palmer said. He pointed to the gable of his house across the lane. "I see you from my window over there, congregating on the wall here every morning."

The wrenlike woman looked at him rather oddly, then

leaped to prevent her daughter from putting out the eyes of the long-suffering setter she was mauling. The pregnant girl smiled a slow, soft smile. Over her shoulder Mr. Palmer saw the thin girl hitch herself up and sit on her hands. The expression on her face said that she knew very well why Mr. Palmer had come down and butted in, and why he watched from his window.

"The sun's so warm out here," the pregnant girl said. "It's a way of killing part of the morning, sitting out here."

"A very good way," Mr. Palmer said. He smoothed the creases in his trousers, finding speech a little difficult. From the shelter of his mother's legs the two-year-old boy down the wall stared at him solemnly. Then the wrenlike woman hopped off the wall and dusted her skirt.

"Here he is!" she said.

They all started across the mouth of the lane, and for some reason, as they waited for the mailman to sort and deliver, Mr. Palmer felt that his first introduction hadn't taken him very far. In a way, as he thought it over, he respected the women for that, too. They were living without their husbands, and had to be careful. After all, Penelope had many suitors. But he could not quite get over wanting to spank the thin girl on her almost-exposed backside, and he couldn't quite shake the sensation of having wandered by mistake into the ladies' rest room.

After that, without feeling that he knew them at all, he respected them and respected their right to privacy. Waiting, after all, put you in an exclusive club. No outsider had any more right on that wall than he had in the company of a bomber crew. But Mr. Palmer felt that he could at least watch from his window, and at the mailboxes he could, almost by osmosis, pick up a little more information.

The red-haired woman's name was Kendall. Her husband was an Army captain, a doctor. The thin girl, Mrs. Fisher, got regular letters bearing a Marine Corps return. The husband of Mrs. Corson, the wrenlike woman, commanded a flotilla of minesweepers in the western Pacific. Of the pregnant girl, Mrs. Vaughn, Mr. Palmer learned little. She got few letters and none with any postmarks that told anything.

From his study window Mr. Palmer went on observing them benignly and making additions to his notes on the profession of waiting. Though the women differed sharply one from another, they seemed to Mr. Palmer to have one thing in common: they were all quiet, peaceful, faithful to the times and seasons of their vigil, almost like convalescents in a hospital. They made no protests or outcries; they merely lived at a reduced tempo, as if pulse rate and respiration rate and metabolic rate and blood pressure were all turned down. Mr. Palmer had a notion how it might be. Sometimes when he awoke very quietly in the night he could feel how quietly and slowly and regularly his heart was pumping, how slow and regular his breathing was, how he lay there mute and cool and inert with everything turned down to idling speed, his old body taking care of itself. And when he woke that way he had a curious feeling that he was waiting for something.

Every morning at ten-thirty, as regular as sun and tide, Mrs. Kendall came out of the beach club apartments and walked across the point, leading her little boy by the hand. She had the child turned down, too, apparently. He never, to Mr. Palmer's knowledge, ran or yelled or cried or made a fuss, but walked quietly beside his mother, and sat with her on the big stump until five minutes to eleven, and then walked with her across to the end of the stone wall. About that time the other women began to gather, until all four of them were there in a quiet, uncommunicative row.

Through the whole spring the tides leaned inward with the same slow inevitability, the gray car came around and stopped by the battery of mailboxes, the women gathered on the wall as crows gather to a rookery at dusk.

Only once in all that drowsy spring was there any breaking of the pattern. That was one Monday after Mr. Palmer had been away for the weekend. When he strolled out at mailtime he found the women not sitting on the wall, but standing in a nervous conversational group. They opened to let him in, for once accepting him silently among them, and he found that the thin girl had moved out suddenly the day before: the Saturday mail had brought word that her husband had gone down in flames over the Marianas.

The news depressed Mr. Palmer in curious ways. It depressed him to see the women shaken from their phlegmatic routine, because the moment they were so shaken they revealed the raw fear under their quiet. And it depressed him that the thin girl's husband had been killed. That tragedy should come to a woman he personally felt to be a snob, a fool, a vain and inconsequent chit, seemed to him sad and incongruous and even exasperating. As long as she was one of the company of Penelopes, Mr. Palmer had refused to dislike her. The moment she made demands upon his pity he disliked her very much.

After that sudden blow, as if a hawk had struck among the quiet birds on the wall, Mr. Palmer found it less pleasant to watch the slow, heavy-bodied walking of Mrs. Kendall, her child always tight by the hand, from apartment to stump to wall. Unless spoken to, she never spoke. She wore gingham dresses that were utterly out of place in the white sun above the white beach. She was plain, unattractive, patient, the most remote, the most tuned-down, the quietest and saddest and most patient and most exasperating of the Penelopes. She too began to make wry demands on Mr. Palmer's pity, and he found himself almost disliking her. He was guilty of a little prayer that Mrs. Kendall's husband would be spared, so that his pity would not have to go any farther than it did.

Then one morning Mr. Palmer became aware of another kind of interruption on the point. Somebody there had apparently bought a new dog. Whoever had acquired it must have fed it, though Mr. Palmer never saw anyone do so, and must have exercised it, though he never saw that either. All he saw was that the dog, a half-grown cocker, was tied to the end of a rose trellis in the club-house yard. And all he heard, for two solid days, was the uproar the dog made.

It did not like being tied up. It barked, and after a while its voice would break into a kind of hysterical howling mixed with shuddering diminuendo groans. Nobody ever came and told it to be still, or took care of it, or let it loose. It stayed there and yanked on its rope and chewed at the trellis post and barked and howled and groaned until Mr. Palmer's teeth were on edge and he was tempted to call the Humane Society.

Actually he didn't, because on the third morning the noise had stopped, and as he came into his study to begin working he saw that the dog was gone. Mrs. Corson was sitting in a lawn chair under one of the cypresses, and her daughter was digging in the sandpile. There was no sign either of Mrs. Kendall or Mrs. Vaughn. The owner of the house was raking leaves on the lawn above the sea-wall.

Mr. Palmer looked at his watch. It was nine-thirty. On

an impulse he slipped on a jacket and went down and out across the lawn and down across the lane and up the other side past the trellis. Where the dog had lain the ground was strewn with chewed green splinters.

Mrs. Corson looked up from her chair. Her cheeks were painted with a hatchwork of tiny ruddy veins, and her eyes looked as if she hadn't slept. They had a stary blankness like blind eyes, and Mr. Palmer noticed that the pupils were dilated, even in the bright light. She took a towel and a pack of cigarettes and a bar of coco-butter off the chair next to her.

"Good morning," she said in her husky voice. "Sit down."

"Thank you," Mr. Palmer said. He let himself down into the steeply slanting wooden chair and adjusted the knees of his slacks. "It *is* a good morning," he said slyly. "So quiet."

Mrs. Corson's thin neck jerked upward and backward in a curious gesture. Her throaty laughter was loud and unrestrained, and the eyes she turned on Mr. Palmer were red with mirth.

"That damned dog," she said. "Wasn't that something?"

"I thought I'd go crazy," Mr. Palmer said. "Whose dog was it, anyway?"

Mrs. Corson's rather withered, red-nailed hand, with a big diamond and a wedding ring on the fourth finger, reached down and picked up the cigarettes. The hand trembled as it held the pack out.

"No thank you," he said.

Mrs. Corson took one. "It was Mrs. Kendall's dog," she said. "She took it back."

"Thank God!" said Mr. Palmer.

Her hands nervous with the matchbox in her lap, Mrs.

Corson sat and smoked. Mr. Palmer saw that her lips, under the lipstick, were chapped, and that there was a dried, almost leathery look to her tanned and freckled skin.

He slid deeper into the chair and looked out over the water, calm as a lake, the long light swells breaking below him with a quiet, lulling swish. Up the coast heavier surf was breaking farther out. Its noise came like a pulsating tremble on the air, hardly a sound at all. Everything tuned down, Mr. Palmer was thinking. Even the lowest frequency of waves on the beach. Even the ocean waited.

"I should think you'd bless your stars, having a place like this to wait in," he said.

One of Mrs. Corson's eyebrows bent. She shot him a sideward look.

"Think of the women who are waiting in boarding-house rooms," Mr. Palmer said, a little irritated at her manner. "Think of the ones who are working and leaving their children in nurseries."

"Oh, sure," Mrs. Corson said. "It's fine for Anne, with the beach and yard."

Mr. Palmer leaned on the arm of the chair and looked at her quizzically. He wished any of these women would ever put away their reticence and talk about their waiting, because that was where their life lay, that was where they had authority. "How long has your husband been gone?" he asked.

"Little over two years."

"That's a long time," Mr. Palmer said, thinking of Penelope and her wait. Ten years while the war went on at Troy, ten more years while Ulysses wandered through every peril in the Mediterranean, past Scylla and Charybdis and Circe and the Cyclops and the iron terrors of

Hades and the soft temptations of Nausicaa. But that was
poetry. Twenty years was too much. Two, in all con-
science, was enough.

"I shouldn't kick," the woman said. "Mrs. Kendall's husband has been gone for over three."

"I've noticed her," Mr. Palmer said. "She seems rather
sad and repressed."

For a moment Mrs. Corson's eyes, slightly bloodshot,
the pupils dilated darkly, were fixed questioningly on Mr.
Palmer's. Then the woman shook herself almost as a dog
does. "I guess," she said. She rose with a nervous snap and
glanced at her watch. From the sandpile the little girl
called, "Is it time, Mommy?"

"I guess so," Mrs. Corson said. She laid the back of her
hand across her eyes and made a face.

"I'll be getting along," Mr. Palmer said.

"I was just taking Anne down for her pony ride. Why
don't you ride down with us?"

"Well . . . "

"Come on," Mrs. Corson said. "We'll be back in less
than an hour."

The child ran ahead of them and opened the car doors,
down in the widened part of the lane. As Mr. Palmer
helped Mrs. Corson in she turned her face a little, and he
smelled the stale alcohol on her breath. Obviously Mrs.
Corson had been drinking the night before, and obviously
she was a little hung over.

But my Lord, why not? he said to himself. Two years
of waiting, nothing to do but sit and watch and do nothing
and be patient. He didn't like Mrs. Corson any less for
occasional drinking. She was higher-strung than either
Mrs. Vaughn or Mrs. Kendall. You could almost lift up
the cover board and pluck her nerves like the strings of a
piano. Even so, she played the game well. He liked her.

At the pony track Anne raced down the fenced runway at a pink fluttering gallop, and Mr. Palmer and Mrs. Corson, following more slowly, found her debating between a black and a pinto pony.

"Okay," the man in charge said. "Which'll it be today, young lady?"

"I don't know," the girl said. Her forehead wrinkled. "Mommy, which do you think?"

"I don't care, hon," her mother said. "Either one is nice."

Pretty, her blonde braids hanging in front and framing her odd pre-Raphaelite face, Anne stood indecisive. She turned her eyes up to Mr. Palmer speculatively. "The black one's nice," she said, "but so's the . . ."

"Oh, Anne," her mother said. "For heaven's sake make up your mind."

"Well . . . the black one, then," Anne said. She reached out a hand and touched the pony's nose, pulling her fingers back sharply and looking up at her mother with a smile that Mr. Palmer found himself almost yearning over.

"You're a nitwit," her mother said. "Hop on, so we can get back for the mailman."

The attendant swung her up, but with one leg over the saddle Anne kicked and screamed to get down. "I've changed my mind," she said. "Not this one, the pinto one."

The attendant put her up on the pinto and Mrs. Corson, her chapped lips trembling, said, "Another outburst like that and you won't get on any, you little . . . !"

The pony started, led by the attendant who rocked on one thick-soled shoe. For a moment Mrs. Corson and Mr. Palmer stood in the sun under the sign that said "Pony Rides, 10 Cents, 12 for $1.00." They were, Mr. Palmer

noticed, in the Mexican part of town. Small houses, some
of them almost shacks, with geraniums climbing all over
them, strung out along the street. Down on the corner
beyond the car was a tavern with a dusty tin sign. Mrs.
Corson unsnapped her purse and fished out a wadded bill
and held it vaguely in her hand, looking off up the street
past the track and the pinto pony and the pink little
huddle on its back and the attendant rocking along ahead
on his one thick shoe.

"I wonder," she said. "Would you do me a favor?"

"Anything."

"Would you stay here five minutes while I go to the
store? Just keep an eye on her?"

"Of course," he said. "I'd be glad to go to the store for
you, if you'd like."

"No," she said. "No, I'd better get it." She put the
crumpled bill into his hand. "Let her have all the rides
she wants. I'll be back in a few minutes."

Mr. Palmer settled himself on a chair against the stable
wall and waited. When Anne and the attendant got back
he waved the bill at them. "Want another ride?"

"Yes!" Anne said. Her hands were clenched tightly in
the pony's mane, and her eyes danced and her mouth was
a little open. The attendant turned and started down the
track again. "Run!" Anne cried to him. "Make him run!"

The crippled hostler broke into a clumsy hop-skip-and-
jump for a few yards, pulling the pony into a trot. The
girl screamed with delight. Mr. Palmer yawned, tapped
his mouth, smiled a little as he smelled the powder-and-
perfume smell on the dollar bill, yawned again. Say what
you would, it was decent of the woman to come out with
a hangover and take her child to the pony track. She
must feel pretty rocky, if her eyes were any criterion.

He waited for some time. Anne finished a second ride,

took a third, finished that and had a fourth. The attendant
was sweating a little. From the fence along the sidewalk
two Negro children and a handful of little Mexicans
watched. "How about it?" Mr. Palmer said. "Want another?"

She nodded, shaken with giggles and sudden shyness
when she looked around and found her mother gone.

"Sure you're not getting sore?" Mr. Palmer patted his
haunch suggestively.

She shook her head.

"Okay," the hostler said. "Here we go again, then."

At the end of the fifth ride Anne let herself be lifted off.
The hostler went inside and sat down, the pony joined its
companion at the rail, cocked its hip and tipped its right
hoof and closed its eyes. Anne climbed up into Mr.
Palmer's lap.

"Where's Mommy?"

"She went to buy something."

"Darn her," Anne said. "She does that all the time. She
better hurry up, it's getting mailtime."

"Don't you like to miss the mail?"

"Sometimes there's packages and things from Daddy,"
Anne said. "I got a grass skirt once."

Mr. Palmer rounded his mouth and eyes. "You must
like your daddy."

"I do. Mommy doesn't, though."

"What?"

"Mommy gets mad," Anne said. "She thinks Daddy
could have had shore duty a long time ago, he's had so
much combat, but she says he likes the Navy better than
home. He's a commander."

"Yes, I know," Mr. Palmer said. He looked up the street,
beginning to be fretful. The fact that the woman spent
her whole life waiting shouldn't make her quite so callous

to how long she kept other people waiting. "We *are* going to miss the mailman if your Mommy doesn't hurry," he said.

Anne jumped off his lap and puckered her lips like her mother. "And today's a package!"

Mr. Palmer raised his eyebrows. "How do you know?"

"The fortune teller told Mommy."

"I see," the old man said. "Does your mother go to fortune tellers often?"

"Every Saturday," Anne said. "I went with her once. You know what she said? And it came true, too."

Mr. Palmer saw the girl's mother coming down the sidewalk, and stood up. "Here comes Mommy," he said. "We'd better meet her at the car."

"She said we'd get good news, and right away Daddy was promoted," Anne said. "And she said we'd get a package, and that week we got *three!*"

Mrs. Corson was out of breath. In the bright sun her eyes burned with a curious sightless brilliance. The smell of alcohol on her was fresher and stronger.

"I'm sorry," she said as she got in. "I met a friend, and it was so hot we stopped for a beer."

On the open highway, going back home, she stepped down hard on the throttle, and her fingers kept clasping and unclasping the wheel. Her body seemed possessed of electric energy. She radiated something, she gave off sparks. Her eyes, with the immense dark pupils and suffused whites, were almost scary.

When they pulled up and parked in front of Mr. Palmer's gate, opposite the mailboxes, the little red flags on some of the boxes were still up. On the stone wall sat Mrs. Kendall, her son Tommy, and the pregnant girl, Mrs. Vaughn. "Late again," Mrs. Corson said. "Damn that man."

"Can I play, Mommy?" Anne said.

"Okay." As the child climbed out, the mother said, "Don't get into any fixes with Tommy. Remember what I told you."

"I will," Anne said. Her setter came up and she stooped to pull its ears.

Her mother's face went pinched and mean. "And stop abusing that dog!" she said.

Mr. Palmer hesitated. He was beginning to feel uncomfortable, and he thought of the pages he might have filled that morning, and the hour that still remained before noon. But Mrs. Corson was leaning back with the back of her hand across her eyes. Through the windshield Mr. Palmer could see the two women and the child on the wall, like a multiple Patience on a monument. When he looked back at Mrs. Corson he saw that she too was watching them between her fingers. Quite suddenly she began to laugh.

She laughed for a good minute, not loudly but with curious violence, her whole body shaking. She dabbed her eyes and caught her breath and shook her head and tried to speak. Mr. Palmer attended uneasily, wanting to be gone.

"Lord," Mrs. Corson said finally. "Look at 'em. Vultures on a limb. Me too. Three mama vultures and one baby vulture."

"You're a little hard on yourself," Mr. Palmer said, smiling. "And Anne, I'd hardly call her a vulture."

"I didn't include her," Mrs. Corson said. She turned her hot red eyes on him. "She's got sense enough to run and play, and I hope I've got sense enough to let her."

"Well, but little Tommy . . . "

"Hasn't had his hand out of mamma's since they came here," Mrs. Corson said. "Did you ever see him play with anybody?"

Mr. Palmer confessed that he hadn't, now that he thought of it.

"Because if you ever do," Mrs. Corson said, "call out all the preachers. It'll be Christ come the second time. Honest to God, sometimes that woman . . ."

Bending forward, Mr. Palmer could see Mrs. Kendall smoothing the blue sweater around her son's waist. "I've wondered about her," he said, and stopped. Mrs. Corson had started to laugh again.

When she had finished her spasm of tight, violent mirth, she said, "It isn't her child, you know."

"No?" he said, surprised. "She takes such care of it."

"You're not kidding," Mrs. Corson said. "She won't let him play with Anne. Anne's too dirty. She digs in the ground and stuff. Seven months we've lived in the same house, and those kids haven't played together once. Can you imagine that?"

"No," Mr. Palmer confessed. "I can't."

"She adopted it when it was six months old," Mrs. Corson said. "She tells us all it's a love-child." Her laugh began again, a continuous, hiccoughy chuckle. "Never lets go its hand," she said. "Won't let him play with anybody. Wipes him off like an heirloom. And brags around he's a love-child. My God!"

With her thin, freckled arm along the door and her lips puckered, she fell silent. "Love-child!" she said at last. "Did you ever look at her flat face? It's the last place love would ever settle on."

"Perhaps that explains," Mr. Palmer said uncomfortably. "She's childless, she's unattractive. She pours all that frustrated affection out on this child."

Mrs. Corson twisted to look almost incredulously into his face. "Of course," she said. Her alcoholic breath puffed at him. "Of course. But why toot it up as a love-child?" she said harshly. "What does she think my child is, for God's sake? How does she think babies are made?"

"Well, but there's that old superstition," Mr. Palmer said. He moved his hand sideward. "Children born of passion, you know — they're supposed to be more beautiful . . . "

"And doesn't that tell you anything about her?" Mrs. Corson said. "Doesn't that show you that she never thought of passion in the same world with her husband? She has to go outside herself for any passion, there's none in her."

"Yes," Mr. Palmer said. "Well, of course one can speculate, but one hardly knows . . . "

"And that damned dog," Mrs. Corson said. "Tommy can't play with other kids. They're too dirty. So she gets a dog. Dogs are cleaner than Anne, see? So she buys her child this nice germless dog, and then ties him up and won't let him loose. So the dog howls his head off, and we all go nuts. Finally we told her we couldn't stand it, why didn't she let it loose and let it run. But she said it might run away, and Tommy loved it so she didn't want to take a chance on losing the pup. So I finally called the Society for the Prevention of Cruelty to Animals, and they told her either to give it regular running and exercise or take it back. She took it back last night, and now she hates me."

As she talked, saliva had gathered in the corner of her mouth. She sucked it in and turned her head away, looking out on the street. "Lord God," she said. "So it goes, so it goes."

Through the windshield Mr. Palmer watched the quiet women on the wall, the quiet, well-behaved child. Anne was romping with the setter around the big stump, twenty feet beyond, and the little boy was watching her. It was a peaceful, windless morning steeped in sun. The mingled smell of pines and low tide drifted across the street, and was replaced by the pervading faint fragrance of ceanothus, blooming in shades of blue and white along Mr. Palmer's walk.

"I'm amazed," he said. "She seems so quiet and relaxed and plain."

"That's another thing," Mrs. Corson said. "She's a cover-yourself-up girl, too. Remember Margy Fisher, whose husband was killed a few weeks ago? You know why she never wore anything but a bathing suit? Because this old biddy was always after her about showing herself."

"Well, it's certainly a revelation," Mr. Palmer said. "I see you all from my window, you know, and it seems like a kind of symphony of waiting, all quiet and harmonious. The pregnant girl, too — going on with the slow inevitable business of life while her husband's gone, the rhythm of the generations unchanged. I've enjoyed the whole thing, like a pageant, you know."

"Your window isn't a very good peek-hole," Mrs. Corson said drily.

"Mm?"

"Hope's husband was killed at Dieppe," said Mrs. Corson.

For a moment Mr. Palmer did not catch on. At first he felt only a flash of pity as he remembered the girl's big steady brown eyes, her still, rather sad face, her air of pliant gentleness. Then the words Mrs. Corson had spoken began to take effect. Dieppe — almost three years ago. And the girl six months pregnant.

He wished Mrs. Corson would quit drumming her red nails on the car door. She was really in a state this morning, nervous as a cat. But that poor girl, sitting over there with all that bottled up inside of her, the fear and uncertainty growing as fast as the child in her womb grew . . .

"Some naval lieutenant," Mrs. Corson said. "He's right in the middle of the fighting, gunnery officer on a destroyer. You ought to hear Hope when she gets scared he'll never come back and make a decent woman of her."

"I'd not like to," Mr. Palmer said, and shook his head. Across the lane the placid scene had not changed, except that Mrs. Kendall had let Tommy toddle fifteen feet out from the wall, where he was picking up clusters of dry pine needles and throwing them into the air.

The figures were very clean, sharp-edged in the clear air against the blue backdrop of sea. An Attic grace informed all of them: the girl stooping above the long-eared red setter, the child with his hands in the air, tossing brown needles in a shower, the curving seated forms of the women on the wall. To Mr. Palmer's momentarily tranced eyes they seemed to freeze in attitudes of flowing motion like figures on a vase, cameo-clear in the clear air under the noble trees, with the quiet ocean of their watchfulness stretching blue to the misty edge. Like figures on a Grecian urn they curved in high relief above the white molding of the wall, and a drift of indescribable melancholy washed across the point and pricked goose-pimples on Mr. Palmer's arms. "It's sad," he said, opening the door and stepping down. "The whole thing is very sad."

With the intention of leaving he put his hand on the door and pushed it shut, thinking that he did not want to stay longer and hear Mrs. Corson's bitter tongue and watch the women on the wall. Their waiting now, with the momentary trance broken and the momentary lovely group dispersed in motion, seemed to him a monstrous aberration, their patience a deathly apathy, their hope an obscene self-delusion.

He was filled with a sense of the loveliness of the white

paper and the cleanly sharpened pencils, the notebooks and the quiet and the sense of purpose that waited in his study. Most of all the sense of purpose, the thing to be done that would have an ending and a result.

"It's been very pleasant," he said automatically. At that moment there came a yowl from the point.

He turned. Apparently Anne, romping with the dog, had bumped Tommy and knocked him down. He sat among the pine needles in his blue play-suit and squalled, and Mrs. Kendall came swiftly out from the wall and took Anne by the arm, shaking her.

"You careless child!" she said. "Watch what you're doing!"

Instantly Mrs. Corson was out of the car. Mr. Palmer saw her start for the point, her lips puckered, and was reminded of some mechanical toy lightly wound and tearing erratically around a room giving off sparks of ratchety noise. When she was twenty feet from Mrs. Kendall she shouted hoarsely, "Let go of that child!"

Mrs. Kendall's heavy gingham body turned. Her plain face, the mouth stiff with anger, confronted Mrs. Corson. Her hand still held Anne's arm. "It's possible to train children . . . " she said.

"Yes, and it's possible to mistreat them," Mrs. Corson said. "Let go of her."

For a moment neither moved. Then Mrs. Corson's hands darted down, caught Mrs. Kendall's wrist, and tore her hold from Anne's arm. Even across the lane, fifty feet away, Mr. Palmer could see the white fury in their faces as they confronted each other.

"If I had the bringing up of that child . . . !" Mrs. Kendall said. "I'd . . . "

"You'd tie her to your apron strings like you've tied your own," Mrs. Corson said. "Like you tie up a dog and expect it to get used to three feet of space. My God, a child's a little animal. He's got to run!"

"And knock other children down, I suppose."

"Oh my God!" Mrs. Corson said, and turned her thin face skyward as if to ask God to witness. She was shaking all over: Mr. Palmer could see the trembling of her dress. "Listen!" she said, "I don't know what's the matter with you, and why you can't stand nakedness, and why you think a bastard child is something holier than a legitimate one, and why you hang onto that child as if he was worth his weight in diamonds. But you keep your claws off mine, and if your little bastard can't get out of the way, you can just . . . "

Mrs. Kendall's face was convulsed. She raised both hands above her head, stuttering for words. From the side the pregnant girl slipped in quietly, and Mr. Palmer, rooted uneasily across the lane, heard her quiet voice. "You're beginning to draw a crowd," she said. "For the love of mike, turn it down."

Mrs. Corson swung on her. Her trembling had become an ecstasy. When she spoke she chewed loudly on her words, mangling them almost beyond recognition. "You keep out of this, you pregnant bitch," she said. "Any time I want advice on how to raise love children, I'll come to you too, but right now I haven't got any love children, and I'm raising what I've got my own way."

A window had gone up in the house next to Mr. Palmer's, and three boys were drifting curiously down the street, their pants sagging with the weight of armament they carried. Without hesitating more than a moment, Mr. Palmer crossed the street and cut them off. "I think you'd better beat it," he said, and pushed his hands in the air as if shooing chickens. The boys stopped and eyed him suspiciously, then began edging around the side. It was clear that in any contest of speed, agility, endurance, or anything else Mr. Palmer was no match for them. He put his hand in his pocket and pulled out some change. The boys stopped. Behind him Mr. Palmer heard the saw-edged voice of Mrs. Corson. "I'm not the kind of person that'll stand it, by God! If you want to . . . "

"Here," Mr. Palmer said. "Here's a quarter apiece if you light out and forget anything you saw."

"Okay!" they said, and stepped up one by one and got their quarters and retreated, their heads together and their armed hips clanking together and their faces turning once, together, to stare back at the arguing women on the point. Up the street Mr. Palmer saw a woman and three small children standing in the road craning. Mrs. Corson's voice carried for half a mile.

In the hope that his own presence would bring her to reason, Mr. Palmer walked across the lane. Mrs. Corson's puckered, furious face was thrust into Mrs. Kendall's, and she was saying, "Just tell me to my face I don't raise my child right! Go on, tell me so. Tell me what you told Margy, that Anne's too dirty for your bastard to play with. Tell me, I dare you, and I'll tear your tongue out!"

Mr. Palmer found himself standing next to Mrs. Vaughn. He glanced at her once and shook his head and cleared his throat. Mrs. Corson continued to glare into the pale flat face before her. When Mrs. Kendall turned heavily and walked toward the wall, the wrenlike woman skipped nimbly around her and confronted her from the other side. "You've got a lot of things to criticize in me!" she said. Her voice, suddenly, was so hoarse it was hardly more than a whisper. "Let's hear you say them to my face. I've heard them behind my back too long. Let's hear you say them!"

"Couldn't we get her into the house?" Mr. Palmer said to the pregnant girl. "She'll raise the whole neighborhood."

"Let her disgrace herself," Mrs. Vaughn said, and shrugged.

"But you don't understand," Mr. Palmer said. "She had a beer or so downtown, and I think that, that and the heat . . ."

The girl looked at him with wide brown eyes in which doubt and contempt and something like mirth moved like shadows on water. "I guess *you* don't understand," she said. "She isn't drunk. She's hopped."

"Hopped?"

"I thought you went downtown with her."

"I did."

"Did she leave you at the pony track?"

"Yes, for a few minutes."

"She goes to a joint down there," Mrs. Vaughn said. "Fortune telling in the front, goofballs and reefers in the rear. She's a sucker for all three."

"Goofballs?" Mr. Palmer said. "Reefers?"

"Phenobarb," Mrs. Vaughn said. "Marijuana. Anything. She doesn't care, long as she gets high. She's high as a kite now. Didn't you notice her eyes?"

Mrs. Kendall had got her boy by the hand. She was heavily ignoring Mrs. Corson. Now she lifted the child in her arms and turned sideways, like a cow ducking to the side to slip around a herder, and headed for the stone wall. Mrs. Corson whipped around her flanks, first on one side, then on the other, her hoarse whisper a continuing horror in Mr. Palmer's ears.

"What I ought to do," Mrs. Corson said, "is forbid Anne to even speak to that bastard of yours."

Mrs. Kendall bent and put the child on the ground and stood up. "Don't you call him that!" she shouted. "Oh, you vulgar, vicious, drunken, depraved woman! Leave me alone! Leave me alone, can't you?"

She burst into passionate tears. For a moment Mr.

Palmer was terrified that they would come to blows and
have to be pulled apart. He started forward, intending to
take Mrs. Corson by the arm and lead her, forcefully if
necessary, to the house. This disgraceful exhibition had
gone on long enough. But the pregnant girl was ahead of
him.

She walked past the glaring women and said over her
shoulder, carelessly, "Mail's here."

Mr. Palmer caught his cue. He put out his hand to
Anne, and walked her down across the mouth of the lane.
He did not look back, but his ears were sharp for a re-
newal of the cat-fight. None came. By the time the man
in gray had distributed the papers and magazines to all
the battery of boxes, and was unstrapping the pack of
letters, Mr. Palmer was aware without turning that both
Mrs. Corson and Mrs. Kendall were in the background by
the gray car, waiting quietly.

Buglesong

THERE had been a wind during the night, and all the loneliness of the world had swept up out of the southwest. The boy had heard it wailing through the screens of the sleeping porch where he lay, and he had heard the washtub bang loose from the outside wall and roll down toward the coulee, and the slam of the screen doors, and his mother's padding feet after she rose to fasten things down. Through one half-open eye he had peered up from his pillow to see the moon skimming windily in a luminous sky; in his mind he had seen the prairie outside with its woolly grass and cactus white under the moon, and the wind, whining across that endless oceanic land, sang in the screens, and sang him back to sleep.

Now, after breakfast, when he set out through the west pasture on the morning round of his gopher traps, there was no more wind, but the air smelled somehow recently

swept and dusted, as the house in town sometimes smelled
after his mother's whirlwind cleaning. The sun was gently
warm on the bony shoulder blades of the boy, and he
whistled, and whistling turned to see if the Bearpaws were
in sight to the south. There they were, a ghostly tenuous
outline of white just breaking over the bulge of the world:
the Mountains of the Moon, the place of running streams
and timber and cool heights that he had never seen —
only dreamed of on days when the baked clay of the farmyard cracked in the heat and the sun brought cedar smells
from fence posts long since split and dry and odorless,
when he lay dreaming on the bed in the sleeping porch
with a Sears Roebuck catalogue open before him, picking
out the presents he would buy for his mother and his
father and his friends next Christmas, or the Christmas
after that. On those days he looked often and long at the
snowy mountains to the south, while the dreams rose in
him like heat waves, blurring the reality of the unfinished
shack that was his summer home.

The Bearpaws were there now, and he watched them a
moment, walking, his feet dodging cactus clumps automatically, before he turned his attention again to the traps
before him, their locations marked by a zigzag line of
stakes. He ran the line at a half-trot, whistling.

At the first stake the chain was stretched tightly into the
hole. The pull on its lower end had dug a little channel in
the soft earth of the mound. Gently, so as not to break the
gopher's leg off, the boy eased the trap out of the burrow,
held the chain in his left hand, and loosened the stake
with his right. The gopher lunged against the heavy trap,
but it did not squeal. They squealed, the boy had noticed,
only when at a distance, or when the weasel had them.
Otherwise they kept still.

For a moment the boy debated whether to keep this one

alive for the weasel or to wait till the last trap so that he wouldn't have to carry the live one around. Deciding to wait, he held the chain out, measured the rodent for a moment, and swung. The knobbed end of the stake crushed the animal's skull, and the eyes popped out of the head, round and blue. A trickle of blood started from nose and ears.

Releasing the gopher, the boy lifted it by the tail and snapped its tail-fur off with a dexterous flip. Then he stowed the trophy carefully in the breast pocket of his overalls. For the last two years he had won the grand prize offered by the province of Saskatchewan to the school child who destroyed the most gophers. On the mantel in town were two silver loving cups, and in a shoe box under his bed in the farmhouse there were already eight hundred and forty tails, the catch of three weeks. His whole life on the farm was devoted to the destruction of the rodents. In the wheat fields he distributed poison, but in the pasture, where stock might get the tainted grain, he trapped, snared, or shot them. Any method he preferred to poisoning: that offered no excitement, and he seldom got the tails because the gophers crawled down their holes to die.

Picking up trap and stake, the boy kicked the dead animal down its burrow and scraped dirt over it with his foot. They stunk up the pasture if they weren't buried, and the bugs got into them. Frequently he had stood to windward of a dead and swollen gopher, watching the body shift and move with the movements of the beetles and crawling things working through it. If such an infested corpse were turned over, the beetles would roar out of it, great orange-colored, hard-shelled, scavenging things that made his blood curdle at the thought of their touching him, and after they were gone and he looked again he would see the little black ones, undisturbed, seething through the rotten flesh. So he always buried his dead, now.

Through the gardens of red and yellow cactus blooms he went whistling, half trotting, setting the traps anew whenever a gopher shot upright, squeaked, and ducked down its burrow at his approach. All but two of the first seventeen traps held gophers, and he came to the eighteenth confidently, expecting to take this one alive. But this gopher had gone into the trap head first, and the boy put back into his pocket the salt sack he had brought along as a game bag. He would have to snare or trap one down by the dam.

On the way back he stopped with bent head while he counted his day's catch of tails, mentally adding this lot of sixteen to the eight hundred and forty he already had, trying to remember how many he had had at this time last year. As he finished his mathematics his whistle broke out again, and he galloped down through the pasture, running for very abundance of life, until he came to the chicken house just within the plowed fireguard.

Under the eaves of the chicken house, so close that the hens were constantly pecking up to its very door and then almost losing their wits with fright, was the made-over beer case that contained the weasel. Screen had been tacked tightly under the wooden lid, which latched, and in the screen was cut a tiny wire door. In the front, along the bottom, a single board had been removed and replaced with screen.

The boy lifted the hinged top and looked down into the cage.

"Hello," he said. "Hungry?"

The weasel crouched, its long snaky body humped, its head thrust forward and its malevolent eyes staring with lidless savagery into the boy's.

"Tough, ain't you?" said the boy. "Just wait, you blood-thirsty old stinker, you. Wait'll you turn into an ermine. Won't I skin you quick, hah?"

There was no dislike or emotion in his tone. He took the weasel's malignant ferocity with the same indifference he displayed in his gopher killing. Weasels, if you could keep them long enough, were valuable. He would catch a lot, keep them until they turned white, and sell their hides as ermine. Maybe he could breed them and have an ermine farm. He was the best gopher trapper in Saskatchewan. Once he had even caught a badger. Why not weasels? The trap broke their leg, but nothing could really hurt a weasel permanently. This one, though virtually three-legged, was as savage and lively as ever. Every morning he had a live gopher for his breakfast, in spite of the protests of the boy's mother that it was cruel. But nothing, she had said, was cruel to the boy.

When she argued that the gopher had no chance when thrown into the cage, the boy retorted that he didn't have a chance when the weasel came down the hole after him either. If she said that the real job he should devote himself to was exterminating the weasels, he replied that then the gophers would get so thick they would eat the fields down to stubble. At last she gave up, and the weasel continued to have his warm meals.

For some time the boy stood watching his captive, and then he turned and went into the house, where he opened the oat box in the kitchen and took out a chunk of dried beef. From this he cut a thick slice with the butcher knife, and went munching into the sleeping porch where his mother was making beds.

"Where's that little double naught?" he asked.

"That what?"

"That little wee trap. The one I use for catching live ones for the weasel."

"Hanging out by the laundry bench, I think. Are you going out trapping again now?"

"Lucifer hasn't had his breakfast yet."

"How about your reading?"

"I'n take the book along and read while I wait," the boy said. "I'm just goin' down to the coulee at the edge of the dam."

"I *can*, not 'Ine,' son."

"I can," the boy said. "I am most delighted to comply with your request."

He grinned at his mother. He could always floor her with a quotation from a letter or the Sears Roebuck catalogue.

With the trap swinging from his hand, and under his arm the book — *Narrative and Lyric Poems,* edited by Somebody-or-other — which his mother kept him reading during the summer "so that next year he could be at the head of his class again," the boy walked out into the growing heat.

From the northwest the coulee angled down through the pasture, a shallow swale dammed just above the house to catch the spring run-off of snow water. In the moist dirt of the dam grew ten-foot willows planted as slips by the boy's father. They were the only things resembling trees in sixty miles. Below the dam, watered by the slow seepage from above, the coulee bottom was a parterre of flowers, buttercups in broad sheets, wild sweet pea, and "stinkweed." On the slopes were evening primroses, pale pink and white and delicately fragrant, and on the flats above the yellow and red burgeoning of the cactuses.

Just under the slope of the coulee a female gopher and three half-grown puppies basked on their warm mound. The boy chased them squeaking down their hole and set the trap carefully, embedding it partially in the soft earth.

Then he retired back up the shoulder of the swale, where he lay full length on his stomach, opened the book, shifted so that the glare of the sun across the pages was blocked by the shadow of his head and shoulders, and began to read.

From time to time he stopped reading to roll on his side and stare out across the coulee, across the barren plains pimpled with gopher mounds and bitten with fire and haired with dusty woolly grass. Apparently as flat as a table, the land sloped imperceptibly to the south, so that nothing interfered with his view of the ghostly line of mountains, now more plainly visible as the heat increased. Between the boy's eyes and that smoky outline sixty miles away the heat waves rose writhing like fine wavy hair. He knew that in an hour Pankhurst's farm would lift above the swelling knoll to the west. Many times he had seen that phenomenon — had seen his friend Jason Pankhurst playing in the yard or watering horses when he knew that the whole farm was out of sight. It was the heat waves that did it, his father said.

The gophers below had been thoroughly scared, and for a long time nothing happened. Idly the boy read through his poetry lesson, dreamfully conscious of the hard ground under him, feeling the gouge of a rock under his stomach without making any effort to remove it. The sun was a hot caress between his shoulder blades, and on the bare flesh where his overalls pulled above his sneakers it bit like a burning glass. Still he was comfortable, supremely relaxed and peaceful, lulled into a half-trance by the heat and the steamy flower smells and the mist of yellow in the buttercup coulee below.

And beyond the coulee was the dim profile of the Bearpaws, the Mountains of the Moon.

The boy's eyes, pulled out of focus by his tranced state,

fixed on the page before him. Here was a poem he knew
. . . but it wasn't a poem, it was a song. His mother sang
it often, working at the sewing machine in winter.

It struck him as odd that a poem should also be a song,
and because he found it hard to read without bringing in
the tune, he lay quietly in the full glare of the sun, singing
the page softly to himself. As he sang the trance grew on
him again; he lost himself entirely. The bright hard di-
viding lines between individual senses blurred, and buttercups, smell of primrose, feel of hard gravel under body
and elbows, sight of the ghosts of mountains haunting the
southern horizon, were one intensely felt experience fo-
cused by the song the book had evoked.

And the song was the loveliest thing he had ever known.
He felt the words, tasted them, breathed upon them with
all the ardor of his captivated senses.

> The splendor falls on castle walls
> And snowy summits old in story. . . .

The current of his imagination flowed southward over
the strong gentle shoulder of the world to the ghostly
outline of the Mountains of the Moon, haunting the heat-
distorted horizon.

> Oh hark, oh hear, how thin and clear,
> And thinner, clearer, farther going,
> Oh, sweet and far, from cliff and scar . . .

In the enchanted forests of his mind the horns of elfland
blew, and his breath was held in the slow-falling cadence
of their dying. The weight of the sun had been lifted from
his back. The empty prairie of his home was castled and
pillared with the magnificence of his imagining, and the
sound of horns died thinly in the direction of the Mountains of the Moon.

From the coulee below came the sudden metallic clash

of the trap, and an explosion of frantic squeals smothered almost immediately in the burrow. The boy leaped up, thrusting the book into the wide pocket of his overalls, and ran down to the mound. The chain, stretched down the hole, jerked convulsively, and when the boy took hold of it he felt the terrified life at the end of it strain to escape. Tugging gently, he forced loose the gopher's digging claws, and hauled the squirming captive from the hole.

On the way up to the chicken house the dangling gopher with a tremendous muscular effort convulsed itself upward from the broken and imprisoned leg, and bit with a sharp rasp of teeth on the iron. Its eyes, the boy noticed impersonally, were shining black, like the head of a hatpin. He thought it odd that when they popped out of the head after a blow they were blue.

At the cage by the chicken house he lifted the cover and peered through the screen. The weasel, scenting the blood of the gopher's leg, backed against the far wall of the box, yellow body tense as a spring, teeth showing in a tiny soundless snarl.

Undoing the wire door with his left hand, the boy held the trap over the hole. Then he bore down with all his strength on the spring, releasing the gopher, which dropped on the straw-littered floor and scurried into the corner opposite its enemy.

The weasel's three good feet gathered under it and it circled, very slowly, around the wall, its lips still lifted to expose the soundless snarl. The abject gopher crowded against the boards, turned once and tried to scramble up the side, fell back on its broken leg, and whirled like lightning to face its executioner again. The weasel moved carefully, circling.

Then the gopher screamed, a wild, agonized, despairing

squeal that made the watching boy swallow and wet his lips. Another scream, wilder and louder than before, and before the sound had ended the weasel struck. There was a fierce flurry in the straw of the cage before the killer got its hold just back of the gopher's right ear, and its teeth began tearing ravenously at the still-quivering body. In a few minutes, the boy knew, the gopher's carcass would be as limp as an empty skin, with all its blood sucked out and a hole as big as the ends of his two thumbs where the weasel had dined.

Still the boy remained staring through the screen top of the cage, face rapt and body completely lost. And after a few minutes he went into the sleeping porch, stretched out on the bed, opened the Sears Roebuck catalogue, and dived so deeply into its fascinating pictures and legends that his mother had to shake him to make him hear her call to lunch.

Balance His, Swing Yours

THE PING of tennis rackets was a warm, summer-afternoon sound in the air as Mr. Hart came up through the hedge. He stopped to survey the grounds, the red roof of the hotel, the fans of coco palms graceful beyond the white wall. Past the wall the coral rock broke off in ledges to the beach, and beyond the sand was the incredible peacock water of the Gulf.

February. It was hard to imagine, with that sun, the brown skins of the bathers between the palms, the ping of rackets. The whole place, to Mr. Hart's Colorado eyes, was fantastic — hibiscus and bougainvillea and night-blooming jasmine. He squirmed his shoulders against the itching warmth of his first sunburn, caught the previous afternoon, and ruminated on the hardly believable thought that to many people this summer-in-February paradise was a commonplace thing.

The sound of tennis led him past the shuffleboard courts and around a backstop cascading with scarlet bougain-villea. A girl was playing with the pro, and beyond the court, in lawn chairs, lay two of the three people Mr. Hart had so far met. His reaction was immediate. Good. Good it was the two boys, not the impossible Englishman who had descended on him at breakfast. He cut across the lawn toward them.

The young men in the chairs, one very blond, one dark and impressively profiled, did not stir. They lay in their swimming trunks, inert and sprawling, and when Mr. Hart asked, "Were you saving these other chairs?" they looked up indolently, two loafing demigods with mahogany hides. The blond one lifted his towel out of a chair, and Mr. Hart sat down with a sigh.

"What a place!" he said.

The blond one — Thomas, Mr. Hart remembered — turned his head. He seemed a pleasant sort of boy. "Like it?" he said.

Mr. Hart lifted his hands. "It's incredible. I had no idea — I've never been down before. Even the fishing boats coming in in the evening are a nice institution. Have you tried the fishing?"

"Once or twice," Thomas said. He slumped further down in his chair. Mr. Hart found a pack of cigarettes, stretched to pass them over Thomas' body. He got a shake of the head, no thanks, from the dark one, Tenney, but Thomas took one.

"I've been thinking I might hook up with a party," Mr. Hart said. "This water fascinates me. The water and these silly little mangrove islands. I've read about mangroves all my life — never saw one. Now I find they're not islands at all, not a spoonful of dirt in them, just clumps of ocean-going shrubs."

"Yeah," Thomas said. He lay with the cigarette between

his lips, his eyes lidded like a lizard's against the sun. Tenney seemed to sleep.

"I guess I interrupted your siesta," Hart said. "I just can't get over this place. I'll keep quiet now."

"Not at all," Thomas said, but Mr. Hart leaned back and watched the tennis. He had no desire to intrude on people. And it was good tennis to watch, he admitted. But Eastern tennis, the rhythmical and somehow mechanical tennis of people who learned the game as a social accomplishment. In an obscure way he felt superior to it. He had learned in a different school, municipal hard courts, worn balls. Still, he felt he could lick three out of four of these mechanical marvels.

His eye was caught by Tenney's feet, big naked feet, arched like the feet of a statued Mercury and brown as stained wood, the leather thongs of the sandals coming up between great and second toes. They struck him as arrogant feet. The boy had a lordly air, sure enough. There was something really admirable in the way he and his companion lolled. This was their birthright, and their arrogance was simply acceptance of something perfectly natural and right.

The blond youth turned, and Mr. Hart nodded toward the court. "The girl has nice shots."

"One of these tennis drunkards," Thomas said. "Lives tennis twenty-four hours a day."

"I like to see that," Mr. Hart said. "I like to see people simply dissolve themselves in the thing that interests them. I can remember when I was that way about tennis myself."

"Oh," Thomas said. "You're a tennis player."

Mr. Hart shrugged deprecatingly. "Used to be, in a way. Haven't done much with it since college, just a game now and then."

"What college?"

"I grew up in the West," Mr. Hart said. "Went to the local cow college."

Tenney leaned toward them. "I hate to interrupt," he said, "but look what's bearing down on us."

He jerked a thumb. The impossible little Englishman, in his pink polo shirt, was walking springily on the balls of his feet down the path from the cocktail garden. "Oh, my God," Hart said.

The two were both looking at him. "Has he got to you, too?" Tenney said. His look of distaste had dissolved into cynical amusement.

"For an hour at breakfast," Hart said. "Why can't people like that go to Miami, where they belong? Maybe we ought to run."

They smiled their relaxed, indolent smiles. "Lie and take it," Thomas said. "That's the least painful way."

Mr. Hart slid down in his chair and prepared his muscles for the relaxed indifference with which this interloper would have to be met. "But what a blowhard!" he said. "Did you know he was being bombarded from all sides to write a play for Cornell? My God."

He shut up abruptly. In a moment the British voice — vulgar British voice, Mr. Hart thought — was right above him. "Ah," it said. "Taking a little sun?"

"Hello," Thomas said, pleasantly enough. Tenney looked up and nodded. So did Mr. Hart. It was a cool reception, but it wasn't cool enough, Mr. Hart thought, for this rhinoceros to feel it.

"Topping day for it," the Englishman said. He sat down and took out his pipe, watching the tennis game while he filled and lighted. His fingers, holding the blown-out match, waved gently back and forth.

"She's not bad, you know," he said conversationally. "Pity she doesn't have a sounder backhand."

Mr. Hart regarded him coldly. "What's wrong with her backhand?" he said.

"Not enough follow-through," the Englishman said. "And she's hitting it too much on the rise."

Tenney said, grunting from his slumped chest. "She ought to be told."

The Englishman took his pipe from his mouth. "Eh?"

"You ought to put her right," said Mr. Hart.

All he got was a grin and wag of the head. "Not in front of these pros, you know. The beggars think they know it all."

Mr. Hart impatiently recrossed his neatly creased legs. "You sound as if you were an expert," he said, with just the suggestion of a slur. It was exactly the right tone, ambiguous without being insulting. Sooner or later anybody, confronted by that tone, would begin to wonder if he were wanted.

"Know a bit about it," the Englishman said. He waved his pipe at the court, talking too loud. "Watch her forehand, too. She's cocking her racket up too much at right angles with her wrist." His head moved back and forth, following a fast rally. "So's the pro," he cackled. "So's the pro, swelp me. Look at 'im!"

"The ball," said Mr. Hart, "seems to be going back and forth pretty fast."

"Ping-pong," the Englishman said. "Anybody who hit it instead of slapping it that way would have put it away by now."

Tenney was lying back staring at the sky, where a man-o'-war hawk alternately soared and sped on dark, bent wings. Tenney was like a hawk himself, Mr. Hart thought. Dark and built for speed. The Mercury foot, and the arrogance to go with it. He was built to run down little web-footed gulls like this Englishman and take their fish away from them. But all he did was stare at the sky and wag one foot over the footrest. Thomas, ordinarily more talkative, now seemed to be asleep. Mr. Hart simmered. It had been very pleasant, very quiet, very friendly, till this terrier with the big yap butted in.

". . . thing I miss in America," the Englishman was saying. "Never can get up a good game. Any public-school boy in England plays a good game as a matter of course. Here nobody seems to."

The idea came gently to Mr. Hart's door, and he opened to it. It might boomerang, but he thought not. His mind went scornful. Pestered to write a play for Cornell. Like hell. Bothered to do articles for the *Britannica.* My Aunt Annica. Aldington wanting him to come in on an anthology. In a pig's physiology. British public school likewise. Tennis as well.

"It *is* hard to get a game, sometimes," he said. "If I wasn't afraid of getting out of my class I'd suggest we play."

"Yes," the Englishman said cordially. "Have to do that."

"How about this afternoon, now?"

Tenney started to whistle lightly. The whistle was encouraging to Mr. Hart. It said, Go ahead, pin his ears down.

"This weather might not last, even here," Hart said. "Little exercise'd do us good. That is, if you'd step down to my level."

"Oh, step down!" the Englishman said. "Not at all!"

"Let's have a set then. The court'll be empty in a minute."

The Englishman knocked out his pipe, looked back toward the empty cocktail garden, puckered his lips. He had a pulpy nose and prominent teeth. "I didn't bring a racket," he said. "Perhaps . . ."

"The pro'll have some."

The Englishman rose. "Very well," he said. "I'll go pop into my things." He went toward the hotel, walking springily, a preposterous, lumpy little blowhard, and Mr. Hart dropped a look of grim anticipation at the two lazy, amused youths.

"The International Matches," Tenney said. "Shall I cry 'Well struck, Cow College!' now and again?"

"Don't encourage me," said Mr. Hart. "I might start shooting for the little stinker's belt buckle."

The Englishman looked even more preposterous in shorts than he had in polo shirt and slacks. His muscles were knobbly, his bones stuck out like the elbows of characters in comic strips. Mr. Hart, leading the way onto the court, was aware of the young men watching from their somnolent chairs. It was as if he had made them a promise. Opening the can of balls he made another to himself. He was going to play every shot as if dollars depended on it.

"Here we go," he said cheerily, and wafted a warm-up ball across the net. From the very awkwardness of the Englishman's run he knew his plan was not going to boomerang. The goof looked as if he'd never been on a court before. This, he told himself happily, was murder.

It was a murder that he enjoyed thoroughly. For three quarters of an hour he ran the Englishman's tongue out, tricked him with soft chops that died in the clay, outran him with topped drives into the corners, aced him with flat services, left him going full steam in the wrong direction for an occasional American twist. He was playing carefully himself, not hitting anything too hard until he got a kill, and then plastering it with everything he had. He blessed the high altitude and worn balls of his youth which had made him learn to murder a high ball. The

Englishman's game, when there was any, gave him little to hit except soft high bouncers, big as a basketball and begging to be swatted.

As he went about his methodical mayhem his amazement grew. The Englishman didn't have a thing. Then why in the world would he have the consummate gall to talk the way he had? Mr. Hart could not imagine; but he saw the two watchers in their chairs, and his unspoken compact with them kept him at the butchery. The Englishman got six points the first set, and his face was a little strained as they changed courts. You bloody upstart, Mr. Hart thought. This is where you learn to be humble. He stepped up to the service line prepared to skunk the Englishman completely, never give him a point.

In the middle of the set the two young men rose and stretched and picked up their towels. They lifted their hands and walked off toward the bath-houses, and Mr. Hart, a little disappointed at the loss of his audience, went on finishing the thing off. The Englishman was feeling his shoulder between shots now. Obviously, thought Mr. Hart, he has pulled a muscle. Obviously.

At five-love the Englishman walked up to the net. "I say, do you mind? I seem to have done something to my shoulder here. Can't seem to take a decent swing."

Mr. Hart picked up the ball can and his sweater. Without really wanting to, he let the alibi establish itself. "No use to play with a bad arm," he said. And looking at the grimace pretending to be pain on the little man's face, he said, almost kindly and to his own astonishment, "It was spoiling your game. I could see you weren't up to scratch."

"Makes me damned mad," the Englishman said. "Here I've mucked up your whole afternoon. Couldn't hit a thing after the first game or two."

"Too bad," said Mr. Hart. And so, condoling one another, they went back to the hotel. It was funny. It was,
Mr. Hart decided while he was dressing, so damned funny
he ought to be rolling on the bed stuffing covers in his
mouth. That he was not, he laid to the complete incorrigi-
bility of that dreadful little man. People like that would
never see themselves straight. No innuendo, no humili-
ation, would ever teach them anything. Hopelessly in-
adequate, they must constantly be butting into situations
and places where they didn't belong. Mr. Hart shrugged.
Let him live. The hell with him. If he couldn't be overlooked, he could be avoided.

He brushed off his white shoes, felt his tie, and looked
in the mirror. Nose and forehead pretty red. For an instant of irritation he wished he wouldn't always burn and
peel before he tanned. There was some system — tannic
acid, was it? — but he always forgot till too late. The
regulars around here, he was sure, never peeled.

In the dining room there were flowers bright against the
stiff linen on every table, and the ladderlike shadow of a
palm frond fell across the floor from the west windows.
Mr. Hart answered the headwaiter's bow and stepped
down into the cocktail lounge. There was no one there
except two waiters, the bartender, and some stuffed fish.
Outside, however, several tables were occupied. At one
of them sat Thomas and Tenney, and as Mr. Hart started
over he noticed that they still wore sandals and no socks.
Their arrogant feet seemed at home and unembarrassed.
He wondered if they wore socks to dinner, and it crossed
his mind that he might be overdressing. White jacket
might look like ostentation. He didn't want that.

"Well!" said Mr. Hart, and sat down. "What's a good
drink here?"

Tenney shrugged. His amber, remote, hawklike eyes

were away off down the garden, then briefly on Mr. Hart. "Rum collins?"

Mr. Hart signaled a waiter. The three sat quietly while people came in twos and threes into the garden. The young men did not speak of the tennis match. Neither did Mr. Hart. And he did not remember, until a small party came pushing a blue wheelbarrow with a sailfish in it, that he had meant to go down and watch the boats come in.

There were a gray-haired man and a blonde older woman and a wind-blown, pretty girl in the party. They came through the garden in triumph, calling to people to witness. Everybody seemed to know them. Everyone got up and crowded around and admired. Thomas and Tenney went over with their glasses in their hands, and Mr. Hart rose, but did not want to push in. "Fifty-nine pounds," the girl said. "And *I* caught it. Little me." The tempo of the garden had picked up; the lazy afternoon was already accelerating into cocktail hour, dinner hour, the evening dance. Mr. Hart, standing at the edge of the crowd, thought what really pleasant fun it would be to spend a day that way. The fishing party seemed pleasant, agreeable people. And it would be fun to catch a thing like that sailfish. Lovely to see him break the peacock water.

"Come on," the girl said. "I'm buying the drinks on this one." She hooked arms with Tenney and Thomas, the gray-haired man picked up the handles of the wheelbarrow, and they went up the garden to a table under the hedge.

Mr. Hart stood a moment alone. Then he sat down. The chatter, the bright afternoon sounds, went over him, and he heard the fishing girl's brittle tinkle of laughter. The long light of evening lay over the palms and the flowering trees and the golf-green lawn. Waiters tipped the umbrellas sideways and lifted the steel butts from the holes and stacked the canvas against the hedge. Mr. Hart watched them; his eyes went beyond them to the party at the hedge table, Tenney and Thomas leaning forward, no languor about them now, their talk animated.

Beside his own table he saw his immaculate buck foot. It irritated him, somehow, and he put it out of sight. The bronze feet of Tenney and Thomas, he noticed, were in plain view as they tipped their chairs forward to talk to the fishermen. The dead fish's fin stuck up from the blue wheelbarrow like a black-violet lacquered fan. It was while he watched them that the cold finger touched Mr. Hart, and he knew what it was.

The garden was full of people now, brown-faced, casual. They were necessary, Mr. Hart thought, to complete the picture. The whole garden, tipped with light through the palms, was like a Seurat. And he sat alone, outside the picture. There were two rings of moisture on the enameled table, left by the glasses of Tenney and Thomas. Very carefully Mr. Hart squeegeed them off with his thumb and finger and wiped his hands on his handkerchief. When he looked up he saw the Englishman, fantastically white and sluglike in this garden of brown demigods, standing in the doorway of the lounge in white jacket and ascot tie, looking around the tables.

For an instant Mr. Hart hesitated. He heard the brittle chatter and laughter from the other tables. His elbows felt the tug of hands, heard the voices saying, "Come on, let's have a drink on it," his bronze face felt the sun as he went with the others across to a corner table. . . .

His fingers went around the cold glass, raised it. With his other hand he signaled the Englishman standing in the doorway.

✿ ✿ ✿

Saw Gang

THE SUN had not yet risen above the woods when Ernie started, and the grass on the little road up through the hemlocks was crisp with frost. As he topped the stiff climb and came out onto Thurson's meadow, above the town reservoir, the first flat rays hit him in the face.

He put his double-bitted axe through the fence, climbed through after it, crossed the meadow, and jumped the swamp from hummock to hummock until he entered the cedars. Cattle had been among the low growth; their split tracks were sucked deep into the ground and half frozen there.

On the other side of the rail fence belting the cedars he came again into open meadow, still green after a late mowing, and saw the long hill ahead of him, winter-black spruce scattered through the dying color of the maples. October was a very taste in the air of smoke and frost and dried seed pods, and he filled his lungs with it, walking rapidly up toward Pembrook's farm and the crown of woods behind it where George Pembrook was cutting wood.

He did not trouble to stop in the Pembrook's yard, but ducked under the last fence and went on up the skid road George had worn hauling limb wood down to his circle saw. As he climbed, the sun climbed with him, but the air still had its winy sparkle, and there was a smell from grass and weeds as the frost thawed.

Just where the skid road turned left up a little draw toward the sugarbush, he saw Will Livesy and Donald Swain coming across from the other side, both with axes. Their greetings were brief.

"Hi, kid," Donald said.

"Hi, boy," said Will.

They walked along together, not talking. Ernie, matching his behavior to theirs, walked steadily, watching the woods. Only when Donald Swain breathed his lungs full of air, shifted his axe to the other shoulder, and said, "Good workin' weather," the boy looked at him and they grinned. It was what he had wanted to say himself.

Ahead of them, back in the woods, the saw engine started, and a minute later they heard the blade rip across the first log. Will Livesy took out a turnip watch, turned it for the others to see. It was seven-thirty. "Ain't wastin' no time," Will said.

The saw was set up in a clearing at the bottom of a slope. Behind it was a skidway piled ten feet high with logs. George Pembrook was there, and his brother Howard, and John LaPere, the sawyer. George, dogging a log forward under the upraised saw, spat sideways on the ground, unsmiling.

"Up late last night?"

"'y God," Will Livesy said, "I was up all night. Got any wood to chop to keep me awake?"

George looked at the mountainous skidway behind him. "Just a mite," he said.

Ernie stood his axe against a tree and jumped to roll a chunk, solid and squat as a meat block, from under the saw. Donald and Will squared away. Donald spat on his hands, swung: the blade bounded from the hard wood. A second later Will's axe came down on the other side, in the mathematical center of the chunk, and got a bite. Donald swung again, his blade biting into the crack his first blow had made, a quarter of an inch from Will's axe, and the chunk fell cleanly in two.

Everybody found a job and went at it. Howard Pembrook rolled logs down onto the track, George dogged them through and braced them, LaPere dropped the saw onto them and whacked them into stove lengths, Ernie cleared them away, Donald and Will split. In the leaf-and-chip-strewn clearing, under the thinning maples, the pulse of the saw went up like the panting of a man.

Every hour or two, without talking about it, they changed off jobs, all except LaPere and Donald Swain. The work went on without pause while the sun climbed higher above the hill and the air warmed. Once in a while, seeing the lower part of the skidway bare, Ernie left his job and helped roll a new supply of logs down the skids with cant hooks. Nobody said anything.

About eleven, as Will was poking a six-inch pole under the saw, LaPere raised his denim cap and looked down his nose at the thing. Most of the logs they had been sawing were birch and beech and maple anywhere from eighteen to thirty inches through.

"Call that a log?" he said.

Will grinned. "George lost his fishpole."

A few minutes later, as Ernie rolled a big twisted knotty rot-sided maple log onto the tracks and Will dogged it forward, LaPere let the saw down experimentally and raked it across the crumbling bark. "Kind of gone by, ain't it?"

"Best George could find," Will said. He dropped the bracing lever across the log and threw his weight on it. LaPere bore down on the clutch and the jerking blade came down. Halfway through the pulpy log it hit a hard knot, the blade bent almost double, the log kicked sideways off the track as Will's lever slipped on the rotten bark and flipped upward like a swung bat. By the time LaPere could raise the saw the blade had jumped free and hung quivering, shaking shredded pulp from its two-inch teeth. Will was standing with his head down, feeling his jaw.

"Thunderation!" George Pembrook said. "That was a whack."

"Lever kicked up," Donald Swain said, watching Will. He said it for nobody in particular; they had all looked up instantly at the warning howl of the saw. "Took him right under the chin," Donald said.

Will felt his jaw tenderly. His hat had fallen off, and his thin red hair stuck up on end. Looking down from the platform, LaPere chuckled.

"Lose any teeth, Will?"

Will shook his head to clear it, felt his chin again, and cackled with sudden laughter. " 'y God, I didn't have 'em in!" he said. He rolled the log back with a hook, and they were working again so abruptly that Ernie had to jump to get the chunk from under the saw.

At noon, without comment, LaPere cut the switch and the engine stopped with three lunging coughs. Donald and George sank their axes in the chunk they had been splitting, they all collected their frocks from the trees where they had hung them, and within three minutes they were strung out along the trail on their way to the farmhouse.

Ernie did not push himself up with the others. Though he had known them all his life, he knew better at fifteen than to take it for granted he was one of them. In silence he followed the silent file until they came into the open opposite George's sugarhouse. There John LaPere, walking with George Pembrook, stopped and stared, and the rest piled up behind him.

"Great God, George!" LaPere said.

A little clump of spruces had been chopped down by the side of the road, and Ernie, coming up behind the clot of men, saw that the trees had been whittled and chewed and mangled with a dull axe and finally broken off instead of being chopped off clean.

"That city kid I had this summer," George said. "I think he used his teeth."

One by one, as they started again, the men looked at the mangled butts, then at each other. They whistled, grinning a little, and walked on. Will Livesy, a black smear of blood like a beard under his chin, turned and shook his head at Ernie, calling his attention to the stumps.

The table was set at the Pembrooks'. George changed from gum boots to slippers and turned on the radio while the men went one by one to the sink to wash. Ernie went last. By the time he sat down, the governor from Montpelier was discussing with the state the provisions he was making for coal supplies, and they listened to him in silence for twenty minutes, steadily consuming two plates apiece of Mrs. Pembrook's meat loaf, baked potatoes, hot biscuits, string beans, carrots, and sweet pickle.

They finished neck and neck with the governor, loitered briefly outside in the sun while George got back into gum boots, and then went silently back up the skid road past the sugarhouse and the gnawed spruce stumps and into the woods. Before LaPere had his engine started Howard Pembrook and Donald Swain were swinging splitting hammers on the tough and knotty chunks that they had rolled aside earlier.

In midafternoon George's hound wandered up muddy-footed from chasing through a swamp. It went around to each man, and each stopped for a second to scratch its ears, until it came to LaPere, up on the shaking platform. Then the hound sat down. "Hi, Sport," LaPere said.

About three-thirty, with the saw halfway through a big yellow birch log, the engine died. LaPere looked surprised. " 'Nuts,' said McGinty," he said. He opened the gas cap, stuck a twig down, raised his eyebrows, and reached for the gas can. Ernie, straightening up to ease his aching back, saw that none of the others was stopping. Howard and Will were rolling down a new supply of logs, Donald and George stacking stovewood against the spreading pile to keep it from engulfing the splitting space. Ernie got the shovel and cleaned the sawdust out from under the track.

Through the whole afternoon, while the sun rolled down the long slope of the western hills and the hound got bored and wandered away and the stack of split wood got head high, and more than head high, they worked steadily and in silence. Ernie, his back and his belly sore from leaning and lifting, kept his mouth shut and worked with them. He knew they would never have worked like this for any employer, that they kept up the pace only because they all owed George help and would give nothing but their best day's work in exchange. Still, he kept listening, half hopeful that the engine would die again. The great pile of logs had receded twenty feet up the skidway, and sawdust was ankle deep all around the saw.

About four George began jacking the logs thirty inches forward instead of fifteen. "Got about enough stovewood," he said.

The erratic, tearing rhythm of the saw, the panting of the engine, went on, punctuated by the solid, wet *chunk* of the splitters' axes. Behind the splitters another pile began to grow, furnace chunks this time. The hound came back, found no one to scratch its ears, and disappeared again. The logs came faster off the skids now; George's hand on the dogging lever was almost as regular as a hand on a pump handle.

The sun was shining through the maples, almost flat over the hill, when LaPere cut the switch. This time the men did not immediately drop what they were doing. Ernie, looking around gratefully in the expectation that the day was finally over, saw Donald and Howard finishing up a dozen blocks. Donald, who had been splitting steadily, without change or rest, since seven-thirty, was cleaning up all the gnarled and knotty chunks that had resisted him before. LaPere was gassing and oiling the engine and taking out the blade for sharpening. Will was shoveling out sawdust. Unwillingly, because he couldn't help it, Ernie went and helped George roll down logs from the skids for the next day.

It was fifteen minutes before they all picked up their frocks. For a while George Pembrook stood looking at the two mighty heaps of sawed and split wood. "I'm obliged to you, boys," he said. "Way I felt when I was skiddin' them up, I thought there was a week's sawing there."

LaPere worked his eyebrows. "Can't be more'n about thirty run."

"If there ain't fifty already split I'll eat all the bark and sawdust," George said.

Winking at Donald Swain, LaPere drew his mouth down sorrowfully. "Never make fifty in a day, not without better help'n we had."

"Guess the help got to it fast as you could saw it," Donald said.

LaPere looked at the remaining pile of logs. "Only another half-day," he said. "You'll have about enough to last you till mud time, George."

They shouldered into their coats, grinning a little among themselves. Ernie, following their lead, looked at the piles of wood and knew that they had done a day's work that amounted to something. George already had enough wood there to last him two years.

His back ached as if a log had dropped across it, and a hard sore spot had developed under his left shoulder blade, but he followed them out of the woods feeling good, feeling tired and full of October smell and the smell of fresh-sawed wood and hot oil. As they left the woods he jumped for a limb and shook down a patter of beechnuts around him and Will Livesy. They stopped and gathered their hands full before following the others out.

Ernie, peeling a beechnut and popping it in his mouth, looked at Will, small, skinny, his chin still clotted with dried blood, and it was respect as much as anything else that made him say, "How's your jaw feel, Will?"

"Feels all right," Will said. " 'T ain't as bad as last time I got kicked. Wa'n't any horseshoe on it this time."

In the dusk they strung out into the open above the sugarhouse. Ernie, looking ahead, saw John LaPere stop momentarily beside the chewed and whittled spruce butts, turn his head and stare. His voice boomed in the quiet, tired twilight, loud with wonder and laughter and disbelief.

"Great God!" he said, and walked on shaking his head and laughing.

Goin' To Town

AFTER the night's rain the yard was spongy and soft under
the boy's bare feet. He stood at the edge of the packed
dooryard in the flat thrust of sunrise looking at the ground
washed clean and smooth and trackless, feeling the cool
firm mud under his toes. Experimentally he lifted his
right foot and put it down in a new place, pressed, picked
it up again to look at the neat imprint of straight edge and
curving instep and the five round dots of toes. The air was
so fresh that he sniffed at it as he would have sniffed at the
smell of cinnamon.

Lifting his head backward, he saw how the prairie
beyond the fireguard looked darker than in dry times,
healthier with green-brown tints, smaller and more intimate somehow than it did when the heat waves crawled
over scorched grass and carried the horizons backward
into dim and unseeable distances. And standing in the
yard above his one clean sharp footprint, feeling his own

verticality in all that spread of horizontal land, he sensed
how the prairie shrank on this morning and how he himself grew. He was immense. A little jump would crack
his head on the sky; a few strides would take him to any
horizon.

His eyes turned south, into the low south sky, cloudless,
almost colorless in the strong light. Just above the brown
line of the horizon, faint as a watermark on pale blue
paper, was the wavering tracery of the mountains, tenuous
and far off, but today accessible for the first time. His
mind had played among those ghostly summits for un-
countable lost hours; today, in a few strides, they were
his. And more: under the shadow of those peaks, under
those Bearpaws that he and his mother privately called
the Mountains of the Moon, was Chinook; and in Chinook,
on this Fourth of July, were the band, the lemonade stands,
the crowds, the parade, the ball game, the fireworks, that
his mind had hungered toward in anticipation for three
weeks.

His shepherd pup lay watching, belly down on the
damp ground. In a gleeful spasm the boy stooped down
to flap the pup's ears, then bent and spun like an Indian
in a war dance while the wide-mouthed dog raced around
him. And when his father came to the door in his undershirt, yawning, running a hand up the back of his head
and through his hair, peering out from gummed eyes to
see how the weather looked, the boy watched him, and his
voice was one deep breathing relief from yesterday's rainy
fear.

"It's clear as a bell," he said.

His father yawned again, clopped his jaws, rubbed his
eyes, mumbled something from a mouth furry with sleep.
He stood on the doorstep scratching himself comfortably,
looking down at the boy and the dog.

"Gonna be hot," he said slyly. "Might be too hot to drive."

"Aw, Pa!"

"Gonna be a scorcher. Melt you right down to axle grease riding in that car."

The boy regarded him doubtfully, saw the lurking sly droop of his mouth. "Aw, we are too going!"

At his father's laugh he burst from his immobility like a sprinter starting, raced one complete circle of the house with the dog after him. When he flew around past his father again his voice trailed out behind him at the corner of the house. "Gonna feed the hens," he said. His father looked after him, scratched himself, laughed suddenly, and went back indoors.

Through chores and breakfast the boy moved with the dream of a day's rapture haunting his eyes, but that did not keep him from swift and agile helpfulness. He didn't even wait for commands. He scrubbed himself twice, slicked down his hair, hunted up clean clothes, wiped the mud from his shoes with a wet rag and put them on. While his mother packed the shoe box of lunch he stood at her elbows proffering aid. He flew to stow things in the topless old Ford. He got a cloth and polished the brass radiator. Once or twice, jumping around to help, he looked up to catch his parents watching him, or looking at each other with the knowing, smiling expression in the eyes that said they were calling each other's attention to him.

"Just like a race horse," his father said once, and the boy felt foolish, swaggered, twisted his mouth down in a leer, said "Awww!" But in a moment he was hustling them again. They ought to get going, with fifty miles to drive. And long before they were ready he was standing beside the Ford, licked and immaculate and so excited that his feet jumped him up and down without his volition or knowledge.

It was eight o'clock before his father came out, lifted off the front seat, poked the flat stick down into the gas tank, and pulled it out again dripping. "Pretty near full," he said. "If we're gonna drive up to the mountains we better take a can along, though. Fill that two-gallon one with the spout."

The boy ran, dug the can out of the shed, filled it from the spigot of the sixty-gallon drum that stood on a plank support to the north of the farmhouse. When he came back, his left arm stuck straight out and the can knocking against his legs, his mother was settling herself into the back seat among the parcels and water bags.

"Goodness!" she said. "This is the first time I've been the first ready since I don't know when. I should think you'd have got all this done last night."

"Plenty time." The father stood looking down at the boy, grinning. "All right, race horse. You want to go to this shindig, you better hop in."

The boy was up into the front seat like a squirrel. His father walked around in front of the car. "Okay," he said. "You look sharp now. When she kicks over, switch her onto magneto and pull the spark down."

The boy said nothing. He looked upon the car, as his father did, with respect and a little awe. They didn't use it much, and starting it was a ritual like a fire drill. The father unscrewed the four-eared brass plug, looked down into the radiator, screwed the cap back on, and bent to take hold of the crank. "Watch it now," he said.

The boy felt the gentle heave of the springs, up and down, as his father wound the crank. He heard the gentle hiss in the bowels of the engine as the choke wire was pulled out, and his nostrils filled with the strong, volatile odor of gasoline. Over the slope of the radiator his father's brown strained face lifted up. "Is she turned on all right?"

"Yup. She's on battery."

"Must of flooded her. Have to let her rest a minute."

They waited — and then after a few minutes the wave-like heaving of the springs again, the rise and fall of the blue shirt and bent head over the radiator, the sighing swish of the choke, a stronger smell of gasoline. The motor had not even coughed.

The two voices came simultaneously from the car. "What's the matter with it?"

His brow puckered in an intent and serious scowl, the father stood blowing mighty breaths. "Son of a gun," he said. Coming around, he pulled at the switch to make sure it was clear over, adjusted the spark and gas levers. A fine mist of sweat made his face shine like oiled leather in the sun.

"There isn't anything really wrong with it, is there?" the mother said, and her voice wavered uncertainly on the edge of fear.

"I don't see how there could be," he said. "She's always started right off, and she was running all right when I drove her in here."

The boy looked at his mother where she sat erect among the things in the seat. She looked all dressed up, a flowered dress, a hat with hard red varnished cherries on it pinned to her red hair. For a moment she sat, stiff and nervous. "What'll you have to do?" she said.

"I don't know. Look into the motor."

"Well, I guess I'll get in out of the sun while you do it," she said, and, opening the door, she fumbled her way out of the clutter.

The boy felt her exodus like a surrender, a betrayal. If they didn't hurry up they'd miss the parade. In one motion he bounced out of the car. "Gee whiz!" he said. "Let's do something. We got to get started."

"Keep your shirt on," his father grunted. Lifting the hood, he bent his head inside, studying the engine. His hand went out to test wires, wiggle spark-plug connections, make tentative pulls at the choke. The weakly hinged hood slipped and came down across his wrist, and he swore, pushing it back. "Get me the pliers," he said.

For ten minutes he probed and monkeyed. "Might be the spark plugs," he said. "She don't seem to be getting any fire through her."

The mother, sitting on a box in the shade, smoothed her flowered voile dress nervously. "Will it take long?"

"Half-hour."

"Any day but this!" she said. "I don't see why you didn't make sure last night."

He breathed through his nose and bent over the engine again. "Don't go laying on any blame," he said. "It was raining last night."

One by one the plugs came out, were squinted at, scraped with a knife blade, the gap tested with a thin dime. The boy stood on one foot, then on the other, time pouring like a flood of uncatchable silver dollars through his hands. He kept looking at the sun, estimating how much time there was left. If they got it started right away they might still make it for the parade, but it would be close. Maybe they'd drive right up the street while the parade was on, and be part of it. . . .

"Is she ready?" he said.

"Pretty quick."

He wandered over by his mother, and she reached out and put an arm around his shoulders, hugging him quickly.

"Well, anyway we'll get there for the band and the ball game and the fireworks," he said. "If she doesn't start till noon we c'n make it for those."

"Sure," she said. "Pa'll get it going in a minute. We won't miss anything, hardly."

"You ever seen skyrockets, Ma?"

"Once."

"Are they fun?"

"Wonderful," she said. "Just like a million stars, all colors, exploding all at once."

His feet took him back to his father, who straightened up with a belligerent grunt. "Now!" he said. "If the sucker doesn't start now . . ."

And once more the heaving of the springs, the groaning of the turning engine, the hiss of choke. He tried short, sharp half-turns, as if to catch the motor off guard. Then he went back to the stubborn laboring spin. The back of his blue shirt was stained darkly, the curving dikes of muscle along the spine's hollow showing cleanly where the cloth stuck. Over and over, heaving, stubborn at first, then furious, until he staggered back panting.

"God damn!" he said. "What you suppose is the matter with the damn thing?"

"She didn't even cough once," the boy said, and, staring up at his father's face full of angry bafflement, he felt the cold fear touch him. What if it didn't start at all? What if they never got to any of it? What if, all ready to go, they had to turn around and unload the Ford and not even get out of the yard? His mother came over and they stood close together, looking at the Ford and avoiding each other's eyes.

"Maybe something got wet last night," she said.

"Well, it's had plenty time to dry out," said his father.

"Isn't there anything else you could try?"

"We can jack up the hind wheel, I guess. But there's no damn reason we ought to have to."

"Well, if you have to, you'll have to," she said briskly. "After planning it for three weeks we can't just get stuck like this. Can we, son?"

His answer was mechanical, his eyes steady on his father. "Sure not," he said.

The father opened his mouth to say something, saw the boy's lugubrious face, and shut his lips again. Without a word he pulled off the seat and got out the jack.

The sun climbed steadily while they jacked up one hind wheel and blocked the car carefully so that it wouldn't run over anybody when it started. The boy helped, and when they were ready again he sat in the front seat so full of hope and fear that his whole body was one taut concentration. His father stooped, his cheek pressed against the radiator as a milker's cheek touches the flank of a cow. His shoulder dropped, jerked up. Nothing. Another jerk. Nothing. Then he was rolling in a furious spasm of energy, the wet dark back of his shirt rising and falling. And inside the motor only the futile swish of the choke and the half sound, half feel of cavernous motion as the crankshaft turned over. The Ford bounced on its springs as if the front wheels were coming off the ground on every upstroke. Then it stopped, and the boy's father was hanging on the radiator, breathless, dripping wet, swearing: "Son of a dirty, lousy, stinking, corrupted . . ."

The boy, his eyes dark, stared from his father's angry wet face to his mother's, pinched with worry. The pup lay down in the shade and put his head on his paws. "Gee whiz," the boy said. "Gee whiz!" He looked at the sky, and the morning was half gone.

His shoulders jerking with anger, the father threw the crank halfway across the yard and took a step or two toward the house. "The hell with the damn thing!"

"Harry, you can't!"

He stopped, glared at her, took an oblique look at the boy, bared his teeth in an irresolute, silent swearword. "Well, God, if it won't go!"

"Maybe if you hitched the horses to it," she said.

His laugh was short and choppy. "That'd be fine!" he said. "Why don't we just hitch up and let the team haul this damned old boat into Chinook?"

"But we've got to get it started! Why wouldn't it be all right to let them pull it around? You push it sometimes on a hill and it starts."

He looked at the boy again, jerked his eyes away with an exasperated gesture, as if he held the boy somehow accountable. The boy stared, mournful, defeated, ready to cry, and his father's head swung back unwillingly. Then abruptly he winked, mopped his head and neck, and grinned. "Think you want to go, uh?"

The boy nodded. "All right!" his father's voice snapped crisply. "Fly up in the pasture and get the team. Hustle!"

On the high lope the boy was off up the coulee bank. Just down under the lip of the swale, a quarter-mile west, the bay backs of the horses and the black dot of the colt showed. Usually he ran circumspectly across that pasture, because of the cactus, but now he flew. With shoes it was all right, and even without shoes he would have run — across burnouts, over stretches so undermined with gopher holes that sometimes he broke through to the ankle, staggering. Skimming over patches of cactus, soaring over a badger hole, plunging down into the coulee and up the other side, he ran as if bears were after him. The black colt, spotting him, hoisted his tail and took off in a spectacular, stiff-legged sprint across the flats, but the bays merely lifted their heads to watch him. He slowed, came up walking, laid a hand on the mare's neck and untied the looped halter rope. She stood for him while he scrambled and wriggled and kicked his way to her back, and then they were off, the mare in an easy lope, the gelding trotting after, the colt stopping his wild showoff career and wobbling hastily and ignominiously after his departing mother.

They pulled up before the Ford, the boy sliding off to throw the halter rope to his father. "Shall I get the harness?" he said, and before anyone could answer he was off running, to come back lugging one heavy harness, tugs trailing little furrows in the damp bare earth. He dropped it, turned to run again, his breath laboring in his lungs. "I'll get the other'n," he said.

With a short, almost incredulous laugh his father looked at his mother and shook his head before he threw the harness on the mare. When the second one came he laid it over the gelding, pushed against the heavy shoulder to get the horse into place. The gelding resisted, pranced a little, got a curse and a crack with the rope across his nose, jerked back and trembled and lifted his feet nervously, and set one shod hoof on his owner's instep. The father, unstrung by the hurry and the heat and the labor and the exasperation of a morning when nothing went right, kicked the horse savagely in the belly. "Get in there, you damned big blundering ox! Back! Back, you bastard! Whoa! Whoa, now!"

With a heavy rope for a towline he hitched the now-skittish team to the axle. Without a word he stooped and lifted the boy to the mare's back. "All right," he said, and his face relaxed in a quick grin. "This is where we start her. Ride 'em around in a circle, not too fast."

Then he climbed into the Ford, turned on the switch to magneto, fussed with the levers. "Let her go!" he said.

The boy kicked the mare ahead, twisting as he rode to watch the Ford heave forward as a tired, heavy man heaves to his feet, begin rolling after him, lurching on the uneven ground, jerking and kicking and making growling noises when his father let the emergency brake off and put it in gear. The horses settled as the added pull came on them, flattened into their collars, swung in a circle, bumped each other, skittered. The mare reared, and the boy shut his eyes and clung. When he came down, her leg was entangled in the towline and his father was climbing cursing out of the Ford to straighten it out. His father was mad again, and yelled at him. "Keep 'em apart! There ain't any tongue. You got to keep Dick kicked over on his own side."

And again the start, the flattening into the collars, the snapping tight of the tugs under his legs. This time it went smoothly, the Ford galloped after the team in lumbering, plunging jerks. The mare's eyes rolled white, and she broke into a trot, pulling the gelding after her. Desperately the boy clung to the knotted and shortened reins, his ears alert for the grumble of the Ford starting behind him. The pup ran beside the team yapping in a high, falsetto, idiot monotone, crazy with excitement.

They made three complete circles of the back yard between house and chicken coop before the boy looked back again. "Won't she start?" he shouted. He saw his father rigid behind the wheel, heard his ripping burst of swearwords, saw him bend and glare down into the mysterious inwards of the engine through the pulled-up floorboards. Guiding the car with one hand, he fumbled down below, one glaring eye just visible over the cowl.

"Shall I stop?" the boy shouted. Excitement and near-despair made his voice a tearful scream. But his father's wild arm waved him on. "Go on, go on! Gallop 'em! Pull the guts out of this thing. Run 'em, run 'em!"

And the galloping — the furious, mud-flinging, rolling-eyed galloping around the circle already rutted like a road, the Ford, now in savagely held low, growling and surging and plowing behind; the mad yapping of the dog, the erratic scared bursts of runaway from the colt, the mother in sight briefly for a quarter of each circle, her hands to her mouth and her eyes hurt, and behind him in the Ford his father in a strangling rage, yelling him on, his lips back over his teeth and his face purple.

Until finally they stopped, the horses blown, the boy white and tearful and still, the father dangerous with unexpended wrath. The boy slipped off, his lip bitten between his teeth, not crying now but ready to at any moment, the corners of his eyes prickling with it, and his teeth tight on his misery. His father climbed over the side of the car and stood looking as if he wanted to tear the thing apart with his bare hands.

Shoulders sagging, tears trembling to fall, his jaw aching with the need to cry, the boy started toward his mother. As he came near his father he looked up, their eyes met, and he saw his father's blank with impotent rage. Dull hopelessness swallowed him. Not any of it, his mind said. Not even any of it — no parade, no ball game, no band, no fireworks. No lemonade or ice cream or paper horns or firecrackers. No close sight of the mountains that throughout every summer called like a legend from his horizons. No trip, no adventure — none of it, nothing.

Everything he was feeling was in that one still look. In spite of him his lip trembled, and he choked off a sob, his eyes on his father's face, on the brows pulling down and the eyes narrowing.

"Well, don't blubber!" his father shouted at him. "Don't stand there looking at me as if it was me that was keeping you from your picnic!"

"I can't — help it," the boy said, and with a kind of

terror he felt the grief swelling up, overwhelming him, driving the voice out of him in a wail. Through the blur of his crying he saw the convulsive tightening of his father's face, and then all the fury of a maddening morning concentrated itself in a swift backhand blow that knocked the boy staggering.

He bawled aloud, from pain, from surprise, from outrage, from pure desolation, and ran to bury his face in his mother's skirts. From that muffled sanctuary he heard her angry voice. "No," she said. "It won't do any good to try to make up to him now. Go on away somewhere till he gets over it."

She rocked him against her, but the voice she had for his father was bitter with anger. "As if he wasn't hurt enough already!" she said.

He heard the heavy, quick footsteps going away, and for a long time he lay crying into the voile flowers. And when he had cried himself out, and had listened apathetically to his mother's soothing promises that they would go in the first chance they got, go to the mountains, have a picnic under some waterfall, maybe be able to find a ball game going on in town, some Saturday — when he had listened and become quiet, wanting to believe it but not believing it at all, he went inside to take off his good clothes and his shoes and put on his old overalls again.

It was almost noon when he came out to stand in the front yard looking southward toward the impossible land where the Mountains of the Moon lifted above the plains, and where, in the town at the foot of the peaks, crowds would now be eating picnic lunches, drinking pop, getting ready to go out to the ball field and watch heroes in real uniforms play ball. The band would be braying now from a bunting-wrapped stand, kids would be tossing firecrackers, playing in a cool grove. . . .

In the still heat his face went sorrowful and defeated, and his eyes searched the horizon for the telltale watermark. But there was nothing but waves of heat crawling and lifting like invisible flames; the horizon was a blurred and writhing flatness where earth and sky met in an indistinct band of haze. This morning two strides would have taken him there; now it was gone.

Looking down, he saw at his feet the clean footprint that he had made in the early morning. Aimlessly he put his right foot down and pressed. The mud was drying, but in a low place he found a spot that would still take an imprint. Very carefully, as if he were performing some ritual for his life, he went around, stepping and leaning, stepping and leaning, until he had a circle six feet in diameter of delicately exact footprints, straight edge and curving instep and the five round dots of toes.

The View From the Balcony

THE FRATERNITY HOUSE where they lived that summer was a good deal like a barracks, with its dormitory cut up into eight little plywood cells each with one dormer window, and its two shower rooms divided between the men and the women. They communized their cooking in the one big kitchen and ate together at a refectory table forty feet long. But the men were all young, all veterans, all serious students, and most of the wives worked part time in the university, so that their home life was a thing that constantly disintegrated and re-formed, and they got along with a minimum of friction.

The lounge, as big as a basketball court, they hardly used. What they did use, daytime and nighttime, the thing that converted the austere barracks life into something sumptuous and country-clubbish, was the rooftop deck that stretched out from the lounge over the ten-car garage.

Directly under the bluff to which the house clung ran
the transcontinental highway, but the deck was hidden
and protected above it. At night the air was murmurous
with insects, and sitting there they would be bumped by
blundering June bugs and feel the velvet kiss of moths. By
standing up they could see the centerline of the highway
palely emergent in the glow of the street lamp at the end
of the drive. Beyond the highway, flowing with it in the
same smooth curve, low-banked and smooth and dark and
touched only with sparks and glimmers of light, was the
Wawasee River.

More than a mile of the far shore was kept wild as a
city park, and across those deep woods on insect-haunted
nights, when traffic noise died for a moment and the night
hung still around them, they could hear the lions roar.

The lions were in the zoo at the other side of the park.
At first it was a shock to the students in the fraternity
house to hear that heavy-chested, coughing, snarling roar,
a more dangerous and ominous sound than should be
heard in any American night, and for a moment any of
them could have believed that the midland heat of the
night was tropical heat and that real and wild lions of an
ancient incorrigible ferocity roamed the black woods
beyond the river. But after a week or two the nightly
roaring had become as commonplace as the sound of
traffic along the highway, and they rarely noticed it.

Altogether the fraternity house was a good place, in
spite of the tasteless ostentation of the big echoing lounge
and the Turkish-bath heat of the sleeping cubicles. They
were lucky to be in it. They felt how lucky they were,
and people who came out to drink beer on weekends kept
telling them how lucky they were. So many less lucky
ones were crammed into backstairs rooms or regimented
into converted barracks. Out here there was a fine

spaciousness, a view, a freedom. They were terribly lucky.

Deep in a sun-struck daydream, drowning in light and heat, the sun like a weight on her back and her body slippery with perspiration and her mouth pushed wetly out of shape against her wrist, Lucy Graham lay alone on the deck in the sultry paralysis of afternoon. Her eyes looked into an empty red darkness; in her mind the vague voluptuous uncoiling of memory and fantasy was slowed almost to a stop, stunned almost to sleep.

All around her the afternoon was thick, humid, stirring with the slow fecundities of Midwestern summer — locust-shrill and bird-cheep and fly-buzz, child-shout and the distant chime of four o'clock from the university's clock tower. Cars on the highway grew from hum to buzz-saw whine and slapped past and diminished, coning away to a point of sound, a humming speck. Deep inside the house a door banged, and she heard the scratch of her own eyelashes against her wrist as she blinked, thinking groggily that it was time to get up and shower. Everyone would be coming home soon; Tommy Probst would be through with his exams by four-thirty, and tonight there would be a celebration and a keg of beer.

For a while longer she lay thinking of Tommy, wishing Charley were as far along as that, with his thesis done and nothing but the formalities left. Then it struck her as odd, the life they all lived: this sheltered, protected present tipping ever so slightly toward the assured future. After what they had been, navigator and bombardier, Signal Corps major, artillery captain, Navy lieutenant and yeoman and signalman first class, herself a WAAF and two or three of the other wives WACS or WAVES — after being these things it was almost comic of them to be so seriously and deeply involved in becoming psychologists, professors, pharmacists, historians.

She sat up, her head swimming and the whole world a sheeted glare. Lifting the hair from her neck, she let the cooling air in and shook her head at the absurdity of lying in the sun until her brains were addled and her eyes almost fried from her head. But in England there had never been the time, rarely the place, seldom the sun. She was piggy about the sun as she had been at first about the food. From here England seemed very scrawny and very dear, but very far away. Looking at her arm, she could not believe the pagan color of her own skin.

Quick steps came across the terrazzo floor of the lounge, and Phyllis Probst stepped out, hesitating in the door. "Have you seen anything of Tommy?"

"No," Lucy said. "Is he through his exams already?"

An extraordinarily complex look came over Phyllis' face. She looked hot, her hair was stringy, she seemed half out of breath. Her brows frowned and her mouth smiled a quick weak smile and her eyes jumped from Lucy out across the highway and back again.

Lucy stood up. "Is something wrong?"

"No," Phyllis said. "No, it's just . . . You haven't seen him at all?"

"Nobody's been home. I did hear a door bang just a minute ago, though."

"That was me," Phyllis said. "I thought he might have come home and gone to bed."

"Phyllis, is he sick?" Lucy said, and took Phyllis' arm. She felt the arm tremble. Still with the terrified, anxious, distressed expression on her face, Phyllis began to cry.

"I've got to find him," she said, and tried to pull away.

"We'll find him," Lucy said. "What happened? Tell me."

"He . . . I don't know. Helen Fast called me from the Graduate School office about two. I don't know whether he got sick, or whether the questions were too hard, or what. Helen said he came out once and asked for a typewriter, because he's left-handed and he smudges so when he writes, and she gave him a portable. But in a few minutes he came out again and put the portable on her desk and gave her a queer desperate look and walked out."

"Oh, what a shame," Lucy said, and with her arm around Phyllis sought for something else to say.

"But where *is* he?" Phyllis asked. "I called the police and the hospital and I went to every beer joint in town."

"Don't worry," Lucy said, and pushed her gently inside. "You come and take a cool shower and relax. We'll send the boys hunting when they come."

They came, half a household of them, before the two girls were halfway up the stairs, and they brought Tommy with them. He walked through the door like a prisoner among deputies, quietly, his dark smooth head bent a little as if in thought. Lucy saw his eyes lift and meet his wife's in an indescribable look. "Thanks for the lift," Tommy said to Charley Graham, and went up the stairs and took his wife's arm and together they went down the corridor.

Lucy came back down to where her husband stood. "What on earth happened?"

He pursed up his lips, lifted his shoulders delicately, looked at the others who were dispersing toward dormitory and shower room. "We cruised the park on a hunch and found him over there tossing sticks in the river," Charley said.

"Why didn't he take the exams?"

Her husband lifted his shoulders again.

"But it's so absurd!" she said. "He could have written

the Lord's Prayer backward and they would have passed
him. It was just a ritual, like an initiation. Everyone said
so."

"Of course," he said. "It was a cinch." He put an arm
across her shoulders, made a face as if disgusted by the
coco-butter gooiness and kissed her from a great distance.
"Kind of dampens the party."

"We'd better not have it."

"Why not? I'm going to ask Richards and Latour to
come over. They can straighten Tommy out."

"Will they give him another chance, do you think?"

"*Give* him?" Charley said. "They'll force it on him."

In the lounge after dinner the atmosphere was weighted
and awkward. Lucy had a feeling that somehow, without
in any way agreeing on it, the whole lot of them had arrived at a policy of elaborately ignoring what had happened to Tommy. Faced with the uncomfortable alterna-
tives of ignoring it or of slapping him on the back, encouraging him, they had chosen the passive way. It was still
too hot on the deck for sitting; in the lounge they were too
aware of each other. Some hunted up corners and dove
into books. The others lounged and waited. Watching
them, Lucy saw how the eyes strayed to Tommy when his
back was turned, judging him. She saw that look even in
Charley's face, the contempt that narrowed the eyes and
fluttered the nostrils. As if geared up to play a part,
Tommy stayed, looking self-consciously tragic. His wife
was around him like an anxious hen.

Donna Earp stood up suddenly into a silence. "Lord,
it's sultry," she said. "I wish it would rain."

She went out on deck, and Lucy and Charley followed
her. The sun was dazzling and immense behind the maple
tree that overhung the corner. Shadows stretched almost
across the quiet river. The roof was warm through Lucy's
shoes, and the railing was hot to her hand.

"Has anyone talked to him at all?" she said.

Charley shook his head, shrugged in that Frenchy little way he had.

"Won't it look queer?"

"Richards and Latour are coming. They'll talk to him."

"What about getting the beer, then? It's like a funeral in there."

"Funeral!" Charley said, and snorted. "That's another thing that happened today. Quite a day." He looked at the sun, disintegrating behind the trees.

"Whose funeral?"

"Kay Cedarquist's."

"Who's she?"

"She's a girl," he said. "Maybe I'd better get the beer, I'll tell you later about the funeral. It's a howl."

"Sounds like a peculiar funeral."

"Peculiar is a small word for it," he said. In the doorway he met Art Morris, and haled him along to get the beer.

After the glare, the shade of the tree was wonderful. Lucy sat on the railing looking over the river, and a car pulled into the drive and parked with its nose against the bluff. Paul Latour, the psychology professor, and Clark Richards, head of the department of social science, got out and held assisting hands for Myra, Richards' young wife. For several seconds the three stood looking up, smiling. They seemed struck by something; none of them spoke until Professor Richards with his hand in his bosom took a stance and said:

> O! she doth teach the torches to burn bright.
> It seems she hangs upon the cheek of night
> Like a rich jewel in an Ethiop's ear . . .

He was a rather chesty man, neat in a white suit; in the

violet shadow of the court his close-clipped mustache smudged his mouth. Latour's grim and difficult smile was upturned beside him, Myra Richards' schoolgirl face swam below there like a lily on a pond. "Hi, lucky people," Myra said. "What repulsively romantic surroundings!"

"Come up," Lucy said. "It's cooler at this altitude."

They made her feel pretty, they took away the gloom that Tommy Probst's failure had dropped upon them all. When you were all working through the assured present to the assured future, it was more than a personal matter when someone failed. Ever since dinner they had been acting as if the foundations were shaken, and she knew why. She was glad Richards and Latour were here, outsiders, older, with better perspective.

As she sat waiting for them the lion roared, harsh and heavy across the twilight river. "Down, Bruno!" Henry Earp said automatically, and there was a laugh. The door banged open, and Charley and Art staggered the keg through, to set it up on a table. The talk lifted suddenly in tempo. The guests stepped out onto the deck in a chorus of greeting, the lounge emptied itself, lugubrious Probsts and all, into the open air. Gloom dissolved in the promise of festivity. Charley drew the first soapy glasses from the keg. Far across several wooded bends the university's clock tower, lacy and soaring, was pinned suddenly against the sky by the floodlights.

She saw them working on Tommy during the evening. Within the first half-hour, Clark Richards took him over in the corner, and Lucy saw them talking there, an attractive picture of *magister* and *studens*, Tommy with his dark head bent and his face smoothed perfectly expressionless, Richards solid and confident and reassuring. She saw him leave Tommy with a clap on the shoulder, and saw

Tommy's smile that was like spoken thanks, and then Phyllis came slipping over to where Tommy stood, wanting to be told of the second chance. Some time later, when the whole party had been loosened by beer and a carful of other students had arrived, and the twilight was so far gone into dusk that the river was only a faint metallic shine along the foot of the woods, Paul Latour hooked his arm into Tommy's and unsmiling, looking glum as a detective, led him inside. By that time the party was loud.

Lucy stayed on the fringes of it, alert to her duties as hostess, knowing that the other girls forgot any such responsibilities as soon as they had a couple of drinks. She rescued glasses for people who set them down, kept edging through the crowd around the keg to get glasses filled, talked with new arrivals; circulated quietly, seeing that no bashful student got shoved off into a corner, making sure that Myra Richards didn't get stranded anywhere. But after a half-hour she quit worrying about Myra; Myra was drinking a good deal and having a fine gay time.

It did not cool off much with the dark. The deck was breathless and sticky, and they drank their beer fast because it warmed so rapidly in the glass. Inside, as she paused by the keg, Lucy saw Latour and Tommy still talking head to head in the lighted lounge. Cocking her head a little, she listened to the sound of the party, appraising it. She heard Myra's laugh and a series of groans and hoots from the boys, apparently at someone's joke.

She moved away from the brittle concentration of noise and out toward the rail, and as she passed through the crowd she heard Art Morris say, ". . . got the Westminster Choir and a full symphony orchestra to do singing commercials. That's what Hollywood is, one big assembled empty Technique. They hunt mosquitoes with .155's."

No one was constrained any more; everything was loose and bibulous. As she leaned on the rail a voice spoke at her shoulder, and she turned to see Professor Richards with a glass of beer in his hand and his coat off. But he still looked dignified because he had kept his tie on and his sleeves rolled down. Most of the boys were down to T shirts, and a girl who had come with the carload of students was in a halter that was hardly more than a bra. She was out in an open space now, twirling, showing the full ballerina skirt she had made out of an India print bedspread.

"Find any breeze?" Richards said.

"No, just looking at the river."

"It's very peaceful," he said. "You're lucky to have this place."

"I know." She brushed an insect from her sticky cheek. It was pleasant to her to be near this man, with his confidence and his rich resonant voice, and a privilege that they could all know him on such informal terms. Until six months ago he had been something big and important in the American Military Government in Germany.

He was saying, "How do you like it by now? It's a good bit different from England."

"I'm liking it wonderfully," she said. "People have been lovely."

"Thoroughly acclimated?"

"Not quite to this heat."

"This just makes the corn grow," he said, and she heard in his voice, with forgiving amusement that it should be there in the voice of this so-distinguished man, the thing she had heard in so many American voices — the confidence they had that everything American was bigger and better and taller and colder and hotter and wider and deeper than anything else. "I've seen it a hundred degrees at two in the morning," Richards said. "Inside a house, of course."

"It must be frightful."

He shrugged, smiling with his smudged mouth in the semidarkness. "Myra and I slept three nights on the golf course last time we had that kind of weather."

"We've already slept out here a night or two," Lucy said. She looked across the shadowy, crowded, noisy deck. "Where is Myra? I haven't had a chance to talk to her at all."

"A while ago she was arguing Zionism with a bunch of the boys," Richards said. He chuckled with his full-chested laugh, indulgent and avuncular. "She knows nothing whatever about Zionism."

Lucy had a brief moment of wondering how a professor really looked upon his students. Could he feel completely at ease among men and women of so much less experience and learning, or did he always have a bit of the paternal in his attitude? And when he married a girl out of one of his classes, as Professor Richards had, did he ever — and did *she* ever — get over feeling that he was God omnipotent?

"I imagine you must feel a little as I did when I got back from Germany," he was saying. "After living under such a cloud of fear and shortages and loss, suddenly to come out into the sun."

"Yes," she said. "I've felt it. I take the sun like medicine."

"It's too bad we can't sweep that cloud away for the whole world," Richards said. He looked out over the river, and she thought his voice had a stern, austere ring. "England particularly. England looked straight in the face of disaster and recognized it for what it was and fought on. It's a pity the cloud is still there. They've earned something better."

"Yes," she said again, for some reason vaguely embarrassed. Talk about England's grit always bothered her. You didn't talk about it when you were in any of it. Why should it be talked about outside? To dispel the slight pompous silence she said, "I saw you talking to Tommy Probst."

Richards laughed. "Momentary funk," he said. "It's preposterous. He's one of the best students we've had in years. He'll come up and take it again tomorrow and pass it like a shot."

He touched her shoulder with a pat that was almost fatherly, almost courtly, and lifted his empty glass in explanation and drifted away.

In the corner by the beer keg, people were jammed in a tight group. A yell of laughter went up, hoots, wolf calls. As the lounge door let a brief beam of light across the deck Lucy saw Myra in the middle of the crowd. Her blond hair glinted silver white, her eyes had a sparkle, her mouth laughed. A vivid face. No wonder Professor Richards had picked her out of a whole class.

Charley broke out of the crowd shaking his head and grinning, bony-shouldered in the T shirt. He put a damp arm around her and held his glass for her to sip. "How's my Limey bride?"

"Steamed like a pudding," she said. "It sounds like a good party over here."

He gave her a sidelong down-mouthed look. "Doak was just telling the saga of the funeral."

Laughter broke out again, and Myra's voice said, "Doak, I think that's the most awful thing I've ever . . ."

"Tell me," Lucy said, "what's so screamingly funny about a girl's funeral?"

"Didn't you ever hear about Kay Cedarquist?"

"No."

"She was an institution. Schoenkampf's lab assistant, over in Biology. She had cancer. That's what she died of, day before yesterday."

Lucy waited. "Is it just that I'm British?"

Wiping beer from his lips with his knuckles, Charley grinned at her in the shadow. "Nothing is so funny to Americans as a corpse," he said. "Unless it's a decaying corpse, or one that falls out of the coffin. Read Faulkner, read Caldwell. Kay sort of fell out of the coffin."

"Oh my God," Lucy said, appalled.

"Oh, not really. See, she was Schoenkampf's mistress as well as his assistant. He's got a wife and four kids and they're all nudists. I'll tell you about them too some time. But Schoenkampf also had Kay, and he set her up in an apartment."

He drank again, raised a long admonishing finger. "*But*," he said. "When Schoenkampf was home with Mrs. Schoenkampf and the four nudist children, Kay had a painter from Terre Haute. He spent a lot of time in our town and painted murals all over Kay's walls . . . haven't I ever told you about those murals?"

"No."

"Gentle Wawasee River scenes," Charley said. "Happy farm children in wood lot and pasture, quiet creeks, steepled towns. Kay told Schoenkampf she had it done because art rested her nerves. She had this double feature going right up to the time she died, practically."

"You're making this all up," Lucy said.

He put his hands around her waist and lifted her to the rail. "Sit up here." Confidential and grinning, he leaned over her, letting her in on the inside. It was a pose she had loved in him when they walked all over Salisbury talking and talking and talking, when they were both in uniform.

"But if she had cancer," she said, "wasn't she ill, in bed?"

"Not till the last month." He knocked the bottom of his glass lightly against the stone and seemed to brood, half amused. "She was a good deal of a mess," he said. "Also, she had dozens of short subjects besides her double feature. Graduate students, married or single, she wasn't fussy. Nobody took her cancer very seriously. Then all of a sudden she up and died."

Lucy stirred almost angrily, moving her arm away from his sticky bare skin. "I don't think all that's funny, Charley."

"Maybe not. But Kay had no relatives at all, so Schoenkampf had to arrange the funeral. To keep himself out of it as much as possible, he got a bunch of students to act as pallbearers. Every one of them had passed his qualifying exams. That was what got the snickers."

"Graduate students?" Lucy said. "What have their qualifying exams to do . . . ?" Then she saw, and giggled involuntarily, and was angry at herself for giggling. Over the heads of the crowd she saw the group of students still clustered in the corner. They had linked arms in a circle and were singing "I Wanted Wings." Myra was still among them, between Doak and the girl in the bra and the India print bedspread.

"Who?" she said. "Doak and Jackson and that crowd?"

"They led the parade," Charley said and snorted like a horse into his glass. "I guess there were three or four unfortunates who couldn't find an empty handle on the coffin."

Sitting quietly, the stone still faintly warm through her dress, she felt as if a greasy film had spread over her mind. It was such a nasty little sordid story from beginning to end, sneaking and betrayal and double betrayal and fear and that awful waiting, and finally death and heartless grins. "Well," Charley said, "I see you don't like my tale."

She turned toward him, vaguely and impulsively wanting reassurance. "Charley, was she pretty?"

"No," he said. "Not pretty at all, just easy."

What she wanted, the understanding, wasn't there. "I think it's wry," she said. "Just wry and awful."

"It ought to be," he said, "but somehow it isn't. Not if you knew Kay. You didn't."

With a kind of dismay she heard herself say, not knowing until she said it that there was that much distress and that much venom in her, the thing that leaped abruptly and unfairly to her mind. "Did *you*?"

He stared at her, frowned, looked amazed, and then grinned, and the moment he grinned it was all right again, she could laugh and they were together and not apart. But when he waved his glass and suggested that they go see how the beer was holding out she shook her head and stayed behind on the railing. As he worked his way tall through the jam of shadowy people she had an impulse to jump down and follow him so that not even twenty feet of separation could come desperately between, but the bray of talk and laughter from the deck was like a current that pinned her back against the faintly warm stone, threatening to push her off, and she looked behind her once into the dark pit of the court and tightened her hands on the railing.

She disliked everyone there for being strangers, aliens to her and to her ways of feeling, unable from their vast

plateau of security to see or understand the desperation
and fear down below. And even while she hated them for
it, she felt a pang of black and bitter envy of that un-
troubled assurance they all had, that way of shrugging off
trouble because no trouble that could not be cured had
ever come within their experience. Even the war — a tem-
porary unpleasantness. *Their* homes hadn't leaped into
unquenchable flame or shaken down in rubble and dust.
They had known no families in Coventry. Fighting the
war, they could still feel not desperate but magnanimous,
like good friends who reached out to help an acquaintance
in a scuffle.

She hated them, and as she saw Paul Latour approach-
ing her and knew she could not get away, she hated him
worst of all. His face was like the face of a predatory bird,
beaked, grim-lipped; because of some eye trouble he
always wore dark glasses, and his prying, intent, hidden
stare was an agony to encounter. His mouth was hooked
back in a constant sardonic smile. He not merely un-
dressed her with his eyes; he dissected her most intimate
organs, and she knew he was a cruel man, no matter how
consistently and amazingly kind he had been to Charley,
almost like a father, all the way through school. Charley
said he had a mind like a fine watch. But she wished he
would not come over, and she trembled, unaccountably
emotional, feeling trapped.

Then he was in front of her, big-shouldered for his
height, not burly but somehow giving the impression of
great strength, and his face like the cold face of a great
bird thrust toward her and the hidden stare stabbed into
her and the thin smile tightened. "Nobody to play with?"
he asked. There was every unpleasant and cutting suggestion in the remark. A wallflower. Maybe halitosis. Perhaps B.O.

She came back quickly enough. "Too hot to play." To
steer the talk away from her she said, "You've been conferring with Tommy."

"Yes," he said, and a spasm of what seemed almost contempt twisted across his mouth. "I've been conferring with
Tommy."

"Is he all right now?"

"What do you mean, all right?"

"Is he over his . . . trouble?"

"He is if he can make up his mind to grow up."

Now it was her turn. "What do you mean?"

The dark circles of his glasses stared at her blankly, and
then she realized that Latour was laughing. "I thought
you were an intelligent woman."

"I'm not," she said half bitterly. "I'm stupid."

His laugh was still there, an almost soundless chuckle.
Beyond him the circle of singers had widened to include
almost everyone on the deck, and thirty people were bellowing, "We were sailing a-lo-o-o-ng, on Moonlight Bay
. . ."

Latour came closer, to be heard. "You mean to tell me
you haven't even yet got wise to Tommy?"

"I don't know what you mean. He's a very good student ——"

"Oh, student!" Latour said. "Sure, he's a student.
There's nothing wrong with his brains. He's just a child,
that's all, he never grew up."

A counterattraction to the singing had started in the
lounge. A few of the energetic had turned on the radio
and were dancing on the smooth terrazzo floor. Lucy saw
figures float by the lighted door: Donna and Henry Earp,
the Kinseys, Doak and Myra Richards, Tommy and
Phyllis. The radio cut quick and active across the drag-
ging tempo of the singing.

"But he was in the air force three years," she said. "He's a grown man, he's been through a lot. I never saw anything childish in him."

He turned his head; his profile was cruel and iron against the light. "You're disgustingly obtuse," his mocking voice said. "What did *you* make of that show he put on today?"

"I don't know," she said, hesitating. "That he was afraid, I suppose."

"Afraid of what?"

"Of what? That he'd fail, that he wouldn't make it after all."

"Go to the foot of the class."

"Pardon?"

"Go to the foot of the class," Latour said. "Look at the record. Only child, doting mother. I knew him as an undergraduate, and he's been trying for five or six years to break loose. Or he thought he was. If it hadn't been for the war he'd have found out sooner that he wasn't. The war came just as he graduated, just right so he could hide in it. He could even make a show like a hero, like a flyboy. But not as a pilot, notice. He busted out in pilot training. Somebody else would have the real responsibility. After the war, back to school where he's still safe, with GI benefits and no real decisions to make. And then all of a sudden he wakes up and he's pretty near through. In about three hours he'll be out in the bright light all by himself with a Ph.D. in his hand and a career to make and no mother, no Army, no university, to cuddle him. He wasn't afraid of that exam, he was afraid of passing it."

Lucy was silent. She believed him completely, the pattern matched at every edge, but she rebelled at the triumph and contempt in his voice. Suppose he was completely right: Tommy Probst was still his student and pre-

sumably his friend, somebody to like and help, not someone to triumph over. Sticky with the slow ooze of perspiration, feeling the hot night dense and smothering
around her, she moved restlessly on the rail. Latour
reached into the pocket of his seersucker jacket and
brought out a pint bottle.

"Drink? I've been avoiding the bellywash everyone else
is drinking."

"No thank you," Lucy said. "Couldn't I get you a glass
and some ice?"

"I like it warm," he said. "Keeps me reminded that it's
poison."

She saw then what she had not seen before, that he was
quite drunk, but out of her vague rebelliousness she said,
"Mr. Latour, all the boys are in Tommy's position almost
exactly, aren't they? They're right at that edge where
they have to be fully responsible adults. They all work
much too hard. Any of them could crack just the way
Tommy did. Charley could do it. It isn't a disgrace."

Latour's head went back, the bottle to his lips, and for
a moment he was a bird drinking, his iron beak in the air,
at once terrible and ridiculous. "You needn't worry about
Charley," he said when he had brought the bottle down.
"Charley's another breed of rat. He's the kind that wants
to wear the old man's breeches even before they're off the
old man's legs. Tommy's never got over calling me 'Sir.'
Charley'd eat me tomorrow if he thought he could get
away with it."

"Who'd do what?" Charley said. He had appeared behind Latour with two glasses in his hands. He passed one
to Lucy with a quick lift of the eyebrows and she loved
him again for having seen that she was trapped.

"You, you ungrateful whelp," Latour said. He dropped
the bottle in his pocket; his blank stare and forward-

thrusting face seemed to challenge Charley. "I'll tell you
what you think. You think you're younger than I am.
That's right. You think you're better-looking than I am.
Maybe that's right too. You think you could put me
down. That's a foolish mistake. You think you're as smart
as I am, and that's even more foolish." His thumb jerked
up under Charley's wishbone like a disemboweling knife,
and Charley grunted. "Given half a chance," Latour said,
"you'd open your wolfish jaws and swallow me. You're like
the cannibals who think it gives them virtue to eat their
enemy's heart. You'd eat mine."

"He's distraught," Charley said to Lucy. "Maybe we
should get him into a tepid bath."

"You and who else?" Latour said, like a belligerent kid.
His sardonic fixed grin turned on Lucy. "You can see how
it goes in his mind. I develop a lot of apparatus for testing perception, and I fight the whole damn university till
I get a lab equipped with sound equipment and Phonele-
scopes and oscillographs and electronic microscopes, and
then punks like this one come along and pick my brains
and think they know as much as the old man. I give them
the equipment and provide them with ideas and supervise
their work and let them add their names to mine on schol-
arly articles, and they think they're all ready to put on the
old man's breeches."

"Why Paul," Charley said, "you've got an absolute
anxiety neurosis. You should see a psychiatrist. You'll
brood yourself into paranoia and begin to have persecu-
tion complexes. You've got one now. Here I've been holding you up all year, and you think I'm secretly plotting to
eat you. You really should talk to a good psychologist."

"Like who?" Latour said, grinning. "Some punk like
you whose soft spot hasn't hardened yet?"

"There are one or two others almost as good," Charley
said, "but Graham is the best."

Latour took the bottle from his pocket and drank again and screwed on the cap and dropped the bottle back in the pocket. His stare never left Charley's face; his soundless chuckle broke out into a snort.

"A punk," he said. "A callow juvenile, a pubescent boy, a beardless youth. You're still in the spanking stage."

Winking at Lucy, Charley said, "Takes a good man."

"Oh, not so good," Latour said. "Any *man* could do it."

His hand shot out for Charley's wrist, and Charley jerked back, slopping his beer. It seemed to Lucy that something bright and alert had leaped up in both of them, and she wanted to tell them to drop it, but the noise of singing and the moan of dance music from the lounge made such a current of noise that she didn't trust her voice against it. But Latour's edged foolery bothered her; she didn't think he was entirely joking, and she didn't think Charley thought so either. She watched them scuffle and shove each other, assuming exaggeratedly the starting pose for a wrestling match. Latour reached in his pocket and handed her the almost empty whisky bottle; he removed his glasses and passed them to her, and she saw his eyes like dark holes with a glint of light at the bottom.

"For heaven's sake," she said, "you're not going to . . . "

Latour exploded into violent movement, reached and leaned and jerked in a flash, and suddenly Charley's length was across his shoulder, held by crotch and neck, and Latour with braced legs was staggering forward. He was headed directly for the rail. Charley's legs kicked frantically, his arm whipped around Latour's neck in a headlock, but Latour was brutally strong. Face twisted under Charley's arm, he staggered ahead.

Lucy screamed, certain for a moment that Latour was going to throw Charley over. But her husband's legs kicked free, and he swung sideward to get his feet on the floor. Latour let go his neck hold, and his palms slapped

against Charley's body as he shifted. Charley was clinging to his headlock, twisting the blockier Latour into a
crouch. Then somehow Latour dove under him, and they
crashed.

The whole crowd was around them, shutting off the
light from the lounge so that the contestants grunted and
struggled in almost total darkness. Lucy bent over them,
screaming at Charley to quit it, let go. Someone moved in
the crowd, and in a brief streak of light she saw Latour's
hands, iron strong, tearing Charley's locked fingers apart,
and the veins ridged on Charley's neck as he clung to his
hold.

"Stop it!" she screamed at them. "You'll get all dirty,
you'll get hurt, stop it, please Charley!"

Latour broke free and spun Charley like a straw man,
trying to get a hold for a slam. But as they went to the
floor again Charley's legs caught him in a head scissors
and bent him harshly back.

"Great God," Henry Earp said beside Lucy. "What is
this, fun or fight?"

"I don't know," she said. "Fun. But make them stop."
She grabbed the arm of Clark Richards. "Make them stop,
please!"

Richards bent over the wrestlers, quiet now, Latour's
head forced back and Charley lying still, just keeping the
pressure on. "Come on," Richards said. He slapped them
both on the back. "Bout's a draw. Let go, Charley."

Latour's body arched with a convulsive spring, but
Charley's legs clenched tighter and crushed him down
again.

"Okay with me," Charley said. "You satisfied with a
draw, Paul?"

Latour said nothing. "All right," Richards said. "Let's
call it off, Paul. Someone might get hurt."

As Charley unlocked his legs and rolled free, Latour was up and after him like a wolf, but Richards and Henry and several others held him back. IIe put a hand to his neck and stood panting. "That was a dirty hold, Graham."

"Not so dirty as getting dumped twenty feet into a courtyard," Charley said. His T shirt was ripped half off him. He grinned fixedly at Latour. Sick and fluttery at what had happened, Lucy took his hand, knowing that it was over now, the support was gone, the rest of the way was against difficulties all the way. "You foolish people," she said. "You'll spoil a good party."

Somehow, by the time she had got herself together after her scare, the party had disintegrated. The unmarried graduate students who had been noisily there all evening had vanished, several of the house couples had gone quietly to bed. The keg was empty, and a half-bottle of whisky stood unwanted on the table. A whole carful of people had gone out the Terre Haute road for sandwiches, taking Paul Latour with them. The court below the rail was empty except for Charley's jeep and Clark Richards' sedan, and the deck was almost deserted, when Richards stepped out of the lounge with his white coat on, ready to go home.

He came from light into darkness, so that for a moment he stood turning his head, peering. "Myra?" he said. "We should be getting on."

"She isn't out here," Lucy said, and jumped down from the railing where she had been sitting talking to Charley. "Isn't she in the lounge?"

"I just looked," Richards said. "Maybe she's gone up to the ladies' room."

He came out to lean against the rail near them, looking out across the darkness to the floodlighted clock tower

floating in the sky. "It's a little like the spire of Salisbury
Cathedral, isn't it?" he said. "Salisbury Cathedral across
the Avon." He turned his face toward Lucy. "Isn't that
where you're from, Salisbury?"

"Yes," she said, "it is rather like."

Then an odd thing happened. The southwest horizon
leaped up suddenly, black and jagged, hill and tree and
floating tower, with the green glow of heat lightning behind it, and when the lightning winked out, the tower
went with it, leaving only the unbroken dark. "Wasn't
that queer?" she said. "They must have turned off the
floodlights just at that instant. It was almost as if the
lightning wiped it out."

They were all tired, yawning, languid with the late hour
and the beer and the unremitting, oozing heat. Richards
looked at his watch, holding it so that light from the
lounge fell on it. "Where can Myra be?" he said. "It's one
o'clock."

Slowly Charley slid off the rail, groaning. "Could she be
sick? Did she have too much, you think?"

"I don't know," Richards said. His voice was faintly
snappish, irritated. "I don't think so, but she could have,
I suppose."

"Let me just look up in the shower room," Lucy said,
and slipped away from them, through the immense hot
lounge. Art Morris was asleep in the big sofa, looking
greasy with sweat under the bluish light. Down the long
wide hall she felt like a tiny lost figure in a nightmare and
thought what a really queer place this was to live in, after
all. So big it forgot about you. She pushed the door, felt
for the switch. Light leaped on the water-beaded tile, the
silence opened to the lonely drip of a tap. No one was in
the shower room, no shoes showed under the row of toilet
doors.

When she got back to the deck, someone had turned on the powerful light above the door, and the party lay in wreckage there, a surly shambles of slopped beer and glasses and wadded napkins and trampled cigarette butts. In that light the Earps and Charley and Richards were looking at each other abashed.

"It's almost a cinch she went with the others out to the Casino," Charley was saying. "There was a whole swarm of them went together."

"You'd think she would have said something," Richards said. His voice was so harsh that Lucy looked at him in surprise and saw his mouth tight and thin, his face drawn with inordinate anxiety. "She wasn't upstairs?"

Lucy shook her head. For an instant Richards stood with his hands opening and closing at his sides. Abruptly he strode to the rail and looked over it, following it around to the corner and peering over into the tangle of weeds and rubbish at the side. He spun around as if he feared guns were pointed at his back. "Who saw her last? What was she doing? Who was she with?"

No one spoke for a moment, until Henry Earp said cautiously, "She was dancing a while ago, a whole bunch of us were. But that was a half-hour ago, at least."

"Who with?" Richards said, and then slapped at the air with his hand and said, "No, that wouldn't tell us anything. She must have gone for a sandwich."

"We can go see," Charley said. "Matter of fact, I'd like a sandwich myself. Why don't we run up the road and see if she's at the Casino? She probably didn't notice what time it was."

"No," Richards said grimly. Lucy found it hard to look at him, she was so troubled with sympathy and embarrassment. "Probably she didn't." He looked at Charley almost vaguely, and sweat was up on his forehead. "Would you

mind?" he said. "Perhaps I ought to stay here, in case
she . . . "

"I'll stay here," Lucy said. The distraught vague eyes
touched her.

"You'll want something to eat too. You go along."

"No," she said. "I'd rather stay. I would anyway." To
Charley she said, "Why don't you and Henry and Donna
go? You could look in at the Casino and the Tavern and
all those places along there."

With his arm around her he walked her to the lounge
door, and everything that had passed that evening was in
their look just before he kissed her. When she turned
around Richards was watching. In the bald light, swarming with insects that crawled and leaped and fluttered
toward the globe above the doors, his eyes seemed to
glare. Lucy clicked off the light and dropped them back
into darkness.

"Should you like a drink?" she said into the black. After
a moment he answered, "No, thank you."

Gradually his white-suited figure emerged again as her
eyes adjusted. He was on the rail looking out across the
river and woods. Heat lightning flared fitfully again along
the staring black horizon. The jeep started down below
them, the lights jumped against the bluff, turned twisting
the shadows, and were gone with the diminishing motor.

"Don't worry," Lucy said. "I'm sure she just forgot
about the time and went for something to eat. We should
have had something here, but somehow with so many to
plan things, nothing ever gets planned."

"I don't like that river," Richards said. "It's so absolutely
black down there . . . " He swung around at her. "Have
you got a flashlight?"

"I think so," she said, "but don't you suppose —— "

"Could I borrow it, please?" he said. "I'm going down

along the bank to look. If you'd stay here — if she should come back . . . "

She slipped in and past the still-sleeping Art Morris and found a flashlight in the kitchen drawer, and now suddenly it was as if she were five years back in time, the cool tube in her hand, the intense blackout darkness around, the sense of oppression, the waiting, the search. That sense was even stronger a few minutes later as she sat on the rail and saw the thin slash of the light down along the riverbank, moving slowly, cutting on and off, eventually disappearing in the trees.

It was very still. Perched on the rail, she looked out from the deck they were so lucky to have, over the night-obliterated view that gave them such a sense of freedom and space, and in all the dark there was no sound louder than the brush of a moth's wings or the tick of an armored bug against the driveway light. Then far up the highway a point of sound bored into the silence and grew and rounded, boring through layers of dark and soundless air, until it was a rush and a threat and a roar, and headlights burst violently around the corner of the bluff and reached across the shine of water and picked out, casual and instantaneous, a canoe with a couple in it.

It was there, starkly white, for only a split instant, and then the road swung, the curtain came down. She found it hard to believe that it had been there at all; she even felt a little knife-prick of terror that it could have been there — so silent, so secret, so swallowed in the black, as unseen and unfelt and unsuspected as a crocodile at a jungle ford.

The heat lightning flared again like the flare of distant explosions or the light of burning towns. Instinctively, out of a habit long outgrown, and even while her eyes remained fixed on the place where the canoe had been, she waited for the sound of the blast, but nothing came; she found herself waiting almost ridiculously, with held breath, and that was the time when the lion chose to roar again.

That challenge, coming immediately after the shock of seeing the silent and somehow stealthy canoe, brought a thought that stopped her pulse: "What if he should be loose?" She felt the adrenalin pump into her blood as she might have felt an electric shock. Her heart pounded and her breath came fast through her open mouth. What if he should be loose?

What if, in these Indiana woods by this quiet river where all of them lived and worked for a future full of casual expectation, far from the jungles and the velds where lions could be expected and where darkness was full of danger, what if here too fear prowled on quiet pads and made its snarling noise in the night? This fraternity house where they lived amicably was ringed with dark water and darker woods where the threat lay in wait. This elevated balcony which she could flood with light at the flip of a finger, this fellowship of youth and study and common experience and common hopes, this common belief in the future, were as friable as walls of cane, as vulnerable as grass huts, and she did not need the things that had happened that evening, or the sight of Clark Richards' tiny light flicking and darting back toward her along the riverbank, to know that what she had lived through for six years was not over and would perhaps never be over for any of them, that in their hearts they were alone, terrified, and at bay, each with his ears attuned to some roar across the woods, some ripple of the water, some whisper of a footstep in the dark.

✲ ✲ ✲

The Volcano

ONCE they had turned off the asphalt onto the rough graded road the driver nursed the car along carefully, creeping across bridges and through arroyos and along rocky stretches. While lighting a cigarette he explained to his American passenger.

"It is a car which cost seven thousand pesos," he said. "One does not treat it as if it were a burro."

"Truly," the American said.

"Partly it is the tires," the driver said. "Tires one cannot buy without paying too much to those who sell them illegally. But partly it is the engine. In the dust an engine suffers."

"I believe it," the American said politely. He was watching out the closed window, seeing how the ash had deepened in the last mile or two, how the bridge rails now were mounded with it, and how the pines, growing thickly

on the sides of the countless little volcanic hills, rose list-
less and gray out of a gray blanket as smooth as new snow
and as light under the wind as feathers. Across the west
the cloud of smoke was blacker and angrier, funneling
down so that its compact lower plume was hidden behind
the hills. The sun, at the upper edge of the cloud, was an
immense golden orange.

A horn blatted behind them, and the driver pulled half
off the road. A car went by them fast, pouring back a
choking, impenetrable fog of dust. The driver stopped
philosophically to let it blow away before he started
again. "Loco," he said. "That one has no respect either
for his passengers or his engine."

The American did not answer. He was leaning back in
the seat watching the blasted country outside. Occasionally they crept past adobe huts half buried in the ash,
their corrals drifted deep, their roofs weighted down, the
fields which had once grown corn and beans stretching
away on both sides without a track to break their even,
slaty gray. He thought of the little animals that had lived
in these woods, and whether they had got out before the
ash became deep, or had quietly smothered in their holes.
A wildcat might make headway through it, perhaps, but
not the smaller things, the mice and rabbits and lizards,
and it was the small things that one thought of.

"What has become of the people from here?" he asked.

The driver half turned. Some, he said, had gone, many
to the United States, being taken away in buses and trains
to work as *braceros* in the fields of Arizona and California.

"Where they may be cheated and abused," the American
said. "What of those who stay?"

"I will show you one," the driver said. A little further
on he pointed to a gray hut under the ash-laden shelter

of the pines, a few yards off the road. Peering, the American saw a woman standing in the door, her *rebozo* wrapped across her face, and back of her the cavelike interior and the gleam of a charcoal fire.

"Some, like that one, will not leave," the driver said. "The governor's men have been here and urged them, but they are foolish. It is where they were born; they do not want to leave."

"But what do they live on? They can't grow anything here."

"There are those who cut wood," the driver said. "Though the trees are dying, they are a thing that can be saved. Others, in San Juan, rent horses and burros for the trip to the *boca*. That one, she has nothing. She will die."

The road turned, and the American lost sight of the hut and the still woman in the doorway. Somehow, though the windows were tight shut and the motor and the punished springs filled the car with sound, he had an impression of great silence.

They curved left along a ridge and dropped into a valley, and the volcano was directly ahead of them, not more than two miles away. From its vent monstrous puffs of black smoke mushroomed upward, were whipped ragged by the wind, belched up again. The side of the cone, looking as straight at that distance as if drawn with a ruler, ran down into a curving lava stream that stopped in a broken wall two hundred yards short of the road. The west side of the cone was lost in smoke.

The driver stopped and pointed. Under the lava, he said, was the village of Paricutin. It was not possible to walk across the lava yet, because it had not cooled completely and there were poisonous fumes, but this was a good place to watch from, with the wind the way it was.

"In San Juan it will be dirty," he said. "One will not be able to see much for the smoke."

"The horses leave from San Juan?"

"At about this time every afternoon."

"And there are people in San Juan still?"

"*Si.*"

"*Vamanos,*" the American said. "If we wish we can come back here later."

He sat forward in the seat, watching the volcano throw up its gobbets of smoke. Through and behind the smoke, like distant flying specks, he could see the rocks and boulders that were thrown up and fell swiftly again.

"This trip by horse," he said. "What is it like?"

"It is something to be remembered," the driver said. "One goes up in daylight, but on the return it is very dark, so dark that one cannot see the horse's ears. And behind, as one comes down this black trail that one knew a year ago as a cornfield, is always this noise and this glare on the sky as if hell were open." He took his hand off the wheel and raised it over his head. "There is always this feeling of something behind," he said. "It is like fleeing the end of the world."

"You could wait for me if I went up?"

"Why not?" the driver said. "It is an experience."

They passed a corral, a hut, a clutter of sheds, another corral, its gates hanging open under a gray drift. Then the houses closed in suddenly and they were in a street. In the perpetual twilight of this town of San Juan men and women, wrapped to the eyes in *rebozos* and *serapes,* their bare feet gray and silent in the ashes, walked along under the overhang of thatch, and children leaned against the walls, only their eyes showing under the sombrero rims, and watched the car pass.

In the plaza three buses and a half-dozen cars were

parked. Only when the motor was cut did the American realize that the silence he had been constantly aware of outside had given place to a thin, gritty patter on the roof. The driver gestured upward. "Here it rains cinders," he said. "It is necessary to keep the head well covered, and something over the mouth and nose." He tied a bandanna across his face and climbed out. "I shall see about these horses," he said.

The American waited. On the far side of the plaza a group of Americans, men and women, were already mounting. In odd mismatched clothes, suit trousers and leather jackets and sombreros and bandannas, the women in riding breeches or levis, all of them with their faces muffled, they looked like members of a comic-opera outlaw gang. The driver was having a conference with two Mexicans who were adjusting stirrups for the women. After five minutes he came back.

"It is a pity," he said. "This crowd which is to go immediately has taken all the horses available."

"It is not important," the American said. "Actually I am not so interested in the insides of this volcano."

He tied his handkerchief across his nose, pulled down his hat, and stepped out into the feathery ash. The air was thick with smoke, and cinders pattered on his hat and shoulders. He slitted his eyes against the gritty rain.

"If you would like me to show you around ——" the driver said.

"It is not necessary," the American said. He went poking off up a street that opened on the plaza, his nose filled with the odor that he realized he had been smelling for some time, a sour, acrid, vinegarish odor like fresh-sawn oak. He saw many people, shrouded and silent, but they did not break the stillness in which the falling cinders whispered dryly. Even the handkerchief-muffled calls of the Americans riding off toward the crater, and the tooting of the bus horns in farewell, came through the air as through a thick pillow, and he did not hear his own footsteps in the dust.

Once, as he walked past a doorway into which a trail led through the deep ash, the accumulated ashes on a roof let go and avalanched behind him. He turned to see the last runnels trickling from the thatch, and two little Indian girls, each with a small baby hung over her back in the looped *rebozo,* came out of the doorway and waded experimentally in the knee-deep powder.

The end of the street trailed off into ashen fields, and for a moment the American stood in the unnatural gray dusk looking across toward the cone of Paricutin under its lowering cloud of smoke. At intervals of about a minute there was a grumble like far-off blasting, but because of the smoke which blew directly over the town he could not see the rocks flying up. The cinders were an insistent, sibilant rain on his head and shoulders, and his mouth was bitter with the vinegarish taste.

It was not a place he liked. The village of Paricutin, on the other side, had been buried completely under the lava. That was death both definite and sudden. But this slow death that fell like light rain, this gradual smothering that drooped the pines and covered the holes of the little animals and mounded the roofs and choked the streets, this dying village through which ghosts went in silence, was something else. It was a thing Mexicans had always known, in one form or another, else there would not be in so many of their paintings the figure of the robed skeleton, the walking Death. They were patient under it, they accepted it — but the American did not like to remember how alive the eyes of the Indian girls had been as they waded through the ashes with their little sisters on their backs.

On the way back to the plaza he met a pig that wandered in from a side street. The pig looked at him, wrinkling its snout. Its bristly back was floured with gray ash, and its eyes were red. It grunted softly, querulously, and put its snout to the ground, rooted without hope in the foot-deep powder, walked a few steps with its nose plowing the dry and unprofitable dust.

The American left it and went back to the car. In a moment the driver came from the bus where he had been gossiping. "Let's go," the American said. "Perhaps where we stopped first it is clearer."

They went back through the choked streets, leaving the silent Indians who moved softly as shadows through the dead town and the hog which rooted without hope in the ashes, and pulled off the road in deep ash at the end of the valley. For a few minutes they sat, talking desultorily in polite Spanish and watching the irregular spouting of the cone, opening the windows so that they could hear the ominous low grumble and the faint clatter of falling rocks. The cone was blue-black now, and the lava bed across the foreground was a somber, smoking cliff. It was a landscape without shadows, submerged in gray twilight.

"I have conceived a great hatred for this thing," the American said finally. "It is a thing I have always known and always hated. It is something which kills."

"Truly," the driver said. "I have felt it, as those who are in the war must feel the war."

"Yes," the American said.

"You have friends in the war?"

"Sons," the American said. "One is now a prisoner in Germany."

"Ai," the driver said, with sympathy. He hesitated a minute, as if hunting for the correct thing to say to one whose sons were captives of the enemy. "You hear from him?" he said. "How does he endure his captivity?"

"How does one endure anything?" the American said. "I suppose he hates it and endures it, that is all." He looked out the window, raised his shoulders. "I have heard once only," he said for politeness' sake.

They looked across the gray waste that had once been a *milpa,* toward the smoking front of the lava bed. The light had changed. It was darker, more threatening, like the last ominous moments before a thunderstorm. The west was almost as black as night, but across the field spread a steely dusk that rendered every object sharp-edged and distinct. The American raised his head and looked at the ceiling of the car. The stealthy, light finger-ing had begun there.

"You see?" he said. "That is what I mean. It is some-thing which follows. It is like a doom."

The driver made a deprecating gesture. "The wind has shifted," he said.

"It always shifts," the American said.

He stepped out of the car and stood shin-deep in the gray death, listening to the stealthy whisper and the silence that lay over and under and around. The crater rumbled far off, and boulders fell back with a distant clatter, but the silence still hung like something tangible over the valley.

As he watched, the heavy dusk lightened, and he looked up. By a freak of wind the smoke had been blown high, and though no sign of the setting sun came through the obscured west, a pale, pinkish wash of light came through under the cloud and let an unearthly illumination over the field of ash and the smoking cliff of lava.

Into that lurid dusk an Indian in white pajamas, with a bundle of wood on his back and an axe across his shoulder, came out of the pines at the upper edge of the lava and walked along the clifflike front. Little puffs of dust rose from under his feet. After him, fifteen yards behind, came another, and after him another.

The three strung out across the field, walking as silently in the rosy, metallic light as dream figures. The ones behind did not try to close the gap and walk companionably with the one ahead; the one ahead did not wait for them. They walked in single file, fifteen yards apart, each with his burden of wood on his back, and the little puffs of dust rose under their feet and the punched-hole tracks lengthened behind them across the field.

The American watched them, feeling the silence that weighed on these little figures more heavily than the loads upon their backs, and as he watched he heard the man ahead whistle a brief snatch of tune, drop it, start something else. He went whistling, a ghost in a dead land, toward some hut half buried in ash where a charcoal fire would be burning, and his wife would have ready for him tortillas and beans, with cinders in them, perhaps, like everything else, but still tortillas and beans that would fill a man's belly against the work that must be done tomorrow.

The American watched the three until they were out of sight around the shoulder of the hill. When he climbed into the car and motioned for the driver to start back he was not thinking of the steady smothering fall of the cinders or the death that lay over the streets and cornfields of San Juan. He was thinking of the eyes of the little Indian girls, which were so very alive above the muffling *rebozos*.

"It is a strange thing," he said. "This whistling."

The driver, reaching to turn the ignition key, shrugged and smiled. "Why not?" he said. "The mouth is not made merely to spit with or curse with. At times it may be used for whistling, or even for kissing, *verdad?*"

꘎ ꘎ ꘎

Two Rivers

His father's voice awakened him. Stretching his back, arching against the mattress, he looked over at his parents' end of the sleeping porch. His mother was up too, though he could tell from the flatness of the light outside that it was still early. He lay on his back quietly, letting complete wakefulness come on, watching a spider that dangled on a golden, shining thread from the rolled canvas of the blinds. The spider came down in tiny jerks, his legs wriggling, then went up again in the beam of sun. From the other room the father's voice rose loud and cheerful:

> Oh I'd give every man in the army a quarter
> If they'd all take a shot at my mother-in-law.

The boy slid his legs out of bed and yanked the night-shirt over his head. He didn't want his father's face poking around the door, saying, "I plough deep while sluggards sleep!" He didn't want to be joked with. Yesterday was too sore a spot in his mind. He had been avoiding his father ever since the morning before, and he was not yet ready to accept any joking or attempts to make up. Nobody had a right hitting a person for nothing, and you bet they weren't going to be friends. Let him whistle and sing out there, pretending nothing was the matter. The whole business yesterday was the matter, the Ford that wouldn't start was the matter, the whole lost Fourth of July was the matter, the missed parade, the missed fireworks, the missed ball game in Chinook were the matter. The cuff on the ear his father had given him when he got so mad at the Ford he had to have something to hit was the matter.

In the other room, as he pulled on his overalls, the bacon was snapping in the pan, and he smelled its good morning smell. His father whistled, sang:

> In the town of O'Geary lived Paddy O'Flannagan,
> Battered away till he hadn't a pound,
> His father he died and he made him a man again,
> Left him a farm of tin acres o' ground. . . .

The boy pulled the overall straps over his shoulders and went into the main room. His father stopped singing and looked at him. "Hello, Cheerful," he said. "You look like you'd bit into a wormy apple."

The boy mumbled something and went outside to wash at the bench. It wasn't any fun waking up today. You kept thinking about yesterday, and how much fun it had been waking up then, when you were going to do something special and exciting, drive fifty miles to Chinook and spend the whole day just having fun. Now there wasn't anything but the same old thing to do you did every day. Run the trap line, put out some poison for the gophers, read the Sears Roebuck catalogue.

At breakfast he was glum, and his father joked him. Even his mother smiled, as if she had forgotten already how much wrong had been done the day before. "You look as if you'd been sent for and couldn't come," she said. "Cheer up."

"I don't want to cheer up."

They just smiled at each other, and he hated them both.

After breakfast his father said, "You help your ma with the dishes, now. See how useful you can make yourself around here."

Unwillingly, wanting to get out of the house and away from them, he got the towel and swabbed off the plates. He was rubbing a glass when he heard the Ford sputter and race and roar and then calm down into a steady mutter. His mouth opened, and he looked at his mother. Her eyes were crinkled up with smiling.

"It goes!" he said.

"Sure it goes." She pulled both his ears, rocking his head. "Know what we're going to do?"

"What?"

"We're going to the mountains anyway. Not to Chinook — there wouldn't be anything doing today. But to the mountains, for a picnic. Pa got the car going yesterday afternoon, when you were down in the field, so we decided to go today. If you want to, of course."

"Yay!" he said. "Shall I dress up?"

"Put on your shoes, you'd better. We might climb a mountain."

The boy was out into the porch in three steps. With one shoe on and the other in his hand he hopped to the door. "When?" he said.

"Soon as you can get ready."

He was trying to run and tie his shoelaces at the same time as he went out of the house. There in the Ford, smoking his pipe, with one leg over the door and his weight on the back of his neck, his father sat. "What detained you?" he said. "I've been waiting a half-hour. You must not want to go very bad."

"Aw!" the boy said. He looked inside the Ford. There was the lunch all packed, the fat wet canvas waterbag, even Spot with his tongue out and his ears up. Looking at his father, all his sullenness gone now, the boy said, "When did you get all this ready?"

His father grinned. "While you slept like a sluggard we worked like a buggard," he said. Then the boy knew that everything was perfect, nothing could go wrong. When his father started rhyming things he was in his very best mood, and not even breakdowns and flat tires could make him do more than puff and blow and play-act.

He clambered into the front seat and felt the motor shaking under the floorboards. "Hey, Ma!" he yelled. "Hurry up! We're all ready to go!"

Their own road was a barely marked trail that wriggled out over the burnouts along the east side of the wheat field. At the line it ran into another coming down from the homesteads to the east, and at Cree, a mile inside the Montana boundary, they hit the straight section-line road to Chinook. On that road they passed a trotting team pulling an empty wagon, and the boy waved and yelled, feeling superior, feeling as if he were charioted on pure speed and all the rest of the world were earth-footed.

"Let's see how fast this old boat will go," the father said. He nursed it down through a coulee and onto the flat. His fingers pulled the gas lever down, and the motor roared. Looking back with the wind-stung tears in his eyes, the boy saw his mother hanging to her hat, and the artificial cherries on the hat bouncing. The Ford leaped and bucked, the picnic box tipped over, the dog leaned out and the wind blew his eyes shut and his ears straight back. Turning around, the boy saw the blue sparks leaping from the magneto box and heard his father wahoo. He hung onto the side and leaned out to let the wind tear at him, tried to count the fence posts going by, but they were ahead of him before he got to ten.

The road roughened, and they slowed down. "Good land!" his mother said from the back seat. "We want to get to the Bearpaws, not wind up in a ditch."

"How fast were we going, Pa?"

"Forty or so, I guess. If we'd been going any faster you'd have hollered 'nuff. You were looking pretty peaked."

"I was not."

"Looked pretty scared to me. I guess Ma was hopping around back there like corn in a popper. How'd you like it, Ma?"

"I liked it all right," she said, "but don't do it again."

They passed a farm, and the boy waved at three open-mouthed kids in the yard. It was pretty good to be going somewhere, all right. The mountains were plainer now in the south. He could see dark canyons cutting into the slopes and there was snow on the upper peaks.

"How soon'll we get there, Pa?"

His father tapped the pipe out and put it away and laughed. Without bothering to answer, he began to sing:

> Oh, I dug Snoqualmie River,
> And Lake Samamish too,
> And paddled down to Kirkland
> In a little birch canoe.
>
> I built the Rocky Mountains,
> And placed them where they are,
> Sold whiskey to the Ind-i-ans
> From behind a little bar.

It was then, with the empty flat country wheeling by like a great turntable, the wheat fields and the fences and the far red peaks of barns rotating slowly as if in a dignified dance, wheeling and slipping behind and gone, and his father singing, that the strangeness first came over the boy. Somewhere, sometime . . . and there were mountains in it, and a stream, and a swing that he had fallen out of and cried, and he had mashed ripe blackberries in his hand and his mother had wiped him off, straightening his stiff fingers and wiping hard. . . . His mind caught on that memory from a time before there was any memory, he rubbed his finger tips against his palm and slid a little down in the seat.

His father tramped on both pedals hard and leaned out of the car, looking. He swung to stare at the boy as a startled idiot might have looked, and in a voice heavy with German gutturals he said, "Vot it iss in de crass?"

"What?"

"Iss in de crass somedings. Besser you bleiben right here."

He climbed out, and the boy climbed out after him. The dog jumped over the side and rushed, and in the grass by the side of the road the boy saw the biggest snake he had ever seen, long and fat and sleepy. When it pulled itself in and faced the stiff-legged dog he saw that the hind legs and tail of a gopher stuck out of the stretched mouth.

"Jiminy!" the boy said. "He eats gophers whole."

His father stopped with hands on knees to stare at the snake, looked at the boy, and wagged his head. "Himmel," he said. "Dot iss a schlange vot iss a schlange!"

"What is it?" the mother said from the car and the boy yelled back, "A snake, a great big snake, and he's got a whole gopher in his mouth!"

The father chased the pup away, found a rock, and with

one careful throw crushed the big flat head. The body, as
big around as the boy's ankle, tightened into a ridged
convulsion of muscles, and the tail whipped back and
forth. Stooping, the father pulled on the gopher's tail.
There was a wet, slupping noise, and the gopher slid out,
coated with slime and twice as long as he ought to have
been.

"Head first," the father said. "That's a hell of a way to
die."

He lifted the snake by the tail and held it up. "Look,"
he said. "He's longer than I am." But the mother made a
face and turned her head while he fastened it in the
forked top of a fence post. It trailed almost two feet on
the ground. The tail still twitched.

"He'll twitch till the sun goes down," the father said.
"First guy that comes along here drunk is going to think
he's got D.T.'s." He climbed into the car again, and the
boy followed.

"What was it, Pa?"

"Milk snake. They come into barns sometimes and milk
the cows dry. You saw what he did to that gopher. Milk
a cow dry as powder in ten minutes."

"Gee," the boy said. He sat back and thought about
how long and slick the gopher had been, and how the
snake's mouth was all stretched, and it was a good feeling
to have been along and to have shared something like
that with his father. It was a trophy, a thing you would
remember all your life, and you could tell about it. And
while he was thinking that already, even before they got
to the mountains at all, he had something to remember
about the trip, he remembered that just before they saw
the snake he had been remembering something else, and
he puckered his eyes in the sun thinking. He had been
right on the edge of it, it was right on the tip of his tongue,

and then his father had tramped on the pedals. But it was something a long time ago, and there was a strangeness about it, something bothersome and a little scary, and it hurt his head the way it hurt his head sometimes to do arithmetical sums without pencil and paper. When you did them in your head something went round and round, and you had to keep looking inside to make sure you didn't lose sight of the figures that were pasted up there somewhere, and if you did it very long at a time you got a sick headache out of it. It was something like that when he had almost remembered just a while ago, only he hadn't quite been able to see what he knew was there. . . .

By ten o'clock they had left the graded road and were chugging up a winding trail with toothed rocks embedded in the ruts. Ahead of them the mountains looked low and disappointing, treeless, brown. The trail ducked into a narrow gulch and the sides rose up around them, reddish gravel covered with bunch grass and sage.

"Gee whiz," the boy said. "These don't look like mountains."

"What'd you expect?" his father said. "Expect to step out onto a glacier or something?"

"But there aren't any trees," the boy said. "Gee whiz, there isn't even any water."

He stood up to look ahead. His father's foot went down on the low pedal, and the Ford growled at the grade. "Come on, Lena," his father said. He hitched himself back and forward in the seat, helping the car over the hill, and then, as they barely pulled over the hump and the sides of the gully fell away, there were the real mountains, high as heaven, the high slopes spiked and tufted with trees, and directly ahead of them a magnificent V-shaped door with the sun touching gray cliffs far back in,

and a straight-edged violet shadow streaming down from
the eastern peak clear to the canyon floor.

"Well?" the father's voice said. "I guess if you don't
like it we can drop you off here and pick you up on the
way back."

The boy turned to his mother. She was sitting far forward on the edge of the seat. "I guess we want to come
along, all right," she said, and laughed as if she might cry.
"Anything as beautiful as that! Don't we, sonny?"

"You bet," he said. He remained standing all the way
up over the gentle slope of the alluvial fan that aproned
out from the canyon's mouth, and when they passed under
the violet shadow, not violet any more but cool gray, he
tipped his head back and looked up miles and miles to the
broken rock above.

The road got rougher. "Sit down," his father said.
"First thing you know you'll fall out on your head and
sprain both your ankles."

He was in his very best mood. He said funny things to
the car, coaxing it over steep pitches. He talked to it like
a horse, patted it on the dashboard, promised it an apple
when they got there. Above them the canyon walls opened
out and back, went up steeply high and high and high,
beyond the first walls that the boy had thought so terrific,
away beyond those, piling peak on peak, and the sun
touched and missed and touched again.

The trail steepened. A jet of steam burst from the brass
radiator cap, the car throbbed and labored, they all sat
forward and urged it on. But it slowed, shook, stopped
and stood there steaming and shaking, and the motor
died with a last, lunging gasp.

"Is this as far as we can get?" the boy said. The thought
that they might be broken down, right here on the
threshold of wonder, put him in a panic. He looked

around. They were in a bare rocky gorge. Not even any trees yet, though a stream tumbled down a bouldered channel on the left. But to get to trees and the real mountains they had to go further, much further. "Can't we get any further?" he said.

His father grunted. "Skin down to the creek and get a bucket of water." The boy ran, came stumbling and staggering back with the pail. His mother had already climbed out and put a rock under the back wheel, and they stood close together while the father with a rag made quick, stabbing turns at the radiator cap. The cap blew off and steam went up for six feet and they all jumped back. There was a sullen subterranean boiling deep under the hood.

"Now!" the father said. He poured a little water in, stepped back. In a minute the water came bubbling out again. He poured again, and the motor spit it out again. "Can't seem to keep anything on her stomach," the father said, and winked at the boy. He didn't seem worried.

The fourth dose stayed down. They filled up the radiator till it ran over, screwed the plug in, and threw the pail in the back end. "You two stay out," the father said. "I'll see if she'll go over unloaded."

She wouldn't. She moved two feet, strangled and died. The boy watched with his jaw hanging, remembering yesterday, remembering when something like this had happened and the whole day had gone wrong. But his father wasn't the same today. He just got out of the car and didn't swear at all, but winked at the boy again, and made a closing motion with his hand under his chin. "Better shut that mouth," he said. "Some bird'll fly in there and build a nest."

To the mother he said, "Can you kick that rock out from under the wheel?"

"Sure," she said. "But do you think . . . Maybe we could walk from here."

"Hell with it," he said cheerfully. "I'll get her up if I have to lug her on my back."

She kicked the stone away and he rolled backward down the hill, craning, steering with one hand. At the bottom he cramped the wheels, got out and cranked the motor, got in again, and turned around in the narrow road, taking three or four angled tries before he made it. Then his hand waved, and there was the Ford coming up the hill backwards, kicking gravel down from under its straining hind wheels, angling across the road and back and up, and the motor roaring like a threshing engine, until it went by them and on up to the crest and turned around with one quick expert ducking motion, and they got in and were off again.

"Well!" said the mother in relief. "Who'd have thought of going up backwards."

"Got more power in reverse," the father said. "Can't make it one way, try another."

"Yay!" the boy said. He was standing up, watching the deep insides of the earth appear behind the angled rock, and his mind was soaring again, up into the heights where a hawk or eagle circled like a toy bird on a string.

"How do you like it?" his mother shouted at him. He turned around and nodded his head, and she smiled at him, wrinkling her eyes. She looked excited herself. Her face had color in it and the varnished cherries bouncing on her hat gave her a reckless, girlish look.

"Hi, ma," he said, and grinned.

"Hi yourself," she said, and grinned right back. He lifted his face and yelled for the very pressure of happiness inside him.

They lay on a ledge high upon the sunny east slope and looked out to the north through the notch cut as sharply as a wedge out of a pie. Far below them the golden plain spread level, golden-tawny grass and golden-green wheat checkerboarded in a pattern as wide as the world. Back of them the spring they had followed up the slope welled out of the ledge, spread out in a small swampy spot, and trickled off down the hill. There were trees, a thick cluster of spruce against the bulge of the wall above them, a clump of twinkling, sunny aspen down the slope, and in the canyon bottom below them a dense forest of soft maple. The mother had a bouquet of leaves in her hand, a little bunch of pine cones on the ground beside her. The three lay quietly, looking down over the steeply dropping wall to the V-shaped door, and beyond that to the interminable plain.

The boy wriggled his back against the rock, put his hand down to shift himself, brought it up again prickled with broken spruce needles. He picked them off, still staring out over the canyon gateway. They were far above the world he knew. The air was cleaner, thinner. There was cold water running from the rock, and all around there were trees. And over the whole canyon, like a haze in the clear air, was that other thing, that memory or ghost of a memory, a swing he had fallen out of, a feel of his hands sticky with crushed blackberries, his skin drinking cool shade, and his father's anger — the reflection of ecstasy and the shadow of tears.

"I never knew till this minute," his mother said, "how much I've missed the trees."

Nobody answered. They were all stuffed with lunch, pleasantly tired after the climb. The father lay staring off down the canyon, and the sour smell of his pipe, in that air, was pleasant and clean. The boy saw his mother put the stem of a maple leaf in her mouth and make a half-pleased face at the bitter taste.

The father rose and dug a tin cup from the picnic box, walked to the spring and dipped himself a drink. He made a breathy sound of satisfaction. "So cold it hurts your teeth," he said. He brought the mother a cup, and she drank.

"Brucie?" she said, motioning with the cup.

He started to get up, but his father filled the cup and brought it, making believe he was going to pour it on him. The boy ducked and reached for the cup. With his eyes on his father over the cup's rim, he drank, testing the icy water to see if it really did hurt the teeth. The water was cold and silvery in his mouth, and when he swallowed he felt it cold clear down to his stomach.

"It doesn't either hurt your teeth," he said. He poured a little of it on his arm, and something jumped in his skin. It was his skin that remembered. Something numbingly cold, and then warm. He felt it now, the way you waded in it.

"Mom," he said.

"What?"

"Was it in Washington we went on a picnic like this and picked blackberries and I fell out of a swing and there were big trees, and we found a river that was half cold and half warm?"

His father was relighting his pipe. "What do you know about Washington?" he said. "You were only knee-high to a grasshopper when we lived there."

"Well, I remember," the boy said. "I've been remembering it all day long, ever since you sang that song about building the Rocky Mountains. You sang it that day, too. Don't you remember, Mom?"

"I don't know," she said doubtfully. "We went on picnics in Washington."

"What's this about a river with hot and cold running water?" his father said. "You must remember some time you had a bath in a bathtub."

"I do not!" the boy said. "I got blackberries mashed all over my hands and Mom scrubbed me off, and then we found that river and we waded in it and half was hot and half was cold."

"Oh-h-h," his mother said. "I believe I do. . . . Harry, you remember once up in the Cascades, when we went out with the Curtises? And little Bill Curtis fell off the dock into the lake." She turned to the boy. "Was there a summer cottage there, a brown shingled house?"

"I don't know," the boy said. "I don't remember any Curtises. But I remember blackberries and that river and a swing."

"Your head is full of blackberries," his father said. "If it was the time we went out with the Curtises there weren't any blackberries. That was in the spring."

"No," the mother said. "It was in the fall. It was just before we moved to Redmond. And I think there was a place where one river from the mountains ran into another one from the valley, and they ran alongside each other in the same channel. The mountain one was a lot colder. Don't you remember that trip with the Curtises, Harry?"

"Sure I remember it," the father said. "We hired a buckboard and saw a black bear and I won six bits from Joe Curtis pitching horseshoes."

"That's right," the mother said. "You remember the bear, Brucie."

The boy shook his head. There wasn't any bear in what he remembered. Just feelings, and things that made his skin prickle.

His mother was looking at him, a little puzzled wrinkle

between her eyes. "It's funny you should remember such different things than we remember," she said. "Everything means something different to everybody, I guess." She laughed, and the boy thought her eyes looked very odd and bright. "It makes me feel as if I didn't know you at all," she said. She brushed her face with the handful of leaves and looked at the father, gathering up odds and ends and putting them in the picnic box. "I wonder what each of us will remember about today?"

"I wouldn't worry about it," the father said. "You can depend on Bub here to remember a lot of things that didn't happen."

"I don't think he does," she said. "He's got a good memory."

The father picked up the box. "It takes a good memory to remember things that never happened," he said. "I remember once a garter snake crawled into my cradle and I used it for a belt to keep my breechclout on. They took it away from me and I bawled the crib so full of tears I had to swim for shore. I drifted in three days later on a checkerboard raft with a didie for a sail."

The boy stood up and brushed off his pants. "You do too remember that river," he said.

His father grinned at him. "Sure. Only it wasn't quite as hot and cold as you make it out."

It was evening in the canyon, but when they reached the mouth again they emerged into full afternoon, with two hours of sun left them. The father stopped the car before they dipped into the gravelly wash between the foothills, and they all looked back at the steep thrust of the mountains, purpling in the shadows, the rock glowing golden-red far back on the faces of the inner peaks. The mother still held her bouquet of maple leaves in her hand.

"Well, there go the Mountains of the Moon," she said. The moment was almost solemn. In the front seat the boy stood looking back. He felt the sun strong against the side of his face, and the mountains sheering up before him were very real. In a little while, as they went north, they would begin to melt together, and the patches of snow would appear far up on the northern slopes. His eyes went curiously out of focus, and he saw the mountains as they would appear from the homestead on a hot day, a ghostly line on the horizon.

He felt his father twist to look at him, but the trance was so strong on him that he didn't look down for a minute. When he did he caught his mother and father looking at each other, the look they had sometimes when he had pleased them and made them proud of him.

"Okay," his father said, and stabbed him in the ribs with a hard thumb. "Wipe the black bears out of your eyes."

He started the car again, and as they bounced down the rocky trail toward the road he sang at the top of his voice, bellowing into the still, hot afternoon:

> I had a kid and his name was Brucie,
> Squeezed black bears and found them juicy,
> Washed them off in a hot-cold river,
> Now you boil and now you shiver,
> Caught his pants so full of trout
> He couldn't sit down till he got them out.
> Trout were boiled from the hot-side river,
> Trout from the cold side raw as liver.
> Ate the boiled ones, ate the raw,
> And then went howling home to Maw.

The boy looked up at his father, his laughter bubbling up, everything wonderful, the day a swell day, his mother clapping hands in time to his father's fool singing.

"Aw, for gosh sakes," he said, and ducked when his father pretended he was going to swat him one.

Hostage

HE WAS LOOKING at the Foxy Grandpa book that Mr. Richie had given him when he heard the lock click. Instantly he shoved the book under him and crowded back against the wall, his feet just sticking over the edge of the cot, his arms hugged tight around his body. In his terror his body felt small and insufficient, hardly enough to hang onto.

They came in just the way they had come in every day since they brought him here, Mr. Richie first, then the insurance detective from Montpelier, Mr. Richie's sharp little face poked forward, smiling, his eyebrows moving up and down, and the detective behind him tall and solemn, red-nosed, with his handkerchief in his hand. The detective had hay fever and his eyes always looked red-rimmed, like a hound's. Feeling the rough plaster wall through his shirt, and the bulge of the overall straps up his spine, the boy watched them come in and shut the door.

Mr. Richie sat down and thumped his knees. "Well, Bub," he said cheerfully. The detective also sat down, blowing his nose. It was all the same as it had been before. In a minute they would start asking him, and prodding him, and sticking their faces out at him, and trying to twist what he said into something he hadn't said at all.

"Treating you all right?" Mr. Richie said. His little fox-face was grinning, and he twinkled under white eyebrows. He looked, the boy thought with surprise, a good deal like the pictures in the Foxy Grandpa book.

The boy nodded.

"You like being in jail, uh?" the detective said.

The boy shook his head.

"Now looky here, Bub," Mr. Richie said. "We ain't trying to be mean to you. You just tell us the truth about how that fire started and you'll be out of here in a minute."

"I already told you," the boy squeaked.

"You told us something," the detective said. "How about telling us the truth?"

Without taking his sharp, blue, twinkling eyes off the boy's, Mr. Richie dug into his coat pocket, got a cigar, bit off the end and spit it out, found a match, lighted it on his thumb nail, puffed, and said through the smoke, "Still an accident, was it?"

The boy nodded.

"You just went down with a candle to the barn and the swallows flapped around the light and scared you and you dropped the candle and run and that set the barn on fire."

The boy nodded, swallowing.

"You lived on a farm all your life," the detective said heavily, "and you don't know better'n to go into a hay-mow with a candle. You don't know swallows'll fly at a light. You don't know enough to make sure a light's out before you go."

The boy said nothing.

"Why'd they send you down there with a candle?" the detective said harshly, and stuck his face forward.

"There wasn't any coal oil for the lantern."

" 'Tisn't as if Branch Willard was any kin of yours," Mr. Richie said mildly. "He ain't but your stepfather. You don't have to protect him. He never treated you very good anyway, did he?"

The boy did not answer.

"*Did he?*" the detective said.

The boy jumped, but said nothing.

"Why hadn't Willard put any hay in that barn yet?" the detective said.

"He had."

" 'Bout five load," the detective said. "You think we're silly, boy? Everybody's got his hay all in, and there's Willard with a thirty-acre meadow he ain't touched."

"I guess he was busy," the boy said, and drew his knees up under his chin, crowding against the wall. "He was trying to sell the calves."

"And you know why," the detective said. He blew his nose, wrenching the end harshly. "He wanted 'em out of that barn when he burned it down. He wanted his insurance but he didn't want to lose his stock."

The boy hiccoughed. A nerve in his cheek twitched, and he put his hand over the side of his face. He looked at Mr. Richie for help, but Mr. Richie was rolling the cigar in his lips and looking out the window.

"He's a slick one," the detective said. "I never seen any slicker trick. Sending a kid down to the mow with a candle and then saying the swallows scared him. He sent you, didn't he?"

The boy kept still.

"Didn't he?"

"Yes, but . . ."

"What for?"

"The pitchforks."

"What'd he want of them after dark?"

"I don't know."

"Saving his pitchforks too," the detective said. He leaned back and reached for his handkerchief.

Mr. Richie blew half a dozen rings and said, " 'Tisn't as open and shut as all that, Rufe. How in thunder would he know the swallows'd fly down and scare the kid? How'd he know the kid'd drop the candle and run?"

"There's a fifty-fifty chance of a fire whenever you send a kid into a mow with a candle," the detective said.

The boy was looking gratefully at Mr. Richie. Mr. Richie lived in the village, and even if he did sell insurance and even if he had been with the detective when they came to take him to jail, he was somebody familiar, at least. And he wasn't as rough as the detective, and he smiled all the time.

"Just the same," Mr. Richie said, standing up and pointing the cigar at him, "we know Branch Willard burned that barn down a-purpose. You might as well tell us."

"I told you already," the boy said. "Honest, Mr. Richie . . ."

"We might's well go," Mr. Richie said, and put the cigar back in his mouth.

The detective rose, grumbling. "Three days," he said. "Three days already in this damn place where every meadow looks like it'd been planted to goldenrod. You'll never get anything out of this kid."

"Never did expect to," Mr. Richie said cheerfully.

"Then what are we keeping him for?"

"Got a right to hold him," Mr. Richie said. "Long as he

says it was him burned down the barn we got a right to hold him."

"What good will that do?"

"Trouble with you," Mr. Richie said, holding the door open and twinkling past the detective at the boy, as if they shared a joke, "you ain't got enough imagination to bait a hook." The door closed behind him, the lock snapped, and the boy heard Mr. Richie's voice going down the hall. "What would you do, if you was Martha Mount, and you'd married a good-for-nothing like Branch, and he had an insurance fire, and they come and stuck your boy in jail for it? You'd stand it a day or so, maybe, depending on how much . . . "

The voice dwindled and went away, and the boy relaxed a little away from the wall. He pulled the Foxy Grandpa book from under him and looked at it stupidly. What if Branch *had* wanted the barn burned down? But he couldn't have. It was just like he'd told them. Big with terror as that night was, he went over it, trying to remember. He went out with the candle after Branch shook the kerosene can and found it empty, and he went creeping through the blackness that blanketed sky and ground, holding his hand around the candle flame to shield it from the wind that wandered down off the hill toward the swamp. He went in the cow stable and through the milk room and up the ladder to the high drive, and just as he stuck the candle on the beam the Things came, beating at the light, at his head, with fluttering, squeaking noises, and he screamed and ran through the black mow, banging into the double doors, ripping his fingernail trying to get the bars up. Then he ran across the back lot toward the lighted kitchen window, and slammed into a fence post in the dark, knocking his wind out, and the next he remembered was Mumma picking him up off the back stoop and carrying him inside. He was still crying a little, and his chest was still sore, when Branch came in the back door and said the barn was afire, his candle must have dropped off the beam into the hay.

So it had been an accident, plain as that. How was he to know the fluttering things were swallows? The memory of the terrible black loom of the mow above the dim candle-glow, and the squeaking, beating things that swooped down, contracted his whole body in a shiver. He flapped the pages of the Foxy Grandpa book.

He wondered if the detective would put him in jail for a long time. Mr. Richie wouldn't let him. Mr. Richie was too jolly to let a boy get put in jail for an accident. He remembered the way the men in the store at the village had laughed one day when Mr. Richie was telling them a joke he played on a city man. The city man had bought a cow and brought it to Mr. Richie to make sure he hadn't got stung. And Mr. Richie had looked the cow over, opened its mouth and looked in, and said, "My gosh, man, this cow ain't got any teeth in her upper jaw. She'll starve to death in a week." So he ended up by buying a hundred-and-thirty-dollar cow for forty dollars, to make beef out of, and when the city man found out how he'd been fooled, he was so ashamed he sold his camp and moved somewhere else.

Mr. Richie, he assured himself, wouldn't let him get put in jail. Maybe Mumma would come down and get him out. That was what Mr. Richie seemed to expect. Only why should he just wait down here? Mumma was up at the farm. He could go see her if he wanted to. The memory of Mumma hanging onto him and crying and looking around in every direction as if she expected help to come from somewhere, when the detective and Mr.

Richie came and took him away, made the boy swallow.
He shut his eyes tight to squeeze the two big tears that
oozed into his eyes.

Lying down on the cot, he craned under to look at the
rusty springs, put his hand tentatively around the iron leg.
Then he sat up, listening. Somebody was coming again.

The door opened, and it was Mumma. "Andy!" she said.
"Little Andy boy!" She grabbed him in her arms and
hugged him, and he smelled the store smell of her shirt-
waist. "Have they scared you?" she said. "Have they
been mean to you?"

"They keep trying to make me say Branch burned down
the barn a-purpose," he said.

Her arms tightened around him; she kissed the top of
his head and then held him away to look at him. There
were tear streaks in the flour she had used to powder her
face. "Did they feed you?" she said. "Have you had
enough to eat? You look thin."

"Oh yuh," he said vaguely. He looked at the faces of
Mr. Richie and the detective in the doorway. Mr. Richie
winked at him.

"Do you mind staying here a little while longer?"
Mumma said. "I want to talk to Mr. Richie."

"Can't I go?"

"I'd rather you stayed here," she said. He saw her lips
pucker over her upper plate as if they had a drawstring
in them.

"Mumma!" he said. "Don't you tell them anything just
to get me out. They tried to make me say it wasn't an
accident, but it was."

"Don't you worry," Mumma said. Her eyes blinked rapidly and she turned away. "I'll be back in a minute,
Andy." She turned back, took him and shook his shoulders gently. "You won't mind, just for a minute, will you?"

They were a long time coming back, and when they

came in he saw that she had been crying again. The boy
stood up slowly. His mother came across the room very
fast and hugged him tight again. Her voice sounded
choked. "You'll hate your mumma," she said. "That's
what I can't stand, you'll hate your mumma."

He clung to her, trying to look in her face, but she kept
her face turned. Mr. Richie had lighted another cigar.

"They're going to put Mumma in jail," she said.

Andy's eyes went from his mother's averted, twisted
face to Mr. Richie's. "You don't have to pretend any more,
Bub," Mr. Richie said. "Your mumma's told us all about
it."

"But it was the Things!" Andy said. "The swallows,
they came down and knocked the candle out of my
hand . . ."

"And it went out," the detective said. "Branch went
down there afterwards and stuck a match in the hay, like
he'd been planning all the time and then planning to lay
it on you for being careless."

Andy's hands clenched in his mother's coat. "Mumma,
he didn't, did he?"

She nodded.

"But why are they going to put you in jail?" he said.
"You never did it. It was Branch."

"I helped him," she said. "You'll never forgive me,
Andy, but I was even going to help him lay it on you, because I thought if it was an accident, and we didn't blame
you for it, you wouldn't feel too bad. But if there'd been
any other way we could see . . . We were awful hard up,
Andy."

The boy wet his lips. "Why don't they put Branch in
jail?"

"He's left. I don't know where. They'll put him in too
if they can catch him."

He stood very still, letting the detective's long face and

hound-eyes, Mr. Richie's lips with the cigar between them, his mother's pale flour-streaked face twisted with crying, go round him in a confused blur. It was all a part, a continuation, of the terror that had first come on him when he went out into the pitch-darkness with his candle, that had sent him blind and screaming across the high drive under the black loft full of nameless fluttering Things, that had left him throat-dry and frozen when he looked out the door and saw the flames licking high from the open doors of the barn and knew he had done it, that had been with him for three days in the jail while the detective's face and Mr. Richie's face poked out at him, sharp-lipped, saying sharp words.

"I'm ashamed, Andy," his mother said. "I'm so ashamed I could die."

He swallowed, only half hearing her, and a thought came beating down like the terrifying wings from the dark mow. "What'll I do?" he said. "Where'll I go, Mumma?" He looked from her to Mr. Richie, and Mr. Richie smiled and winked.

"Your Mumma and I talked it over," Mr. Richie said. "You're coming to live with me. I ain't so mean I can see a boy thrown out in the world like that. You'll go to school in the village. Think you can make yourself useful enough to earn your keep?" He smiled more widely, and winked again, his fox face full of good humor and friendliness, as if to say, "Sure you can, we'll get along fine."

Andy tugged at his mother's coat, still looking at Mr. Richie. "Mumma?"

"Mr. Richie's very kind to offer it," his mother said. "He'll take good care of you, and you'll be a good boy. Won't you?"

Andy looked at Mr. Richie's lips. Mr. Richie's hand came up and took the cigar out of them, and the lips smiled. Andy stared at him, hardly seeing him at all, seeing only the smiling lips. There was a mist over everything else. He smelled the store smell of his mother's clothes.

"Yes," he said. He laid his face against the store smell, and his fingers dragged at the coat. With his eyes shut tight he screamed into the muffling cloth, "But I'll hate him! I'll hate him as long as I live!"

❦ ❦ ❦

In the Twilight

THE BOY always felt October as a twilight month. Its whole function was the preparation for winter, a getting ready, a drawing-in of the sun like a snail into its shell, a shortening and tightening against the long cold. And that year, after his father bought the sow up on the north bench and brought her in to be fattened up in the corral behind the barn, he felt obscurely the difference between the two kinds of preparation going on. The footbridge came out, was piled up in sections and planks in the loft of the barn. That would go in again next spring, as soon as the danger of the ice and floodwater was over. But the sow was not going to be back next spring. Her preparation was of a more final kind.

He had the job of carrying the swill bucket to the corral every morning, carrying a sharpened stick to poke the frantic beast away from the trough while he poured the sloppy mess of potato peelings and apple peelings and bacon rinds and sour milk and bread crusts. The sow fascinated him, though he disliked her intensely. He hated the smell of the swill, he hated the pig's lumbering, greedy rush when he appeared with the pail, he hated her pig eyes sunk in fat, he hated the rubber snout and the caked filth on her bristly hide. Still, he used to stand and watch her gobbling in the trough, and sometimes he scratched her back with the stick and felt her vast, bestial pleasure in the hunching of her spine and the deep, smacking grunts that rumbled out of her.

In a sense she was his personal enemy. She was responsible for the nasty job he had every day. She was responsible for the stink that offended him when he passed the corral. She was dirty and greedy and monstrous. But she was fascinating all the same, perhaps because all her greed worked against her, and what she ate so ravenously served death, not life. The day she broke loose, and children and dogs and women with flapping aprons headed her off from the river brush and shooed her back toward the corral, the boy and his brother Chet stood at the bars panting with the chase and promised her how soon she'd get hers. In just about a week now she wouldn't be causing any trouble. Chet took aim with an imaginary rifle and shot her just behind the left foreleg, and then Bruce took aim and shot her between the eyes, and they went away satisfied and somehow reconciled to the old sow, ugly and smelly and greedy and troublesome as she was, because she was as good as dead already.

In the big double bed Bruce stirred, yawned, stretched his feet down and pulled them back again quick when they touched a cold spot, opened his eyes and looked up. The mottled ceiling above him, stained by firemen's chemicals when they had the attic fire, was a forest. He

could see a bird with a big, hooked bill sitting on a tree.
He yawned again, squinting his eyes and twisted his head,
and from the different angle, it was not a bird at all, but
an automobile with its top down and smoke coming out
behind. His eyes moved over the whole ceiling, picking
out the shapes he and Chet had settled on definitely: the
wildcat with one white, glaring eye; the man waving a
flag; the woman with big feet and a bundle on her back.
He lay picking them out, letting sleep go away from him
slowly.

Downstairs he heard sounds, bumpings, the clank of a
pan, and his head turned so that he could look out of the
window. It was still early; the sun was barely tipping the
barn roof. The folks didn't usually . . .

Then he stabbed Chet with an elbow. "Hey! Get up.
This is the morning for the pig."

Chet flailed with his arms, grumbled, and half sat up.
His hair was frowsy, and he was mad. "Don't go sticking
your darn elbow into me," he said. "What's the matter?"

"The pig," Bruce said. "Pa's butchering the pig this
morning."

"Heck with the old dirty pig," Chet said, but Bruce
had barely got his long black stockings on before Chet
was on the edge of the bed, dressing, too. Bruce beat him
downstairs by about a minute.

The kitchen was warm. The washtub and the copper
boiler were on the stove, and already sent up wisps of
steam. Both boys, out of habit, huddled their bottoms
close to the open oven door, watching their father finish
his coffee.

He seemed in high spirits, and winked at Chet. "What
are you up so early for?"

"Gonna help butcher the pig."

Their mother, standing by the washstand with a couple

of mush bowls in her hands, looked at them. "You just forget about the pig. Sit down and eat your breakfast. Are you washed?"

"No'm," they said. "But we want to watch."

She waved them to the washstand and set the table for them. While they ate, their father sat sharpening the butcher knife on the edge of a crock, and they watched him.

"How you gonna do it?" Bruce said. "Cut her throat?"

"Bruce!" his mother said.

"Well, is he?" Chet said. He added, "I bet it bleeds like anything," and stared at the glittering edge of the knife.

"You boys better go play in the brush, or go up to the sandhills," their mother said. "You don't want to watch a nasty, bloody mess like this is going to be. I should think you'd feel sorry for the poor old pig."

They jeered. Bruce got the vision of the throat-cutting out of his mind and punched Chet on the shoulder. "No more old slop to carry," he said.

Chet punched him back and said, "No more old ugly sow snuffing around in the manure."

"Sausages for breakfast," Bruce said.

"Pork chops for dinner," said Chet.

They giggled, and their father looked them over, laughing. "Couple of cannibals," he said. He reached out and yanked a hair from Chet's head, held it between thumb and forefinger, and sliced it neatly in two with the knife. Chet watched him with one hand on his violated skull.

"Well, I don't think they should see things like that," the mother said helplessly. "Heaven knows they kill a lot of gophers and things on the farm, but this is worse."

The father stood up. "Oh, rats," he said. "I always watched butcherings when I was a kid. You want to make them so sissy they can't chop the head off a rooster?"

"I still don't think it's right," she said. "When I was little, I had to go out with a bowl and catch the blood for blood pudding. It gave me nightmares for a month after. . . . "

She stopped and turned to the stove, and Bruce saw her shoulders move as if she had had a chill. He imagined her stooping with a bowl under the pig's red, gaping throat, and the thought made him swallow twice at the mouthful he had. But a minute later his father went into the cellarway and got Chet's .22, and they crowded on his heels as he picked up the knife and went out.

"Brucie," his mother said, "don't you go!"

"Aw, heck," he said, and deliberately disobeyed her.

The morning was crisp, sunny, the air tangy with late autumn. In the far corner of the corral the sow heaved to her feet, her hindquarters still sagging loosely on the ground, and stared at them. She did not come near, and Bruce wondered why. Maybe because they didn't have a pail with them. Chet leaned on the corral bars and jeered at her.

"All right for you, old sow. This is where you get yours."

Excitement prickled in Bruce's legs. He couldn't stand still. With his hands on the top bar he jumped up and down and yelled at the ugly beast, and all his hatred of her ugliness and her vast pig appetites came out of him in shrill cries. The sow got clear up, and the father spoke sharply. "Shut up. You'll get her all excited. If you want to help, all right, but if you can't keep quiet you can go back in the house."

They fell quiet while he loaded the single-shot Remington. The sow came forward a few steps, snout wrinkling. She stopped at the edge of the manure pile, under the hole through which it was pitched from the barn, and fronted them suspiciously.

"Where you gonna shoot her?" Chet whispered.

"Head," his father whispered back. "Don't want any holes in her meat."

He leaned the gun over the rail and took aim for what seemed minutes. Then the sow moved, and he took his finger outside the trigger guard and eased up. Bruce let his breath out in a long, wispy plume, thinking: if she hadn't moved just then she'd be dead now, she'd be lying there like a chicken with its head cut off. On a day like this, with the sun just coming up and everything so bright, she'd be dead. He swallowed.

His father reached down and picked up the butcher knife, sticking it into the top bar where it would be handy. "All right now," he said. He seemed excited himself. His breath came short through his nose.

He laid the barrel over the bar again, and his cheek dropped against the stock. The sow lowered her head and snuffed at the manure, and in the instant when she was frozen there, perfectly still except for the little red, upward-peering eyes, the rifle cracked thinly, dryly, like a stick breaking.

The sow leaped straight into the air, her open mouth bursting with sound, came down still squealing to stand for a moment stiff-legged, swinging her head. Then she was running around and around the corral, faster than Bruce had ever believed she could move, around and around, ponderous, galloping, terrified, a sudden and living pain. The constant high shriek of agony, sustained at an unsustainable pitch, cut the nerves like a knife.

The boy stood stiffly with his hands on the bar, watching her. He heard the click of the bolt as his father threw the shell and the snip of metal as he reloaded. Then his father was running, almost as heavily as the sow, but more terribly because he was the killer and she the killed. The boy saw his red face, his open mouth, as he pursued the sow around the corral, trying to stop and corner her for another shot.

The squeal went on, an intolerable sound of death, and the sow charged blindly around the pen. A trickle of red ran down over her snout from between her eyes, and she went on, staggering, a death that did not want to die, a vast, greedy life hurt and dying and shrilling its pain. Even through his own terror Bruce could not miss the way she scrambled to avoid the man with the gun. She plunged up on the manure pile, was cornered there, raced down and around the bars again, and then in one magnificent running leap went clear up over the manure, through the hole and into the barn.

"God Almighty!" the father yelled. "Head her off. *Run!*"

The two boys arrived at the barn door together, slammed the lower half shut and peered over. The pig's wild screaming came from the cow stable, empty now. The horses in the front stalls were trembling and white-eyed, and, as Chet pushed the upper door, the nervous mare lashed out with both hind feet, and splinters flew from the board ceiling.

Their father was beside them now, looking in, the gun in his right hand. His face was so violently red that Bruce shrank away.

"Get on out behind again," the father said. "If she comes out through the hole, yell and keep her inside the fence."

He went inside, and the boys fled around behind, their eyes glued to the manure hole, their ears full of the muffled and unceasing shrilling of the wounded sow. They heard her squealing sharpen, heard the new fear in it, heard their father shouting, and then she arched through the window again, jumping like a horse at a fence, front feet tucked up and hind legs sailing. Her feet hit the edge, and she fell rolling, but the squealing did not stop. She was up in a moment, head swinging desperately from side to side, and in that moment the father, coming around the corner, took quick aim and fired again.

The sow stood still. Her squeal went up and up and up to a cracking pitch. Her whole fat, mud-caked body quivered and began to settle, her legs spraddled as if to keep it from going down. Then the squeal trailed off to a thin whimper, the front legs buckled, the sow's snout plowed into the manure, and the father was over the fence with the knife in his hand. The stoop, the jerk of the shoulder, the rush of bright blood. . . .

"Jeez!" Chet said.

Bruce, strangling, tried to look, tried to say something to show that it had been wonderful and exciting, that it served the dirty old sow right, but he couldn't speak. His eyes, turned away from the corral, were still full of the picture of his father standing over the dead sow, towering, triumphant, the bloody knife in his hand, his back huge and broad and monstrous with power. He gulped and swallowed as a rush of salty liquid filled his mouth.

"My gosh," Chet said. "Did you see her run? Right between the eyes, and it only made her squeal and run."

Bruce turned his head further and clung to the bar. He heard Chet's voice, going away, getting dimmer. "What's the matter? You're white as a sheet."

"I am . . . not," Bruce said. He straightened his shoulders and lifted his head, but a moment later he was hanging on the corral vomiting, heaving, clinging for dear life to keep the black dots in his brain from becoming solid.

And after a minute his father's voice, still breathless and jerky with exertion. "Couldn't stand it, uh? You all right, Chet?"

Chet said he felt fine, swell. Bruce clung to the voices, hung onto them desperately, because as long as he could hear them the terror wasn't total, the black dots weren't solid. "You better get on into the house," his father said, and then raised his voice and called, "Sis!"

His mother came and held him with one arm and led him back to the house and, still frantically clinging to voices, to meanings, he heard her say, "You never should have watched it, it's horrible, I knew all the time. . . . "

There was a while when he lay on the sofa in the parlor with his eyes closed. His mother came in once to see how he felt, but the duties in the kitchen and yard were demanding, and she stayed only a minute. Listening out of his still struggle with nausea, he heard the thumpings in the kitchen, the quick footsteps, the words, and as his nausea ebbed, he wondered what was going on now. Once, when the outside door was opened, he heard the voices of boys out by the barn.

Shame made him turn over and lie face down. What he had done was sissy. Chet hadn't got sick, and the other kids out there watching now weren't sick, or they wouldn't be yelling that way. But they hadn't seen the old sow run, or heard her squeal, or seen his father stooping with the knife. . . .

His mother was out there, though, helping to get it done, and she had said from the start that she hated it. Everybody was helping but him, and he lay inside like a baby because he couldn't stand the sight of blood. What if he'd been told to catch the blood, like Ma? The thought sickened him, and he lay still.

After a while he sat up tentatively, put his feet over the edge of the sofa. He didn't seem dizzy. And he had to go out there and show them that he was as capable of watching a butchering as any of them.

He felt a queer, violent hatred for the old sow. It served her right to be shot and have her throat cut, have her insides ripped out. He would go out and get hold of her insides and pull, and everything would come out in a bundle like the insides of a fish.

He stood up. The dizziness had gone completely. Listening, he heard no sounds in the kitchen. Everybody was outside. Taking three deep breaths, the way he always did before going off the high diving board the first time in the spring, he went out to the back door.

Four boys stood in a ring around his father, who was squatting on the ground. The pig was nowhere in sight, but Bruce saw his mother bending over one of the washtubs, and he saw the rope that went up over a pulley at the corner of the barn and trailed near his father's feet. Then his father took hold of the rope and pulled, and the boys took hold and pulled too, stepping all over each other, and the sow came in sight. But not a sow any longer, not an animal, not the mud-caked, bristly-hided old brute that he had carried slop to all fall. The thing that rose up toward the pulley was clean and pink and hairless, like the carcasses in Heimie Gross's shop, and, as it swung gently on the rope that bound its hind feet, he saw the flapping, opened belly and the clean red meat inside. She hung there, turning gently half around and back again, so innocent and harmless that the boy was no longer sickened or afraid.

His father saw him come out and grinned at him, wiping his red hands on a rag. "Snapped out of it, uh? I thought you were a tough guy."

"Brucie got sick," Chet said. "When Pa cut her throat, Brucie threw up all over the corral."

"Oh, I did not!" Bruce said. He clenched his fists.

"You big liar," Chet said. "I can show you the puddle."

Not daring to look at the other boys, Bruce went over to where his mother was washing a long, whitish mess of stuff in the tubful of bloody water. She held her face to one side, out of the steam that rose from the tub, and worked at arm's length. "Feeling better now?" she said.

He nodded. Conscious of the boys behind him, knowing they must be laughing at him, shaming him, snickering, he pointed to the stuff in the tub. "What's that?"

"Intestines," she said. "They have to be cleaned to stuff sausage in." With a disgusted grimace she went back to working the long, rubbery gut through her fingers.

Bruce stood watching a minute. So sausage was stuffed into intestines. He had always loved sausage, but he could never eat it again, not ever. He couldn't eat any of the old sow. Looking over at the pink, harmless thing swinging gently by its heels, he found it hard to imagine that this was the sow. The eyes were closed, the jowly face was hairless and mild, almost comical. There was nothing to remind anyone of that violence behind the barn, until you looked right between her eyes and saw the two dark dots there, not more than a half inch apart. There were the death wounds, there was the difference. He went up and pushed the stiff front foot, and the carcass swayed. It was funny those two little dots could make all that difference. A half hour ago the old sow had got up full of life, and now she hung like a bag of grain.

"How'd they get her so clean?" he asked Chet.

"Scalded her," Chet said. "You shouldn't've got sick. You'd've seen something."

"What'd her insides look like?"

"Go look yourself," Chet said. He waved at the tub standing against the barn wall.

Slowly Bruce went closer until he could see. The bloody mess appalled him, but he had to see those insides, had to look at them carefully to keep himself reminded that it was really the old sow hanging there. If he didn't keep remembering that, if he forgot the sow and remembered only the clean, butcher-shop carcass, he might forget sometime and eat some of her, and he knew if he ever ate any of her he would die.

His father came up past him, moved him aside. "One side there," he said heartily. "One side for the working men."

He put red hands down into the tub, sorted out the liver and heart. Grinning, he made as if to throw the great, wobbly, purple liver at Bruce, and Bruce felt his stomach go weak.

"What's the matter?" his father said. "Here I thought you were a tough guy, and you go around looking peaked as a ghost."

"I *am* a tough guy!" Bruce said but, looking across at Chet he saw the superior smile, the hands in the pockets and the shoulders insolent. "I'm not getting sick," he said, and made his white face turn fixedly toward the tub of entrails. "I'm not sick at all!" he said, and laughed.

His father looked at him queerly. "You'd better go off and sit down a while," he said finally. "You're not quite in shape yet."

"I am too in shape!" the boy screamed. He wanted to run up and plunge his hands into that red tub of guts, just to show them, but he didn't quite dare. But he stood where he was, and as he stood, the little black dots came back before his eyes, and he stood still and stared through them, fighting them down in hysterical silence. Then his father, still watching him, pulled a flat flap of insides from the tub.

"Show you something," he said to the boys. "This's one that'll surprise you."

He dipped the flap in a clean bucket of water and washed it thoroughly. Bruce, fighting off the black spots, struggling to keep the slaughterhouse smell of blood and scalded hair from turning his stomach inside out, watched with the others. When it came out of the water clean, the thing looked like a flattened bag with a tube the size of a pencil sticking out one side.

"What is it?" Chet said. "Is it her stomach?"

The father laughed. "You've seen that old sow eat, haven't you? Think she could put all that in this little bag?" He flapped it, shaking the water from the end of the tube, and then put the tube to his lips.

At the sight of his father's mouth touching the raw insides of the sow Bruce felt the blood drain from him, and the black dots streamed thicker. He shook his head violently, but they stayed. Through their thickening darkness he saw his father blow into the tube, saw the bladder swell and tighten and grow round, big as a soccer ball. The father pinched the tube, found a piece of string and tied around it, and tossed the bladder out on the ground. It bounced lightly, one side patched with adhesive dust.

His lips tight on his nausea, the blackness almost covering his sight, Bruce stared at the wavering bladder on the ground before him, the tube poking out to one side. The insides of the old sow, the red, dirty insides of the old sow he had hated and seen die. . . .

The vomit was in his very throat. He had to heave, but he couldn't. He wouldn't, with those boys around, his father there, Chet standing around with his superior hands in his pockets. The whole group of boys was staring, momentarily a little stupid, at the bladder the father had tossed out. Without thinking, in a wild leap to save himself and his nausea, Bruce sprang forward and kicked as hard as he could. It soared, and immediately all of

them were after it, yelling, booting it down into the
vacant lot.

Bruce broke into the running crowd again, got a chance,
kicked the bladder hard and far, chased it, missed, chased
again as Preacher-Kid Morrison booted it across the lot.
His nausea was gone, his whole mind centered on that
ritual act of kicking the sow's insides around, dirtying
them in the dust of the field, taking out on them his own
shame and his own fear and hatred and disbelief. And
when they finally broke the bladder, far down the coulee
toward school, he stood over it panting, triumphant, so
full of life that he could have jumped the barn or carried
the woodshed on his back.

Butcher Bird

THAT summer the boy was alone on the farm except for his parents. His brother was working at Orullian's Grocery in town, and there was no one to run the trap line with or swim with in the dark, weed-smelling reservoir where garter snakes made straight rapid lines in the water and the skaters rowed close to shore. So every excursion was an adventure, even if it was only a trip across the three miles of prairie to Larsen's to get mail or groceries. He was excited at the visit to Garfield's as he was excited by everything unusual. The hot midsummer afternoon was still and breathless, the air harder to breathe than usual. He knew there was a change in weather coming because the gingersnaps in their tall cardboard box were soft and bendable when he snitched two to stick in his pocket. He could tell too by his father's grumpiness accu-

mulated through two weeks of drought, his habit of looking off into the southwest, from which either rain or hot
winds might come, that something was brewing. If it was
rain everything would be fine, his father would hum under
his breath getting breakfast, maybe let him drive the
stoneboat or ride the mare down to Larsen's for mail. If it
was hot wind they'd have to walk soft and speak softer,
and it wouldn't be any fun.

They didn't know the Garfields, who had moved in only
the fall before; but people said they had a good big house
and a bigger barn and that Mr. Garfield was an Englishman and a little funny talking about scientific farming
and making the desert blossom like the rose. The boy's
father hadn't wanted to go, but his mother thought it was
unneighborly not to call at least once in a whole year
when people lived only four miles away. She was, the
boy knew, as anxious for a change, as eager to get out of
that atmosphere of waiting to see what the weather would
do — that tense and teeth-gritting expectancy — as he was.

He found more than he looked for at Garfield's. Mr.
Garfield was tall and bald with a big nose, and talked
very softly and politely. The boy's father was determined
not to like him right from the start.

When Mr. Garfield said, "Dear, I think we might have
a glass of lemonade, don't you?" the boy saw his parents
look at each other, saw the beginning of a contemptuous
smile on his father's face, saw his mother purse her lips
and shake her head ever so little. And when Mrs. Garfield, prim and spectacled, with a habit of tucking her
head back and to one side while she listened to anyone
talk, brought in the lemonade, the boy saw his father
taste his and make a little face behind the glass. He hated
any summer drink without ice in it, and had spent two
whole weeks digging a dugout icehouse just so that he

could have ice water and cold beer when the hot weather
came.

But Mr. and Mrs. Garfield were nice people. They sat
down in their new parlor and showed the boy's mother
the rug and the gramophone. When the boy came up
curiously to inspect the little box with the petunia-shaped
horn and the little china dog with "His Master's Voice"
on it, and the Garfields found that he had never seen or
heard a gramophone, they put on a cylinder like a big
spool of tightly wound black thread and lowered a needle
on it, and out came a man's voice singing in Scotch
brogue, and his mother smiled and nodded and said, "My
land, Harry Lauder! I heard him once a long time ago.
Isn't it wonderful, Sonny?"

It was wonderful all right. He inspected it, reached
out his fingers to touch things, wiggled the big horn to
see if it was loose or screwed in. His father warned him
sharply to keep his hands off, but then Mr. Garfield smiled
and said, "Oh, he can't hurt it. Let's play something else,"
and found a record about the saucy little bird on Nelly's
hat that had them all laughing. They let him wind the
machine and play the record over again, all by himself,
and he was very careful. It was a fine machine. He
wished he had one.

About the time he had finished playing his sixth or
seventh record, and George M. Cohan was singing "She's
a grand old rag, she's a high-flying flag, and forever in
peace may she wave," he glanced at his father and discovered that he was grouchy about something. He wasn't
taking any part in the conversation but was sitting with
his chin in his hand staring out of the window. Mr.
Garfield was looking at him a lttle helplessly. His eyes
met the boy's and he motioned him over.

"What do you find to do all summer? Only child, are
you?"

"No, sir. My brother's in Whitemud. He's twelve. He's got a job."

"So you come out on the farm to help," said Mr. Garfield. He had his hand on the boy's shoulder and his voice was so kind that the boy lost his shyness and felt no embarrassment at all in being out there in the middle of the parlor with all of them watching.

"I don't help much," he said. "I'm too little to do anything but drive the stoneboat, Pa says. When I'm twelve he's going to get me a gun and then I can go hunting."

"Hunting?" Mr. Garfield said. "What do you hunt?"

"Oh, gophers and weasels. I got a pet weasel. His name's Lucifer."

"Well," said Mr. Garfield. "You seem to be a pretty manly little chap. What do you feed your weasel?"

"Gophers." The boy thought it best not to say that the gophers were live ones he threw into the weasel's cage. He thought probably Mr. Garfield would be a little shocked at that.

Mr. Garfield straightened up and looking round at the grown folks. "Isn't it a shame," he said, "that there are so many predatory animals and pests in this country that we have to spend our time destroying them? I hate killing things."

"I hate weasels," the boy said. "I'm just saving this one till he turns into an ermine, and then I'm going to skin him. Once I speared a weasel with the pitchfork in the chicken coop and he dropped right off the tine and ran up my leg and bit me after he was speared clean through."

He finished breathlessly, and his mother smiled at him, motioning him not to talk so much. But Mr. Garfield was still looking at him kindly. "So you want to make war on the cruel things, the weasels and the hawks," he said.

"Yes, sir," the boy said. He looked at his mother and it

was all right. He hadn't spoiled anything by telling about the weasels.

"Now that reminds me," Mr. Garfield said, rising. "Maybe I've got something you'd find useful."

He went into another room and came back with a .22 in his hand. "Could you use this?"

"I . . . yes, *sir!*" the boy said. He had almost, in his excitement, said "I hope to whisk in your piskers," because that was what his father always said when he meant anything real hard.

"If your parents want you to have it," Mr. Garfield said and raised his eyebrows at the boy's mother. He didn't look at the father, but the boy did.

"Can I, Pa?"

"I guess so," his father said. "Sure."

"Thank Mr. Garfield nicely," said his mother.

"Gee," the boy breathed. "Thanks, Mr. Garfield, ever so much."

"There's a promise goes with it," Mr. Garfield said. "I'd like you to promise never to shoot anything with it but the bloodthirsty animals — the cruel ones like weasels and hawks. Never anything like birds or prairie dogs."

"How about butcher birds?"

"Butcher birds?" Mr. Garfield said.

"Shrikes," said the boy's mother. "We've got some over by our place. They kill all sorts of things, snakes and gophers and other birds. They're worse than the hawks because they just kill for the fun of it."

"By all means," said Mr. Garfield. "Shoot all the shrikes you see. A thing that kills for the fun of it . . . " He shook his head and his voice got solemn, almost like the voice of Mr. McGregor, the Sunday School Superintendent in town, when he was asking the benediction. "There's something about the way the war drags on, or maybe just this country," he said, "that makes me hate killing. I just can't bear to shoot anything any more, even a weasel."

The boy's father turned cold eyes away from Mr. Garfield and looked out of the window. One big brown hand, a little dirty from the wheel of the car, rubbed against the day-old bristles on his jaws. Then he stood up and stretched. "Well, we got to be going," he said.

"Oh, stay a little while," Mr. Garfield said. "You just came. I wanted to show you my trees."

The boy's mother stared at him. "Trees?"

He smiled. "Sounds a bit odd out here, doesn't it? But I think trees will grow. I've made some plantings down below."

"I'd love to see them," she said. "Sometimes I'd give almost anything to get into a good deep shady woods. Just to smell it, and feel how cool . . . "

"There's a little story connected with these," Mr. Garfield said. He spoke to the mother alone, warmly. "When we first decided to come out here I said to Martha that if trees wouldn't grow we shouldn't stick it. That's just what I said, 'If trees won't grow we shan't stick it.' Trees are almost the breath of life to me."

The boy's father was shaken by a sudden spell of coughing, and the mother shot a quick look at him and looked back at Mr. Garfield with a light flush on her cheekbones. "I'd love to see them," she said. "I was raised in Minnesota, and I never will get used to a place as barren as this."

"When I think of the beeches back home in England," Mr. Garfield said, and shook his head with a puckering smile round his eyes.

The father lifted himself heavily out of his chair and followed the rest of them out to the coulee edge. Below them willows grew profusely along the almost-dry creek, and farther back from the water there was a grove of perhaps twenty trees about a dozen feet high.

"I'm trying cottonwoods first because they can stand dry weather," Mr. Garfield said.

The mother was looking down with all her longings suddenly plain and naked in her eyes. "It's wonderful," she said. "I'd give almost anything to have some on our place."

"I found the willows close by here," said Mr. Garfield. "Just at the south end of the hills they call Old-Man-on-His Back, where the stream comes down."

"Stream?" the boy's father said. "You mean that trickle?"

"It's not much of a stream," Mr. Garfield said apologetically. "But . . ."

"Are there any more there?" the mother said.

"Oh, yes. You could get some. Cut them diagonally and push them into any damp ground. They'll grow."

"They'll grow about six feet high," the father said.

"Yes," said Mr. Garfield. "They're not, properly speaking, trees. Still . . ."

'It's getting pretty smothery," the father said rather loudly. "We better be getting on."

This time Mr. Garfield didn't object, and they went back to the car exchanging promises of visits. The father jerked the crank and climbed into the Ford, where the boy was sighting along his gun. "Put that down," his father said. "Don't you know any better than to point a gun around people?"

"It isn't loaded."

"They never are," his father said. "Put it down now."

The Garfields were standing with their arms round each other's waists, waiting to wave good-bye. Mr. Garfield reached over and picked something from his wife's dress.

"What was it, Alfred?" she said peering.

"Nothing. Just a bit of fluff."

The boy's father coughed violently and the car started with a jerk. With his head down almost to the wheel, still coughing, he waved, and the mother and the boy waved as they went down along the badly set cedar posts of the pasture fence. They were almost a quarter of a mile away before the boy, with a last wave of the gun, turned round again and saw that his father was purple with laughter. He rocked the car with his joy, and when his wife said, "Oh, Harry, you big fool," he pointed helplessly to his shoulder. "Would you mind," he said. "Would you mind brushing that bit o' fluff off me showldah?" He roared again, pounding the wheel. "I shawn't stick it," he said. "I bloody well shawn't stick it, you knaow!"

"It isn't fair to laugh at him," she said. "He can't help being English."

"He can't help being a sanctimonious old mudhen either, braying about his luv-ly luv-ly trees. They'll freeze out the first winter."

"How do you know? Maybe it's like he says — if they get a start they'll grow here as well as anywhere."

"Maybe there's a gold mine in our back yard too, but I'm not gonna dig to see. I couldn't stick it."

"Oh, you're just being stubborn," she said. "Just because you didn't like Mr. Garfield . . . "

He turned on her in heavy amazement. "Well, my God! Did you?"

"I thought he was very nice," she said, and sat straighter in the back seat, speaking loudly above the creak of the springs and cough of the motor. "They're trying to make a home, not just a wheat crop. I liked them."

"Uh, huh." He was not laughing any more now. Sitting beside him, the boy could see that his face had hardened and the cold look had come into his eye again. "So I should start talking like I had a mouthful of bran, and planting trees around the house that'll look like clothesline poles in two months."

"I didn't say that."

"You thought it though." He looked irritably at the sky, misted with the same delusive film of cloud that had fooled him for three days, and spat at the roadside. "You thought it all the time we were there. 'Why aren't you more like Mr. Garfield, he's such a nice man.'" With mincing savagery he swung round and mocked her. "Shall I make it a walnut grove? Or a big maple sugar bush? Or maybe you'd like an orange orchard."

The boy was looking down at his gun, trying not to hear them quarrel, but he knew what his mother's face would be like — hurt and a little flushed, her chin trembling into stubbornness. "I don't suppose you could bear to have a rug on the floor, or a gramophone?" she said.

He smacked the wheel hard. "Of course I could bear it if we could afford it. But I sure as hell would rather do without than be like that old sandhill crane."

"I don't suppose you'd like to take me over to the Old-Man-on-His-Back some day to get some willow slips either."

"What for?"

"To plant down in the coulee, by the dam."

"That dam dries up every August. Your willows wouldn't live till snow flies."

"Well, would it do any harm to try?"

"Oh, shut up!" he said. "Just thinking about that guy and his fluff and his trees gives me the pleefer."

The topless Ford lurched, one wheel at a time, through the deep burnout by their pasture corner, and the boy clambered out with his gun in his hand to slip the loop from the three-strand gate. It was then that he saw the snake, a striped limp ribbon, dangling on the fence, and a moment later the sparrow, neatly butchered and hung by the throat from the barbed wire. He pointed the gun at them. "Lookit!" he said. "Lookit what the butcher bird's been doing."

His father's violent hand waved at him from the seat. "Come on! Get the wire out of the way!"

The boy dragged the gate through the dust, and the Ford went through and up behind the house, perched on the bare edge of the coulee in the midst of its baked yard and framed by the dark fireguard overgrown with Russian thistle. Walking across that yard a few minutes later, the boy felt its hard heat under his sneakers. There was hardly a spear of grass within the fireguard. It was one of his father's prides that the dooryard should be like cement. "Pour your wash water out long enough," he said, "and you'll have a surface so hard it won't even make mud." Religiously he threw his water out three times a day, carrying it sometimes a dozen steps to dump it on a dusty or grassy spot.

The mother had objected at first, asking why they had to live in the middle of an alkali flat, and why they couldn't let grass grow up to the door. But he snorted her down. Everything round the house ought to be bare as a bone. Get a good prairie fire going and it'd jump that guard like nothing, and if they had grass to the door where'd they be? She said why not plow a wider fireguard then, one a fire couldn't jump, but he said he had other things to do besides plowing fifty-foot fireguards.

They were arguing inside when the boy came up on the step to sit down and aim his empty .22 at a fencepost. Apparently his mother had been persistent, and persistence when he was not in a mood for it angered the father worse than anything else. Their talk came vaguely through his

concentration, but he shut his ears on it. If that spot on
the fence post was a coyote now, and he held the sight
steady, right on it, and pulled the trigger, that old coyote
would jump about eighty feet in the air and come down
dead as a mackerel, and he could tack his hide on the barn
the way Mr. Larsen had one, only the dogs had jumped
and torn the tail and hind legs off Mr. Larsen's pelt, and
he wouldn't get more than the three-dollar bounty out of
it. But then Mr. Larsen had shot his with a shotgun anyway, and the hide wasn't worth much even before the
dogs tore it. . . .

"I can't for the life of me see why not," his mother said
inside. "We could do it now. We're not doing anything
else."

"I tell you they wouldn't grow!" said his father with
emphasis on every word. "Why should we run our tongues
out doing everything that mealy-mouthed fool does?"

"I don't want anything but the willows. They're easy."

He made his special sound of contempt, half snort, half
grunt. After a silence she tried again. "They might even
have pussies on them in the spring. Mr. Garfield thinks
they'd grow, and he used to work in a greenhouse, his
wife told me."

"This isn't a greenhouse, for Chrissake."

"Oh, let it go," she said. "I've stood it this long without
any green things around. I guess I can stand it some
more."

The boy, aiming now toward the gate where the butcher
bird, coming back to his prey, would in just a minute fly
right into Deadeye's unerring bullet, heard his father
stand up suddenly.

"Abused, aren't you?" he said.

The mother's voice rose. "No, I'm not abused! Only I
can't see why it would be so awful to get some willows.

Just because Mr. Garfield gave me the idea, and you didn't like him . . . "

"You're right I didn't like Mr. Garfield," the father said. "He gave me a pain right under the crupper."

"Because," the mother's voice said bitterly, "he calls his wife 'dear' and puts his arm around her and likes trees. It wouldn't occur to you to put your arm around your wife, would it?"

The boy aimed and held his breath. His mother ought to keep still, because if she didn't she'd get him real mad and then they'd both have to tiptoe around the rest of the day. He heard his father's breath whistle through his teeth, and his voice, mincing, nasty. "Would you like me to kiss you now, *dear?*"

"I wouldn't let you touch me with a ten-foot pole," his mother said. She sounded just as mad as he did, and it wasn't often she let herself get that way. The boy squirmed over when he heard the quick hard steps come up behind him and pause. Then his father's big hand, brown and meaty and felted with fine black hair, reached down over his shoulder and took the .22.

"Let's see this cannon old Scissor-bill gave you," he said.

It was a single-shot, bolt-action Savage, a little rusty on the barrel, the bolt sticky with hardened grease when the father removed it. Sighting up through the barrel, he grunted. "Takes care of a gun like he takes care of his farm. Probably used it to cultivate his luv-ly trees."

He went out into the sleeping porch, and after a minute came back with a rag and a can of machine oil. Hunching the boy over on the step, he sat down and began rubbing the bolt with the oil-soaked rag.

"I just can't bear to shoot anything any more," he said, and laughed suddenly. "I just cawn't stick it, little man." He leered at the boy, who grinned back uncertainly.

Squinting through the barrel again, the father breathed
through his nose and clamped his lips together, shaking
his head.

The sun lay heavy on the baked yard. Out over the
corner of the pasture a soaring hawk caught wind and
sun at the same time, so that his light breast feathers
flashed as he banked and rose. Just wait, the boy thought.
Wait till I get my gun working and I'll fix you, you hen-
robber. He thought of the three chicks a hawk had struck
earlier in the summer, the three balls of yellow with the
barred mature plumage just coming through. Two of
them dead when he got there and chased the hawk away,
the other gasping with its crop slashed wide open and the
wheat spilling from it on the ground. His mother had
sewed up the crop, and the chicken had lived, but it
always looked droopy, like a plant in drought time, and
sometimes it would stand and work its bill as if it were
choking.

By golly, he thought, I'll shoot every hawk and butcher
bird in twenty miles. I'll . . .

"Rustle around and find me a piece of baling wire," his
father said. "This barrel looks like a henroost."

Behind the house he found a piece of rusty wire,
brought it back and watched his father straighten it, wind
a bit of rag round the end, ram it up and down through
the barrel, and peer through again. "He's leaded her so
you can hardly see the grooves," he said. "But maybe she'll
shoot. We'll fill her with vinegar and cork her up tonight."

The mother was behind them, leaning against the jamb
and watching. She reached down and rumpled the father's
black hair. "The minute you get a gun in your hand you
start feeling better," she said. "It's just a shame you
weren't born fifty years sooner."

"A gun's a good tool," he said. "It hadn't ought to be
misused. Gun like this is enough to make a guy cry."

"Well, you've got to admit it was nice of Mr. Garfield to give it to Sonny," she said. It was the wrong thing to say. The boy had a feeling somehow that she knew it was the wrong thing to say, that she said it just to have one tiny triumph over him. He knew it would make him boiling mad again, even before he heard his father's answer.

"Oh, sure, Mr. Garfield's a fine man. He can preach a better sermon than any homesteader in Saskatchewan. God Almighty! everything he does is better than what I do. All right. All right, *all right!* Why the hell don't you move over there if you like it so well?"

"If you weren't so blind . . . !"

He rose with the .22 in his hand and pushed past her into the house. "I'm not so blind," he said heavily in passing. "You've been throwing that bastard up to me for two hours. It don't take very good eyes to see what that means."

His mother started to say, "All because I want a few little . . . " but the boy cut in on her, anxious to help the situation somehow. "Will it shoot now?" he said.

His father said nothing. His mother looked down at him, shrugged, sighed, smiled bleakly with a tight mouth. She moved aside when the father came back with a box of cartridges in his hand. He ignored his wife, speaking to the boy alone in the particular half-jocular tone he always used with him or the dog when he wasn't mad or exasperated.

"Thought I had these around," he said. "Now we'll see what this smoke-pole will do."

He slipped a cartridge in and locked the bolt, looking round for something to shoot at. Behind him the mother's feet moved on the floor, and her voice came purposefully. "I can't see why you have to act this way," she said. "I'm going over and get some slips myself."

There was a long silence. The angled shade lay sharp

as a knife across the baked front yard. The father's cheek was pressed against the stock of the gun, his arms and hands as steady as stone.

"How'll you get there?" he said, whispering down the barrel.

"I'll walk."

"Five miles and back."

"Yes, five miles and back. Or fifty miles and back. If there was any earthly reason why you should mind . . ."

"I don't mind," he said, and his voice was soft as silk. "Go ahead."

Close to his mother's long skirts in the doorway, the boy felt her stiffen as if she had been slapped. He squirmed anxiously, but his desperation could find only the question he had asked before. His voice squeaked on it: "Will it shoot now?"

"See that sparrow out there?" his father said, still whispering. "Right out by that cactus?"

"Harry!" the mother said. "If you shoot that harmless little bird!"

Fascinated, the boy watched his father's dark face against the rifle stock, the locked, immovable left arm, the thick finger crooked inside the trigger guard almost too small to hold it. He saw the sparrow, gray, white-breasted, hopping obliviously in search of bugs, fifty feet out on the gray earth. "I just . . . can't . . . bear . . . to . . . shoot . . . anything," the father said, his face like dark stone, his lips hardly moving. "I just . . . can't . . . stick it!"

"Harry!" his wife screamed.

The boy's mouth opened, a dark wash of terror shadowed his vision of the baked yard cut by its sharp angle of shade.

"Don't, Pa!"

The rocklike figure of his father never moved. The

thick finger squeezed slowly down on the trigger, there was a thin, sharp report, and the sparrow jerked and collapsed into a shapeless wad on the ground. It was as if, in the instant of the shot, all its clean outlines vanished. Head, feet, the white breast, the perceptible outlines of the folded wings, disappeared all at once, were crumpled together and lost, and the boy sat beside his father on the step with the echo of the shot still in his ears.

He did not look at either of his parents. He looked only at the crumpled sparrow. Step by step, unable to keep away, he went to it, stooped, and picked it up. Blood stained his fingers, and he held the bird by the tail while he wiped the smeared hand on his overalls. He heard the click as the bolt was shot and the empty cartridge ejected, and he saw his mother come swiftly out of the house past his father, who sat still on the step. Her hands were clenched, and she walked with her head down, as if fighting tears.

"Ma!" the boy said dully. "Ma, what'll I do with it?"

She stopped and turned, and for a moment they faced each other. He saw the dead pallor of her face, the burning eyes, the not-quite-controllable quiver of her lips. But her words, when they came, were flat and level, almost casual.

"Leave it right there," she said. "After a while your father will want to hang it on the barbed wire."

The Double Corner

THE SUMMER SUN was fierce and white on the pavement, the station, the tracks, the stucco walls of buildings, but the pepper tree made a domed and curtained cave of shade where they waited — the twins languidly playing catch with a tennis ball, Tom and Janet on the iron bench. Sitting with her head back, looking up into the green dome, Janet saw the swarming flies up among the branches, hanging like smoke against the ceiling of a room. They made a sleepy sound like humming wires.

"I wish I thought you knew what you're doing," Tom said.

She looked at him. He was leaning forward, his hat pushed back, and with his toe he was keeping a frantic ant from going where it wanted to with a crumb. He had worked on cattle ranches as a young man, and she had always said he had cowpuncher's eyes, squinty and faded, the color of much-washed jeans.

"She's your mother," she reminded him.

"I know."

"If I'm glad to have her, I should think you'd be."

The boys were throwing the tennis ball up into the branches, bringing down showers of leaves and twigs. "Hey, kids, cut it out," Tom said. To Janet he said, "We've been all through it. Let it ride."

"But you had some reason," she persisted.

"Reason?" he said, and picked his calloused palm. "She'd be better off in an institution."

That made Janet sit up stiffly and try to hold his eyes. "That's what I can't understand, why you'd be willing to send your mother to an asylum." He was squinting, moving his head slowly back and forth, but he would not look up.

"I wish I could understand you," Janet said, watching the dark cheek, the long jaw, the leathery sunburned neck, the tipped-back rancher's hat that showed the graying temple. "Suppose you died, and I got old and needed care. Would you expect the boys to send me off to an asylum, or would you expect they'd have enough love and gratitude to give me a room in their house?"

"You're not out of your mind," Tom said.

"I would be, if they treated me the way she's been treated. Four or five months with Albert, and then he palmed her off on Margaret; and Margaret kept her a little while and sent her to George; and George keeps her two months and wants to ship her to an institution — would have if we hadn't telephoned."

Tom removed a leaf from a twig. "It isn't that she's not wanted. She just hasn't got all her buttons any more. She can't be fitted into a family."

"Well, I tell you one thing," Janet said. "In our family she's going to feel wanted! She's like a child, Tom. She's got to feel that she has a place."

"Okay," he said. He leaned forward and spit on the ant he had been herding. The boys had given up their ball and were sitting on the edge of the rocked-in well from which the pepper's enormous trunk rose.

Janet watched her husband a minute. She did not like him when his face went wooden and impenetrable. "Tom," she said, "will having her around bother you? Will it make you feel bad?"

His faded blue eyes turned on her, almost amused. "Relax," he said.

The train whistled for the crossing at Santa Clara, and Janet swung around to the boys. "Remember?" she said. "We're all going to be extra nice to Grandma. We're not going to laugh, or pester, or tease. We're going to be as polite and kind as we know how to be. Oliver, can you remember that? Jack, can you?"

The twins stared back at her, identical in T-shirts and jeans, with identical straight brown hair and identical expressions of hypocritical piety. Unsure of what their expressions meant, she waved them out through the curtain of branches, and they stood on the blazing platform in the ovenlike heat until the train rolled in and the Pullmans came abreast of them and the train stopped.

Janet felt above her the cool air-conditioned stares of passengers; she saw porters swing out, down the long train. A redcap pushed a truckload of baggage against the steps of a car. Then, down toward the rear of the train, a man in a blue slack suit stepped down and waited with his hand stretched upward. In a moment he climbed up again and came down leading an old lady by the arm. Janet hurried down the platform.

The man in blue, a fattish man with bare hairy arms, clung to Grandma's elbow and smiled a sickly smile as Janet came up. He had sweated through the armpits of his shirt. Grandma Waldron leaned away from him, her little brown eyes darting constantly, her lips trembling on a soundless stream of talk. She looked agitated, and her arms were folded hard across the breast of her heavy coat as if she were protecting something precious. She wore black shoes and a black hat, and she looked intolerably hot. In her unsuitable clothes amid the white heat and the pastel stucco of a California town, she tugged at Janet's sympathy like a lost and unhappy child.

"Hello, Mom," Tom said and came forward to kiss her, but she twisted away with her arms still clenched across her breast. She appeared to wrestle with something; her face was strained, and drops of perspiration beaded her upper lip. Then the head of a cat thrust violently up above the lapels of the coat, a panting cat, ears back, pink mouth snarling. Under Grandma's clutching arms its body struggled, but it could not work free. It yowled, strangling.

Grandma ducked around Tom and the man in blue and came up to Janet. Her soundless talking became audible as a stream of words so unaccented that Janet wondered if she heard them herself, if she knew when she was speaking aloud and when only thinking with her lips. Paying no attention to the cat writhing weakly under the old lady's coat, she put out her hands and made her voice warm. "Grandma, it's awfully nice to have you here!"

Grandma's voice rode over the greetings, and she did not relax her clutch around the cat to touch the welcoming hands. ". . . never get rid of that man," she said. "Came up before I even got settled in my seat and stuck like a burr all the way I know what he wanted, he wanted into my bag so he could steal my picture of Tom's family, said he wanted to see what they looked like if there'd been a policeman there I'd have had him arrested trying to get into my suitcase I've had to watch every minute."

Her brown, prying eyes lighted on Janet, then on the

staring twins; darted up the platform, swung suspiciously to the man in blue, who was talking quietly to Tom. Janet saw Tom's face, expressionless, and all in an instant she wanted to shout at him, "Don't you think that! She's strange and scared, that's all. This is what shunting her all around has done to her. George should have known better than to send her all the way from Los Angeles with a stranger."

But she could not say this. She barely had time to think it before the long warning cry went up along the train, the porters swung aboard, the train jerked and began to roll. The cat was struggling again in Grandma's arms. The man in blue jumped clumsily and got aboard, waving to them from the steps. Above them the bands of windows with the air-conditioned faces and the stares of strangers moved smoothly past, and then emptiness and a hot wind closed around the last Pullman.

"Well, here we are," Janet said gently. "You remember the twins. Jack and Oliver."

Grandma's eyes darted over the boys. Her talk had gone underground, but her lips still moved. After almost a minute of absolutely soundless vehement talking, the words came to the surface again. ". . . torturing the cat, chasing it through the house. Broke the wandering Jew right off."

One of her hands let go long enough to cram the cat's head down again. "Kept wanting my cat," she said. "That man did. Kept all the time wanting my cat away from me like those other things he took, all my money and my picture and my best mittens. That man took them."

Tom came up and stood smiling into his mother's face. "Don't you know me, Ma?"

Her head shaking slightly, Grandma looked at him.

"Always was wild. Running away to the North Pole. I told my husband all about him, you bet. My husband's the constable." She looked around sharply. "Is that man gone? If we had any proper laws he'd been in jail long ago he got my mittens and my money and he tried to get my cat."

"Come on," Janet said, and took Grandma's elbow with the gentlest of fingers. "Let's get home out of this sun."

After a moment of resistance, Grandma came along. At the car, while Tom was running down the windows to let out the accumulated heat, he caught Janet's eye. The corners of his mouth went down soberly, and she felt that she had been challenged. "Grandma," she said, "don't you think you should let the poor cat out so it can breathe? That man's gone now."

The old lady jerked her shoulders and looked around her hard, but did not relax her arms. Janet helped her into the back seat, climbed in after her, sat down scrupulously on her own side. "Please," she said, and smiled into Grandma's strained face. "It can't get away in the car."

For just a moment, holding the brown intent eyes, she felt that she was being probed and tested. Then Grandma's clenched arms loosened slightly, and the cat shot up under her chin in a convulsive squirming effort, twisted and clawed its way loose, and sprang to the floor, where it crouched with tail flicking. Grandma started half to her feet as if to grab it up again, shot a sidelong look at Janet, and settled back. Outside the car the boys were watching. Jack shoved Oliver, and Oliver returned the shove. "Meowwrrrr!" Jack said. Their eyes glistened, and they giggled.

"Get in," Janet said harshly. The two climbed in beside Tom, and in a bleak admonitory silence they turned into the street. When they had gone a few blocks Jack leaned over the seat to look at the crouching cat.

"Boy, that sure is a beat-up old cat," he said. Oliver turned to look too, and then they huddled down in the front seat. Janet heard their smothered mirth, and catching Tom's eye in the rear-view mirror she thought she saw laughter there too.

For a moment she relaxed, almost ready to laugh herself. But when she turned to Grandma, sitting stiffly with her watchful eyes on the cat, she saw Grandma's open coat. Under it the black dress was plucked and snagged, and the white neck was bloody with scratches.

But what a commentary! Janet thought. What a revelation of the old lady's fear and suspicion, when she would think it necessary to cram her cat into her bosom and cling to it in protection though it clawed her heart out.

She reached out and patted Grandma's arm. The old lady looked at her, and it seemed to Janet that there was no longer suspicion in her eyes, but only inquiry. "It's nice to have you with us," Janet said.

Words flowed over the old lady's lips, but none of them made any sound.

They topped the hill and came into their own valley, the slope falling away below them in orchard and hay meadow, rising again on the far side to the dark chaparral of the coast hills. Little ranches, squares of apricot and almond and pear trees, angular lines of pasture and corral, patterned the valley and the sides of the hills, and the sight of that sheltered country beauty made Janet turn to Grandma to see if she felt it too. But Grandma was soundlessly telling herself something. Of course she couldn't see it. Not yet. Grandma's mind was a terrified little animal trembling in a dark hole while danger walked outside.

"There's our place," Janet said. "The one with the white water tower."

Grandma's eyes darted, but Janet could not be sure whether they really looked or whether they only cunningly pretended to. Then the car turned into the driveway and stopped under the holly oak with the yellow climbing roses incredibly hanging forty feet up among its branches. The fuchsias drooped ripe purple on both sides of the front door; the hill went up behind in a regimented jungle of orchards. The air was hot, heady, full of brandied fruit smell and the intoxication of tarweed. Down at the stable, under the old pear tree by the fence, the two horses stood with their heads companionably over each other's backs, making a two-tailed machine against the flies.

"Isn't it lovely!" Janet said. "Isn't it perfectly lovely!" Very carefully and tenderly she picked up the cat, stroked its fur smooth; and watching Grandma, half expecting the old lady to snatch the cat away, she took it as a small triumph that nothing of the sort happened. Grandma got out, and Janet got out after her. "You'll love it here," she said, and smiled.

Through the whole ritual of arrival she kept that tone. Every gesture was a calculated reassurance; every word soothed. When she led Grandma down into the bedroom wing she threw open the door confidently, feeling that this room, like the valley and the fruit-scented ranch, ought to strike even a sick mind as sheltered and secure. The bed had a blue and white ship quilt for a spread; the cotton rugs were fresh from the laundry; the roses she had put on the bed table that morning breathed sweetly in the room; the curtains moved coolly, secretly at the north windows.

She still had the cat in her arms. It had relaxed there, its eyes half closed. "This is your room," she said to Grandma, and smiled again into the strained brown eyes. She opened the bathroom door and showed the white tile, the towels neat on the racks, the new oval of green soap. Her own quick glance pleased her: it was a room and bath she would have liked to be brought into herself.

"Boys," she said, "I think the kitty would like some milk. Maybe you could bring a dish in here."

They brought it in a minute, their manners still quelled, their eyes speculative. Jack set the dish by the bed and Oliver poured it full. Janet, stooping to set the cat on the floor, glanced up to catch on Grandma's face a look not of suspicion and unfriendliness, but a softened expression that almost erased the hard crease between her eyes. She looked for a moment like anybody's grandmother, soft-faced and gentle.

The cat's feet found the floor, and it crouched, looking up at the people above it. With his toe Oliver moved the dish of milk closer, and the cat fled under the bed. Grandma started forward, the wrinkle hard between her eyes again, her mouth beginning to go, and Janet stopped her with a hand on her arm.

"It's still scared," she said softly to the boys. "It'll be all right after it's got used to us. We'll leave it with Grandma now so they can both take a rest."

As she was herding the twins up the hall Oliver said, "Boy, that cat needs a rest."

"So does Grandma," Tom said from the dining room. "You guys can rest by getting some hay up into the mow."

"Can we ride Peppermint after?"

"She's got a saddlesore."

"We'll ride her bareback."

"All right."

They went out, and Tom looked at Janet with a peculiar sidelong expression. "The eminent psychiatrist," he said.

"It's working, isn't it?" Janet said. "She let me take her cat, and she's already starting to relax a little."

"I hope it's working," he said.

"Tom, don't you want her to be better?"

"Of course. I'd give an arm."

"She's just like her poor cat," Janet said. "She's been so pushed down and crammed under that she —— "

They both began to laugh.

"Probably we shouldn't," Janet said. But she added, "At least it's human to laugh! At least she's part of the family. Isn't that better than some old inhuman institution where she'd just be a number and a case history? They wouldn't laugh at her in a place like that. They wouldn't have the humanity to."

Next morning Grandma came with them to the orchard. She was quite calm, and for five minutes at a time her lips, instead of trembling on a stream of soundless words, were quiet, a little puckered; her eyes followed the preparation for picking with what seemed to Janet interest. Tom set up the ladders and laid out a string of lugs in the shade, and Grandma watched the four of them climb into the foliage among the bright globes of fruit.

Oliver picked a ripe apricot and stood on the ladder ready to toss it. "Here, Grandma," he said, "have an apricot."

He held it out, but the old lady made no move to come near and get it. "Just help yourself off the trees anywhere, Grandma," Janet said, and gave Oliver a sign to go on picking. When they were all up on ladders and busy,

Grandma stooped quickly and snatched up a windfall apricot from the ground.

"No, Grandma," Janet said. "From the trees. Pick all you want. Those on the ground may be spoiled."

Grandma dropped the windfall and wiped her fingers on her dress. After a moment she started at her hurrying, shoulder-forward walk down the orchard toward the lower fence.

"Do you want her taking off across country?" Tom said.

"Who do you think you are, a jailer?" Janet said. "Let her feel free for once."

"I haven't got time to go out every half hour and round her up."

"You won't have to. She'll come back."

"Sure?"

"Absolutely sure," Janet said. "Wait and see."

Thrust up among leaves and branches, they looked down to where Grandma's figure had stopped at the fence. The old lady looked around furtively, then stooped, picked up something from the ground and popped it into her mouth.

"You've got a ways to go," Tom said, and his voice from the other tree was so impersonal and dry that she was angry with him.

"Give her a little time!" she said. "Give her a chance!"

She was confident, yet when Grandma had not returned at eleven her faith began to waver. She did not want Tom to catch her anxiously looking down the orchard, but every time she dumped a pail in the lug she snatched quick looks all around, and she was almost at the point of sending the boys out searching when she saw the gingham figure marching homeward along the upper fence.

She threw an apricot into the tree where Tom was picking. "See?" she said. "What did I tell you?"

Every morning thereafter, Grandma took a walk through the orchards and along the lanes. Every afternoon she settled down in the wicker rocker on the porch, and rocked and talked and told herself things. Janet, working around the house, heard the steady voice going, and sometimes she heard what it said. It said that Simms, the drayman, had his eye on Grandma's house and was trying to get her moved out so that he could move his daughter and her husband in. It said that the minister was angry at her, ever since she sided with the evangelicals, and wanted the Ladies' Aid to leave her out of things. It said that George's wife was trying everything to get George to send Grandma away. Just the other day Grandma had overheard George's wife talking to the cleaning woman, plotting to leave Grandma's room dirty and then blame her in front of George. These were things Grandma knew, and she proved them with great vehemence and circumstantiality.

Sometimes Janet came and sat beside Grandma. When she did, the talk went underground; the lips moved, sometimes fervidly, and the little brown eyes snapped, but there was no conversation between them. Janet might comment on how the air cooled down when fog rolled over the crest of the coast hills, or might point out a hummingbird working the flower beds, but she did not expect replies. She took it as a hopeful sign that her presence did not drive Grandma away or stop her enthusiastic rocking, and sometimes it seemed to her that the rhythmic motion erased the strain from the old lady's face and smoothed the wrinkle between her eyes.

Then one afternoon Janet came quietly on the porch and found Grandma rocking like a child in the big chair, pushing with her toes, lifting off the floor, rocking back down to push with her toes again. She was not talking at all, but was humming a tuneless little song to herself.

It was early August, and dense heat lay over the valley.
The apricots were long gone; in the upper orchard the
prunes were purple among the leaves, the limbs of the
trees propped against the weight of fruit. The unirrigated
pasture was split by cracks three inches wide, and even
in the shade one felt the dry panting of the earth for the
rain that would not come for another three months. Looking out over the heat-hazed valley, Grandma pushed with
her toes, rocking and humming. Her face was mild and
soft, and Janet slipped into the next chair almost holding
her breath for fear of breaking the moment. It was so
easy to make a mistake. Weeks of improvement could be
canceled by one false move that the sick mind could seize
on as it had seized on a harmless conversation between
George's wife and her cleaning woman.

It was Grandma herself who spoke first. She looked
over at Janet brightly and said, "Tom's a handsome man."

"Yes," Janet said.

"He's filled out," Grandma said. "He was a skinny boy."

She went back to her humming. For ten more minutes
Janet sat still, wishing that Tom were there to see his
mother as she had once been, speculating on how the
moment might be stretched, wondering if possibly this
was a turning point, if Grandma had come out of the twilight where she lived and would from now on shake off
the suspicions and the fears. The vines over the porch
moved sluggishly and were still again.

Janet stood up. "It's hot," she said. "Shall we get ourselves a lemonade, Grandma?"

She appraised the quick look, the interrupted humming, the break in the even rocking, and knew that everything was all right, she hadn't broken any spell. Grandma

started to rise but Janet said, "Don't get up. I'll bring it out."

"I'll come along," the old lady said. In the kitchen she stood behind Janet and watched the lemons squeezed, the sugar added, the ice cubes pushed from the rubber tray.

"I like it better with fizz water, don't you?" Janet said. Grandma appeared not to understand, but she watched carefully as Janet filled the glasses. "Now a cherry," Janet said. "We might as well be festive." She looked at Grandma and laughed, surprising a tremble of a smile. Out on the porch she heard steps, and in the hope that Tom might have come in, and that she could demonstrate this miracle to him, she hugged the old lady around the shoulders and walked her through the French doors.

The steps had not been Tom's. Oliver was sprawled in the wicker rocker, his legs clear across the porch, his face sweaty. He looked up limply, brightened at sight of the glasses of lemonade.

"Hey! Can I have one?"

"If you want to fix it yourself. Grandma and I are having a party."

"Aw corn," Oliver said. "I haven't got the strength." He lay out even flatter in the chair, egg-eyed, his tongue hanging out. "This is the way they look when Popeye hits them," he said.

"Weak as you are, you'll have to move," Janet said. "You're in Grandma's chair."

He opened one eye. "Grandma's chair? How come?"

"Oliver!" his mother said. "Haven't you mislaid your manners?"

He rose promptly enough, a little surprised, and Janet ruffled his hair as he went by. But she couldn't miss the way Grandma's mouth had tightened and trembled, and how when she sat down again she sat on the front of the chair, unrelaxed, the mild look that had been briefly on her face replaced by a look of petulance and injury.

Three days later, when they were just beginning to pick the prune crop, Grandma moved.

Janet was preparing lunch when Tom and the boys came in from the orchard and started for the bathroom to clean up. Within a minute Oliver was back. "She's in our room! Mom, she's moved into our room with all her stuff!"

In Oliver's footsteps Janet went down the hall. Grandma sat stiffly on the boy's bed. The end of her suitcase showed under the bed, and the dresser was heaped with her clothing. From across the hall Tom appeared, scrubbing with a towel. Janet, stepping softly, went into the room and said, "Why, Grandma, don't you like your own room?"

The old lady's finger leaped out to point at Jack, who ducked as if the finger were a gun. The finger shifted smartly over to Oliver. "He told me to move. That boy of yours. He didn't want me to have the nice room with the bath when he only had this little one. He told me to get out."

Oliver's brow wrinkled, and his mouth opened. Tom took a step forward, but Janet stopped him with a look and squeezed hard on Oliver's shoulder. "There's just been a mistake," she said. "If either of the boys said that, he didn't mean it. The nice room with the bath is yours."

"He told me."

"If he did he didn't mean it. Did you, Oliver?"

"I never said anything of the kind. I was out in the orchard all morning."

"If you said it you didn't mean it, did you?"

"I never . . . No, I didn't mean it."

"Now let's get Grandma moved back before lunch," Janet said brightly, and motioned Jack to take some clothes from the dresser. When he moved to lift them off, Grandma took them from him with a hard look; he stood back and let her carry her own things to her room.

Back in the kitchen, Oliver said, "Boy, she's crazy as a bedbug. I never said a word to her. Where does she get it I made her move? She's nutty."

"Say she gets notions," Janet said. "I shouldn't have to tell you again. She's had a hard life. If we humor her and treat her nicely maybe she'll get well."

Oliver thoughtfully ate a prune off the work table. "How'd she get that way, fall downstairs or something?"

"I don't know," Janet said. "It just grew on her, I guess."

That was on Friday. On Sunday afternoon, when the prune orchard was dotted with people from the city who had come down to pick their own fruit, and Tom and the boys were out distributing ladders and pails and weighing up baskets and keeping the unpracticed pickers from breaking down limbs, Janet took a cool limeade in to Grandma and found her gone. Her closet was empty; her bureau drawers cleaned out.

Janet went out through the porch, across a road's-width of passionate sun, and under the shade of the oaks, where Tom had his scales. She waited while he weighed two baskets of prunes and carried them to a car. "Grandma's gone," she said when he came back.

She saw his patience bend and crack, and she stood guiltily, granting him the right to blame her but at the same time not admitting that she was in any way wrong. After a moment Tom said, "How long?"

"I don't know. I just took a drink in, and she was gone, with all her stuff. Sometime since dinner. Maybe an hour."

"We'd have seen her if she'd come out through here,"

he said. He looked across into the orchard, where three different parties were picking. "I just about have to stay here till these folks clear out. Can you and the kids look?"

She called the boys and they came at once, intent, sun-blackened, interested like setters being called up for a walk, and she thought as they came under the bronze shade: My nice boys! She thought it with a rush of affection, irrelevantly, grateful to them for their clear eyes and their health.

Trying to forestall in them the impatience that had jumped into Tom's face, she put on a crooked and rueful smile. "Grandma's abandoned us," she said, making it a joke between them.

They groaned, but more to acknowledge the joke than for any other reason, and wobbled their knees and crossed their eyes in dismay. Jack ran up the ladder of the tree house built in the oak and stood like a sailor on the cross-trees, peering into the empty shanty with a hand cupped over his eyes. Oliver sniffed the foot of the tree, followed an imaginary trail into the garage, through the car, around the woodshed, and back to the driveway. "Hey!" they said. "No Grandma. Man overboard. Fireman, save my child."

The three of them went across the brittle oat stubble, stopped to search the pump house, glanced into the chicken house and disturbed some matronly hens. They went through the stable and tackroom, and Janet stayed below while the boys climbed up into the mow. A drift of straw and dust fell from the trapdoor and filled the slant sunbeams with constellations.

The boys came down again. "No Grandma," they said. "Call the St. Bernards; she must be lost in the snow."

They went to the stable door and looked down across the lower orchard and the dry creek bed toward Hillstrom's. There was a breeze coming around the corner, a cool, horsy breath. They stood in it, searching the neighboring orchard and pastures, looking along the quarter-mile of white road that showed on the ridge above Kuhn's.

"She couldn't have gone far, with the suitcase," Janet said. "Did you look carefully in the garage, Oliver?"

"She wasn't there. I looked all over."

At a slight sound behind her, Janet turned. Grandma's cat came out of one of the horse stalls balancing his tail, blinking slit-eyed in the bright doorway, rubbing against her legs.

"Now where'd you come from, kitty?" Janet said. "Where's your mistress?"

"He comes down here to catch mice," Jack said. "I saw him with one the other day."

"But where's your boss?" Janet said, and stooped to let the lifting furry back pass under her hand.

There were footsteps in the tackroom, and Tom came in. "Find her?"

"Not a sign."

Tom stood with his hands in his back pockets, chewing his upper lip. "Oh, damn!" he said, without real anger.

Jack picked up the cat and stood petting it, watching his parents, and the noise of the cat's purring was loud in the stable until the noise of a car ground over it and drowned it out, and a green sedan came around the corner and stopped in the barnyard. "Is this where you can pick your own prunes?" the driver said. A woman and three children were crowding to look through the rear window.

"Up above," Tom said. "If you'll drive back up to the house I'll be with you in a minute." He looked at Janet. "You want me to go hunting, or handle the pickers, or what?"

"The boys and I can cruise around."

Then their voices filled the stable. "Mom! Here she is. Here she is, Mom!"

The sedan started to turn around. Back in against the manger of the second stall there was a threshing and rustling, and as Janet squinted into the shadows she saw Grandma sitting up in the manger. She reared up and scolded the boys, ". . . never get a minute's peace somebody always prying around spying on a person go away you boys or I'll tell your father he sent me down here now you leave me be go 'way."

"For the love of God, Ma, come out of there," Tom said. He went in and half lifted her over the front of the manger. Rigid with anger, muttering, she jerked away and came at a half run out into the doorway. The sedan was just leaving; Janet saw the faces staring, and then she grabbed Grandma and held her until Tom pulled her back inside. Grandma's clothes were slivered with hay, gray with dust. There were oat hulls caught on her lip.

"Oliver," Janet said. "Jump on that man's running board and show him where to go."

"Aw, Ma!"

"Please!" she said. "Get those people out of here!"

Tom hung on to Grandma's arm till the sound of the car had died. "I don't suppose it will do any good to ask you what you thought you were doing down here," he said.

Grandma sniffed. "I know I don't count for anything here," she said. "When I had my own home it was different, before Henry died, but around here I only do as I'm told. If you tell me to live in the stable and eat with the horses that's all right with me. I know I'm on charity, I don't complain."

Abruptly Tom let go of her arm. "You handle this," he said to Janet and went out into the hot light that lay like a sea around the warm dark island of the stable.

"You must trust us, Grandma," Janet said softly. Without really watching him, she was aware how Jack stared with the cat purring in his arms, and she reached out to pull him against her, knowing how Grandma's queerness must trouble his understanding. "You must let us love you and take care of you," she said. "Don't feel that any of us are against you. We all love you. You don't have to move out of your room, or eat out of the horse's box . . ."

Before she could move Grandma had lunged forward and snatched the sleepy tomcat out of Jack's arms. She clenched it against her fiercely, fighting its clawing desperate feet, and turned half around to shield it from their sight. The cat yowled, a frantic squashed sound, as Grandma retreated into the stall from which she had just come.

Janet shook her head at Jack and whispered, "You'd better run up and help Dad and Oliver." She steered him to the edge of the hard sunlight, whispering, "We'll just let her alone a few minutes. She's so excited she shouldn't be pushed around. I'll bring her up in a little while."

"What if she — "

"Run along. She'll be all right."

Her own nerves were on edge; she was trembling. Back in the shadow the cat squalled again, and then the sounds were muffled, as if Grandma had got the animal under her sweater. After a minute or two they stopped entirely. Either the old lady had got over her fright and stopped squeezing the cat, or it had escaped.

Janet waited another five minutes. It was perfectly quiet; she heard the slightest tick of falling straw. She did not like to think of Grandma back there in the shadow, her mouth going on some vehement silent tirade, her mind full of suspicion and crazy notions.

She went to the front of the stall and said casually, "Shall we go back to the house, Grandma?"

Grandma jerked around. She had been bending over

the manger, and now she pulled out the brown suitcase,
the arm or leg of a suit of winter underwear trailing out
of its corner. Janet smiled. "Did the cat get away? Never
mind, he likes it here. He'll be back."

"That boy tried to steal it," Grandma said.

She came out quietly enough, but when Janet offered to
carry the suitcase she swung it far over on one side, guard-
ing it jealously, and Janet sighed. It was so easy to make
a mistake. The slightest gesture of kindness was likely to
rouse suspicion. You had to be as soft and smooth and
easy as cottonwool, or you did harm instead of good. She
watched Grandma marching ahead of her; as the old lady
turned the sun was golden on the oat husks caught on
her lip. Janet smiled, following her up to the house and
into the cool porch, and still smiling followed her down
the hall to her room.

It was not until two hours later, after she had calmed
the old lady and talked her into taking a tepid bath, and
had then started to unpack and put away Grandma's
clothes, that she discovered about the cat. It was jammed
into the suitcase, tangled among long drawers and petti-
coats and damask napkins. And it was desperately and re-
sistantly dead. Its eyes were half open, its mouth wide
so that the needle teeth showed in a grin. Its front legs
were stiffened straight out, as if it had died pushing
against the smothering lid.

That evening after dinner Janet sat on the porch looking across the little valley and feeling how the heat left
the earth as the night came on. The boys were playing
checkers in the living room behind her: she felt their presence in the lamplight that yellowed the windows. Tom
was hammering at something down in the pumphouse.
Grandma was in her room.

Over the ridge of the stable the pasture knoll beyond

the Wilson place shone a lovely fawn color in the last flat sun. But all around, in the valley itself, the earth was already going gray and shadowy. In a little while the light would lift off the last knoll; the clouds would change and darken back of the coast hills; the ranches would begin to melt back into the trees; lights would wink on; the clean sky would be pricked with stars.

It was a most peaceful place and a peaceful life. Half irritably, she thought that Grandma should find healing in every hour of it. But she knew she would have to talk to Tom about Grandma later; for now she put the whole problem away, sitting with her hands turned palm upward in her lap and listening to the lulling rise of the night noises, crickets and tree frogs and the far musical cry of a train down toward San Jose. When it was all but dark she leaned near one of the open lighted windows and said, "Time for bed, boys."

"Just till we finish this game," Oliver said, and looking in she saw them hunched head to head over the card table. There was a rhythm in that too, the same rhythm through which she herself swung, moving evenly through the warm, temperate, repetitive events of a life that was not going anywhere because it was already there; it lived at the center.

She heard Tom coming through the dusk, his steps soft in the disked ground as he crossed a strip of orchard, then grating in the gravel drive, and he came up on the porch and sat down heavily in the wicker chair beside her.

"Boy, I've got you cornered now!" Oliver said from inside. "You give up?"

"Like heck," Jack said. "Not as long as I'm in a double corner."

"Time they were in bed?" Tom said.

"They're just finishing a game."

They sat on without speaking in the dark. Out over the main valley, moving smoothly among the orderly stars, the running lights on the wing tips of an air liner winked on and off. Sometimes, when clouds bridged the main valley trough, the motors of a plane like that could fill their little hollow with sound, but now in the clear night the noise was only a remote and diminishing hum. The lights winked unfailingly far down toward the south until the hills rose and cut them off.

Inside the boys broke up their game and snapped off the light. For a minute or two they stood together at the french doors looking out on the porch. "Well, I guess we'll go to bed now," one of them said, and Janet was amused that in the dark she really couldn't tell which one had spoken.

"I'll look in on you later," she said. "It's so nice out I think I'll sit awhile."

When they had gone, she and Tom sat on. The wicker chair squeaked; she knew he had turned his head.

"Well?" he said.

"Well?" She did not want to make it hard for him to begin; she even wanted with an odd sense of urgency to try again to tell him how she felt, how she knew that even a thing badly done, if it was done with love, was better than a thing done efficiently but without love. But she was in a defensive position, like Jack in his double corner. Tom had to move first . . . "You realize she has to be sent away," Tom said.

"Why?" She would not move until he absolutely forced her.

"My God!" he said. "Why?"

She heard his chair squeak again. Another plane was coming up the valley, its motors a distant even drone.

"I'll tell you why," he said. "Just because she breaks everything up. She can't live with sane people. She'll bust the whole pattern of our lives."

"By pattern you mean comfort," Janet said, and heard her own voice, stiff and resistant, and the irritation that jumped in Tom's voice when he answered.

"No, I don't mean comfort! I mean the way we live, the way the kids grow up. Do you think it does them any good, seeing her batting at empty air?"

Janet had thought of the boys herself, plenty of times. But they were steady and well-balanced. It might even teach them forbearance and kindliness to have the old lady around. It wasn't fair of Tom to bring them into it now.

"I wonder how the boys would like to be responsible for condemning Grandma to prison for life, just to protect their own routine?" she said.

"That's better than letting her break up other people's lives."

"Oh, break up our lives!" Janet said. "The little trouble we've had . . . " She leaned forward trying to reach the vague shadow of her husband with her eyes and voice. "Don't you realize what it would mean if we sent her away? We'd be treating her exactly as strangers might treat her, as if we had no feeling for her at all. We'd be washing our hands of her, just so we could be more comfortable." She sat back, suddenly so angry and hurt that her hands shook. "I'm surprised you don't . . ."

"Don't what?" Tom's voice said.

"Nothing."

"Nazi methods?" Tom said. "That's what you were going to say, isn't it? You're surprised I don't want to cyanide her."

"You know I didn't —— "

"Sometimes you have to do a thing you don't want to do," Tom said. "You can do it kindly, even when it's something hard."

"But that's just what I wish you could see!" Janet cried. "There's no chance of any kindness in an institution, and it's kindness she needs."

There was a pause. "So you don't want to send her away," Tom said. "Not even after that cat business."

"I couldn't forgive myself if we did," she said. "It would be throwing her out when she was crying for help and not knowing how to say the words. That cat was the one thing she had left to love. Remember how afraid she was that the man on the train was going to steal it? That cat was half her life."

"And she killed it."

"Out of fear! We haven't got her over her fear, that's all. She was getting along fine, till this last spell. I've got enough confidence in the way we live to think we can change her pattern instead of her changing ours."

"Then you're crazier than she is."

Janet stood up. Her knees were trembling a little, and the thought crossed her mind that now, without the cat, Grandma was going to be harder than ever to win over. Maybe she would even get the notion that someone in the family had killed it. But that was not the question. The question was whether they could feel right about giving her over to some cold-blooded aseptic hospital that would surely drive her deeper into her persecuted dream.

"I don't see how we could respect ourselves," she said. "It's at least worth a better try than we've given it."

For a time the little night noises were still. Then a cricket started up again, a tinny fiddling under the porch. Tom's face was lost in the dark, but finally he spoke. "Okay. You're the doctor."

"Just the thought of giving up after less than two months."

"Okay, okay."

"I wish you could see it, Tom."

"I see it," he said. "I just don't believe it."

She hesitated. Then she went past him, walking quietly as if he were sleeping and she did not want to disturb him, and opened the screen and let it close softly behind her. The house was still. The padded living-room rug muffled her steps, and she had a feeling that it was very late at night, though she knew it couldn't be past ten. There was a light burning in the hall, and by the diffused glow she made her way to the hall leading down the bedroom wing.

As if a hand had closed around her heart she stopped dead still at the entrance. Halfway down the hall Grandma was standing, looking into the open door of the boys' room. Her head was sunk between her shoulders with the intensity of her stare, and her mouth moved on some secret malevolence. She made no move to enter, but only stood there staring, stooping forward a little. Then she heard Janet and whirled, and all the light that filtered into the hall flashed in her eyeballs, and she scuttled down the hall and into her own room.

Janet fought her breath free, but the cold paralysis of fear was still in her legs. She took four quick steps to the children's door, listened. Their breathing came quiet and steady in the dark, and she sagged against the door in relief. From down the hall there was a muffled click, and she saw the shadowy crack along Grandma's door widen. When she stepped full in to the hall again the crack softly closed.

Janet put her hand down, felt the skeleton key in the lock of the boys' door. That key would work in any of the bedroom doors. She slipped it out and started down the hall, and the stealthy crack which had opened along Grandma's door closed again as she came. Janet stood a moment at the door, listening. There was not a sound. With a quick movement she inserted the skeleton key into the lock and turned it. She leaned against the door with the key in her hand and said, "Oh, Grandma, I'm sorry, I'm so terribly sorry!"

All through the darkened house there was not a sound. Up the hall her boys slept undisturbed, and out on the porch her husband sat in the dark, looking down over the even pattern of his orchards. She thought of the windows that Grandma could climb out of, the screens that should be nailed tight shut, and though the key in her hand was still a rigid reproach, she hurried. She hurried with fear driving her, and she was crying, not entirely from fear, when she called to Tom through the open french doors.

The Colt

It was the swift coming of spring that let things happen. It was spring, and the opening of the roads, that took his father out of town. It was spring that clogged the river with floodwater and ice pans, sent the dogs racing in wild aimless packs, ripped the railroad bridge out and scattered it down the river for exuberant townspeople to fish out piecemeal. It was spring that drove the whole town to the riverbank with pikepoles and coffeepots and boxes of sandwiches for an impromptu picnic, lifting their sober responsibilities out of them and making them whoop blessings on the C.P.R. for a winter's firewood. Nothing might have gone wrong except for the coming of spring. Some of the neighbors might have noticed and let them know; Bruce might not have forgotten; his mother might have remembered and sent him out again after dark.

But the spring came, and the ice went out, and that

night Bruce went to bed drunk and exhausted with excitement. In the restless sleep just before waking he dreamed of wolves and wild hunts, but when he awoke finally he realized that he had not been dreaming the noise. The window, wide open for the first time in months, let in a shivery draught of fresh, damp air, and he heard the faint yelping far down in the bend of the river.

He dressed and went downstairs, crowding his bottom into the warm oven, not because he was cold but because it had been a ritual for so long that not even the sight of the sun outside could convince him it wasn't necessary. The dogs were still yapping; he heard them through the open door.

"What's the matter with all the pooches?" he said. "Where's Spot?"

"He's out with them," his mother said. "They've probably got a porcupine treed. Dogs go crazy in the spring."

"It's dog days they go crazy."

"They go crazy in the spring, too." She hummed a little as she set the table. "You'd better go feed the horses. Breakfast won't be for ten minutes. And see if Daisy is all right."

Bruce stood perfectly still in the middle of the kitchen. "Oh my gosh!" he said. "I left Daisy picketed out all night!"

His mother's head jerked around. "Where?"

"Down in the bend."

"Where those dogs are?"

"Yes," he said, sick and afraid. "Maybe she's had her colt."

"She shouldn't for two or three days," his mother said. But just looking at her he knew that it might be bad, that there was something to be afraid of. In another moment they were both out the door, both running.

But it couldn't be Daisy they were barking at, he thought as he raced around Chance's barn. He'd picketed her higher up, not clear down in the U where the dogs were. His eyes swept the brown, wet, close-cropped meadow, the edge of the brush where the river ran close under the north bench. The mare wasn't there! He opened his mouth and half turned, running, to shout at his mother coming behind him, and then sprinted for the deep curve of the bend.

As soon as he rounded the little clump of brush that fringed the cutbank behind Chance's he saw them. The mare stood planted, a bay spot against the gray brush, and in front of her, on the ground, was another smaller spot. Six or eight dogs were leaping around, barking, sitting. Even at that distance he recognized Spot and the Chapmans' Airedale.

He shouted and pumped on. At a gravelly patch he stooped and clawed and straightened, still running, with a handful of pebbles. In one pausing, straddling, aiming motion he let fly a rock at the distant pack. It fell far short, but they turned their heads, sat on their haunches and let out defiant short barks. Their tongues lolled as if they had run far.

Bruce yelled and threw again, one eye on the dogs and the other on the chestnut colt in front of the mare's feet. The mare's ears were back, and as he ran Bruce saw the colt's head bob up and down. It was all right then. The colt was alive. He slowed and came up quietly. Never move fast or speak loud around an animal, Pa said.

The colt struggled again, raised its head with white eyeballs rolling, spraddled its white-stockinged legs and tried to stand. "Easy, boy," Bruce said. "Take it easy, old fella." His mother arrived, getting her breath, her hair half down, and he turned to her gleefully. "It's all

right, Ma. They didn't hurt anything. Isn't he a beauty,
Ma?"

He stroked Daisy's nose. She was heaving, her ears
pricking forward and back; her flanks were lathered, and
she trembled. Patting her gently, he watched the colt,
sitting now like a dog on its haunches, and his happiness
that nothing had really been hurt bubbled out of him.
"Lookit, Ma," he said. "He's got four white socks. Can I
call him Socks, Ma? He sure is a nice colt, isn't he? Aren't
you, Socks, old boy?" He reached down to touch the
chestnut's forelock, and the colt struggled, pulling away.

Then Bruce saw his mother's face. It was quiet, too
quiet. She hadn't answered a word to all his jabber. Instead she knelt down, about ten feet from the squatting
colt, and stared at it. The boy's eyes followed hers. There
was something funny about . . .

"Ma!" he said. "What's the matter with its front feet?"

He left Daisy's head and came around, staring. The
colt's pasterns looked bent — *were* bent, so that they flattened clear to the ground under its weight. Frightened
by Bruce's movement, the chestnut flopped and floun-
dered to its feet, pressing close to its mother. And it walked,
Bruce saw, flat on its fetlocks, its hooves sticking out in
front like a movie comedian's too-large shoes.

Bruce's mother pressed her lips together, shaking her
head. She moved so gently that she got her hand on the
colt's poll, and he bobbed against the pleasant scratching.
"You poor broken-legged thing," she said with tears in
her eyes. "You poor little friendly ruined thing!"

Still quietly, she turned toward the dogs, and for the
first time in his life Bruce heard her curse. Quietly, almost
in a whisper, she cursed them as they sat with hanging
tongues just out of reach. "God damn you," she said.

"God damn your wild hearts, chasing a mother and a poor little colt."

To Bruce, standing with trembling lip, she said, "Go get Jim Enich. Tell him to bring a wagon. And don't cry. It's not your fault."

His mouth tightened, a sob jerked in his chest. He bit his lip and drew his face down tight to keep from crying, but his eyes filled and ran over.

"It is too my fault!" he said, and turned and ran.

Later, as they came in the wagon up along the cutbank, the colt tied down in the wagon box with his head sometimes lifting, sometimes bumping on the boards, the mare trotting after with chuckling vibrations of solicitude in her throat, Bruce leaned far over and tried to touch the colt's haunch. "Gee whiz!" he said. "Poor old Socks."

His mother's arm was around him, keeping him from leaning over too far. He didn't watch where they were until he heard his mother say in surprise and relief, "Why, there's Pa!"

Instantly he was terrified. He had forgotten and left Daisy staked out all night. It was his fault, the whole thing. He slid back into the seat and crouched between Enich and his mother, watching from that narrow space like a gopher from its hole. He saw the Ford against the barn and his father's big body leaning into it pulling out gunny sacks and straw. There was mud all over the car, mud on his father's pants. He crouched deeper into his crevice and watched his father's face while his mother was telling what had happened.

Then Pa and Jim Enich lifted and slid the colt down to the ground, and Pa stooped to feel its fetlocks. His face was still, red from windburn, and his big square hands were muddy. After a long examination he straightened up.

"Would've been a nice colt," he said. "Damn a pack of mangy mongrels, anyway." He brushed his pants and looked at Bruce's mother. "How come Daisy was out?"

"I told Bruce to take her out. The barn seems so cramped for her, and I thought it would do her good to stretch her legs. And then the ice went out, and the bridge with it, and there was a lot of excitement. . . ." She spoke very fast, and in her voice Bruce heard the echo of his own fear and guilt. She was trying to protect him, but in his mind he knew he was to blame.

"I didn't mean to leave her out, Pa," he said. His voice squeaked, and he swallowed. "I was going to bring her in before supper, only when the bridge . . ."

His father's somber eyes rested on him, and he stopped. But his father didn't fly into a rage. He just seemed tired. He looked at the colt and then at Enich. "Total loss?" he said.

Enich had a leathery, withered face, with two deep creases from beside his nose to the corner of his mouth. A brown mole hid in the left one, and it emerged and disappeared as he chewed a dry grass stem. "Hide," he said.

Bruce closed his dry mouth, swallowed. "Pa!" he said. "It won't have to be shot, will it?"

"What else can you do with it?" his father said. "A crippled horse is no good. It's just plain mercy to shoot it."

"Give it to me, Pa. I'll keep it lying down and heal it up."

"Yeah," his father said, without sarcasm and without mirth. "You could keep it lying down about one hour."

Bruce's mother came up next to him, as if the two of them were standing against the others. "Jim," she said quickly, "isn't there some kind of brace you could put on it? I remember my dad had a horse once that broke a leg below the knee, and he saved it that way."

"Not much chance," Enich said. "Both legs, like that." He plucked a weed and stripped the dry branches from the stalk. "You can't make a horse understand he has to keep still."

"But wouldn't it be worth trying?" she said. "Children's bones heal so fast, I should think a colt's would too."

"I don't know. There's an outside chance, maybe."

"Bo," she said to her husband, "why don't we try it? It seems such a shame, a lovely colt like that."

"I know it's a shame!" he said. "I don't like shooting colts any better than you do. But I never saw a broken-legged colt get well. It'd just be a lot of worry and trouble, and then you'd have to shoot it finally anyway."

"Please," she said. She nodded at him slightly, and then the eyes of both were on Bruce. He felt the tears coming up again, and turned to grope for the colt's ears. It tried to struggle to its feet, and Enich put his foot on its neck. The mare chuckled anxiously.

"How much this hobble brace kind of thing cost?" the father said finally. Bruce turned again, his mouth open with hope.

"Two-three dollars, is all," Enich said.

"You think it's got a chance?"

"One in a thousand, maybe."

"All right. Let's go see MacDonald."

"Oh, good!" Bruce's mother said, and put her arm around him tight.

"I don't know whether it's good or not," the father said. "We might wish we never did it." To Bruce he said, "It's your responsibility. You got to take complete care of it."

"I will!" Bruce said. He took his hand out of his pocket

and rubbed below his eye with his knuckles. "I'll take care of it every day."

Big with contrition and shame and gratitude and the sudden sense of immense responsibility, he watched his father and Enich start for the house to get a tape measure. When they were thirty feet away he said loudly, "Thanks, Pa. Thanks an awful lot."

His father half turned, said something to Enich. Bruce stooped to stroke the colt, looked at his mother, started to laugh and felt it turn horribly into a sob. When he turned away so that his mother wouldn't notice he saw his dog Spot looking inquiringly around the corner of the barn. Spot took three or four tentative steps and paused, wagging his tail. Very slowly (never speak loud or move fast around an animal) the boy bent and found a good-sized stone. He straightened casually, brought his arm back, and threw with all his might. The rock caught Spot squarely in the ribs. He yiped, tucked his tail, and scuttled around the barn, and Bruce chased him, throwing clods and stones and gravel, yelling, "Get out! Go on, get out of here or I'll kick you apart. Get out! Go on!"

So all that spring, while the world dried in the sun and the willows emerged from the floodwater and the mud left by the freshet hardened and caked among their roots, and the grass of the meadow greened and the river brush grew misty with tiny leaves and the dandelions spread yellow among the flats, Bruce tended his colt. While the other boys roamed the bench hills with .22's looking for gophers or rabbits or sage hens, he anxiously superintended the colt's nursing and watched it learn to nibble the grass. While his gang built a darkly secret hide-out in the deep brush beyond Hazard's, he was currying and brushing and trimming the chestnut mane. When packs of boys ran hare and hounds through the town and around the river's slow bends, he perched on the front porch with his sling-shot and a can full of small round stones, waiting for stray dogs to appear. He waged a holy war on the dogs until they learned to detour widely around his house, and he never did completely forgive his own dog, Spot. His whole life was wrapped up in the hobbled, leg-ironed chestnut colt with the slow-motion lunging walk and the affectionate nibbling lips.

Every week or so Enich, who was now working out of town at the Half Diamond Bar, rode in and stopped. Always, with that expressionless quiet that was terrible to the boy, he stood and looked the colt over, bent to feel pastern and fetlock, stood back to watch the plunging walk when the boy held out a handful of grass. His expression said nothing; whatever he thought was hidden back of his leathery face as the dark mole was hidden in the crease beside his mouth. Bruce found himself watching that mole sometimes, as if revelation might lie there. But when he pressed Enich to tell him, when he said, "He's getting better, isn't he? He walks better, doesn't he, Mr. Enich? His ankles don't bend so much, do they?" the wrangler gave him little encouragement.

"Let him be a while. He's growin', sure enough. Maybe give him another month."

May passed. The river was slow and clear again, and some of the boys were already swimming. School was almost over. And still Bruce paid attention to nothing but Socks. He willed so strongly that the colt should get well that he grew furious even at Daisy when she sometimes wouldn't let the colt suck as much as he wanted. He took a butcher knife and cut the long tender grass in the fence corners, where Socks could not reach, and fed it to his pet by the handful. He trained him to nuzzle for sugar-lumps in his pockets. And back in his mind was a fear: in the middle of June they would be going out to the homestead again, and if Socks weren't well by that time he might not be able to go.

"Pa," he said, a week before they planned to leave. "How much of a load are we going to have, going out to the homestead?"

"I don't know, wagonful, I suppose. Why?"

"I just wondered." He ran his fingers in a walking motion along the round edge of the dining table, and strayed into the other room. If they had a wagon load, then there was no way Socks could be loaded in and taken along. And he couldn't walk thirty miles. He'd get left behind before they got up on the bench, hobbling along like the little crippled boy in the Pied Piper, and they'd look back and see him trying to run, trying to keep up.

That picture was so painful that he cried over it in bed that night. But in the morning he dared to ask his father if they couldn't take Socks along to the farm. His father turned on him eyes as sober as Jim Enich's, and when he spoke it was with a kind of tired impatience. "How can he go? He couldn't walk it."

"But I want him to go, Pa!"

"Brucie," his mother said, "don't get your hopes up. You know we'd do it if we could, if it was possible."

"But Ma . . ."

His father said, "What you want us to do, haul a broken-legged colt thirty miles?"

"He'd be well by the end of the summer, and he could walk back."

"Look," his father said. "Why can't you make up your mind to it? He isn't getting well. He isn't going to get well."

"He is too getting well!" Bruce shouted. He half stood

up at the table, and his father looked at his mother and shrugged.

"Please, Bo," she said.

"Well, he's got to make up his mind to it sometime," he said.

Jim Enich's wagon pulled up on Saturday morning, and Bruce was out the door before his father could rise from his chair. "Hi, Mr. Enich," he said.

"Hello, Bub. How's your pony?"

"He's fine," Bruce said. "I think he's got a lot better since you saw him last."

"Uh-huh." Enich wrapped the lines around the whip-stock and climbed down. "Tell me you're leaving next week."

"Yes," Bruce said. "Socks is in the back."

When they got into the back yard Bruce's father was there with his hands behind his back, studying the colt as it hobbled around. He looked at Enich. "What do you think?" he said. "The kid here thinks his colt can walk out to the homestead."

"Uh-huh," Enich said. "Well, I wouldn't say that." He inspected the chestnut, scratched between his ears. Socks bobbed, and snuffled at his pockets. "Kid's made quite a pet of him."

Bruce's father grunted. "That's just the damned trouble."

"I didn't think he could walk out," Bruce said. "I thought we could take him in the wagon, and then he'd be well enough to walk back in in the fall."

"Uh," Enich said. "Let's take his braces off for a minute."

He unbuckled the triple straps on each leg, pulled the braces off, and stood back. The colt stood almost as flat on his fetlocks as he had the morning he was born. Even

Bruce, watching with his whole mind tight and apprehensive, could see that. Enich shook his head.

"You see, Bruce?" his father said. "It's too bad, but he isn't getting better. You'll have to make up your mind. . . . "

"He will get better though!" Bruce said. "It just takes a long time, is all." He looked at his father's face, at Enich's, and neither one had any hope in it. But when Bruce opened his mouth to say something else his father's eyebrows drew down in sudden, unaccountable anger, and his hand made an impatient sawing motion in the air.

"We shouldn't have tried this in the first place," he said. "It just tangles everything up." He patted his coat pockets, felt in his vest. "Run in and get me a couple cigars."

Bruce hesitated, his eyes on Enich. "Run!" his father said harshly.

Reluctantly he released the colt's halter rope and started for the house. At the door he looked back, and his father and Enich were talking together, so low that their words didn't carry to where he stood. He saw his father shake his head, and Enich bend to pluck a grass stem. They were both against him, they both were sure Socks would never get well. Well, he would! There was some way.

He found the cigars, came out, watched them both light up. Disappointment was a sickness in him, and mixed with the disappointment was a question. When he could stand their silence no more he burst out with it. "But what are we going to *do?* He's got to have some place to stay."

"Look, kiddo." His father sat down on a sawhorse and took him by the arm. His face was serious and his voice gentle. "We can't take him out there. He isn't well enough to walk, and we can't haul him. So Jim here has offered to buy him. He'll give you three dollars for him, and when you come back, if you want, you might be able to buy him back. That is if he's well. It'll be better to leave him with Jim."

"Well . . ." Bruce studied the mole on Enich's cheek. "Can you get him better by fall, Mr. Enich?"

"I wouldn't expect it," Enich said. "He ain't got much of a show."

"If anybody can get him better, Jim can," his father said. "How's that deal sound to you?"

"Maybe when I come back he'll be all off his braces and running around like a house afire," Bruce said. "Maybe next time I see him I can ride him." The mole disappeared as Enich tongued his cigar.

"Well, all right then," Bruce said, bothered by their stony-eyed silence. "But I sure hate to leave you behind, Socks, old boy."

"It's the best way all around," his father said. He talked fast, as if he were in a hurry. "Can you take him along now?"

"Oh, gee!" Bruce said. "Today?"

"Come on," his father said. "Let's get it over with."

Bruce stood by while they trussed the colt and hoisted him into the wagon box, and when Jim climbed in he cried out, "Hey, we forgot to put his hobbles back on." Jim and his father looked at each other. His father shrugged. "All right," he said, and started putting the braces back on the trussed front legs. "He might hurt himself if they weren't on," Bruce said. He leaned over the endgate stroking the white blazed face, and as the wagon pulled away he stood with tears in his eyes and the three dollars in his hand, watching the terrified straining of the colt's neck, the bony head raised above the endgate and one white eye rolling.

Five days later, in the sun-slanting, dew-wet spring morning, they stood for the last time that summer on the front porch, the loaded wagon against the front fence. The father tossed the key in his hand and kicked the door-jamb. "Well, good-bye, Old Paint," he said. "See you in the fall."

As they went to the wagon Bruce sang loudly,

> Good-bye, Old Paint, I'm leavin' Cheyenne,
> I'm leavin' Cheyenne, I'm goin' to Montana,
> Good-bye, Old Paint, I'm leavin' Cheyenne.

"Turn it off," his father said. "You want to wake up the whole town?" He boosted Bruce into the back end, where he squirmed and wiggled his way neck-deep into the luggage. His mother, turning to see how he was settled, laughed at him. "You look like a baby owl in a nest," she said.

His father turned and winked at him. "Open your mouth and I'll drop in a mouse."

It was good to be leaving; the thought of the homestead was exciting. If he could have taken Socks along it would have been perfect, but he had to admit, looking around at the jammed wagon box, that there sure wasn't any room for him. He continued to sing softly as they rocked out into the road and turned east toward Mac-Kenna's house, where they were leaving the keys.

At the low, sloughlike spot that had become the town's dump ground the road split, leaving the dump like an island in the middle. The boy sniffed at the old familiar smells of rust and tar-paper and ashes and refuse. He had collected a lot of old iron and tea lead and bottles and broken machinery and clocks, and once a perfectly good amberheaded cane, in that old dumpground. His father turned up the right fork, and as they passed the central part of the dump the wind, coming in from the northeast, brought a rotten, unbearable stench across them.

"Pee-you!" his mother said, and held her nose. Bruce echoed her. "Pee-you! Pee-you-willy!" He clamped his nose shut and pretended to fall dead.

"Guess I better get to windward of that coming back," said his father.

They woke MacKenna up and left the key and started back. The things they passed were very sharp and clear to the boy. He was seeing them for the last time all summer. He noticed things he had never noticed so clearly before: how the hills came down into the river from the north like three folds in a blanket, how the stovepipe on the Chinaman's shack east of town had a little conical hat on it. He chanted at the things he saw. "Goodbye, old Chinaman. Good-bye, old Frenchman River. Good-bye, old Dumpground, good-bye."

"Hold your noses," his father said. He eased the wagon into the other fork around the dump. "Somebody sure dumped something rotten."

He stared ahead, bending a little, and Bruce heard him swear. He slapped the reins on the team till they trotted. "What?" the mother said. Bruce, half rising to see what caused the speed, saw her lips go flat over her teeth, and a look on her face like the woman he had seen in the traveling dentist's chair, when the dentist dug a living nerve out of her tooth and then got down on his knees to hunt for it, and she sat there half raised in her seat, her face lifted.

"For gosh sakes," he said. And then he saw.

He screamed at them. "Ma, it's Socks! Stop, Pa! It's Socks!"

His father drove grimly ahead, not turning, not speaking, and his mother shook her head without looking around. He screamed again, but neither of them turned. And when he dug down into the load, burrowing in and shaking with long smothered sobs, they still said nothing.

So they left town, and as they wound up the dugway to the south bench there was not a word among them except his father's low, "For Christ sakes, I thought he was going to take it out of town." None of them looked back at the view they had always admired, the flat river bottom green with spring, its village snuggled in the loops of river. Bruce's eyes, pressed against the coats and blankets under him until his sight was a red haze, could still see through it the bloated, skinned body of the colt, the chestnut hair left a little way above the hooves, the iron braces still on the broken front legs.

❦ ❦ ❦

The Chink

IT IS an odd trick of memory that after almost a quarter of a century I still remember Mah Li better than I can remember anyone else in that town. The people I grew up among, many of the children I played with every day, are vague names without faces, or faces without names. Maybe I remember him well because he was so ambiguous a figure in the town's life. He and his brother Mah Jim, who ran the restaurant, were the only Chinese in town, and though Mah Li did our laundry, worked for us, delivered our vegetables punctually at seven in the morning three days a week, he was as much outside human society as an animal would have been. Sometimes I catch myself remembering him in the same way I remember the black colt my father gave me when I was nine. I loved Mah Li as I loved the colt, but neither was part of the life that seemed meaningful at the time.

He called me O-Fi', because O-5, our laundry mark, was easier for him to say than Lederer. Every Monday morning he appeared at the back door with his basket, got the laundry, grinned and bobbed so that his pigtail twitched like a limber black snake, and said, "Velly good, O-Fi'. Leddy Fliday." I have a picture of him in my mind, shuffling up the worn path along the irrigation ditch, dogtrotting in his hurry as if daylight were going out on him while he still had a lot to do, and his black baggy pants and loose blouse blowing against his body.

I have other pictures, too. Whenever I think of him a swarm of things come up: Mah Li and Mah Jim sitting in the bare kitchen of the restaurant, a candle between them on the table with its flame as straight as a blade, playing fan-tan in intent, serious, interminable silence. Somehow that picture seems sad now, like a symbol of their home-lessness. They had no women, no friends, no intercourse with the townspeople except when men kidded them along in the way they kid half-wits, condescendingly, with an edge of malice in their jokes.

I remember Mah Li meeting someone on the street in winter, the white man stopping him to say hello, rubbing his stomach and saying, "Belly cold today," and Mah Li beaming his wide smile, jabbering, and the white man saying, "Put your shirt inside your pants and your belly won't be cold," and slapping Mah Li on the back and guf-fawing. Old jokes like that, always the same ones. And the kids who hung around Mah Jim's restaurant jerking the Chinks' pigtails and asking them if it was true that they kneaded their bread in big tubs with their bare feet, or if they really spit in the soup of people they didn't like.

The town accepted them, worked them like slaves for little pay, I suppose even liked them after a fashion, but it never adopted them, just as Mah Jim and Mah Li never adopted white man's clothes, but always wore their black baggy pants and blouses. They never got the white man's habit of loafing, either. Mah Li, for instance, when he worked for us in summers down at the potato field, tended his own garden from daylight till about seven, worked our potatoes till almost dark, and then came into town to wash and iron till midnight on the laundry Mah Jim had taken in for him during the day. Maybe they liked to work that hard; maybe it helped them against their loneliness. My father always said that a Chinaman would outwork a white man two to one, and do it on a cupful of rice a day.

It is around the potato field and the garden that most of my recollections of the Chink center. The second year he worked for us he asked my father if he could rent a little piece of land to put in vegetables, and father let him have the ground free. Mah Li never thanked him — I don't think he ever knew what the word for thanks was. He just looked at him a minute with impassive slant eyes, bobbed his pigtail, and went dogtrotting down to go to work. But in July of that summer he appeared at our back door one morning just after I'd brought the milk in from the barn. He had a basket over his arm.

"Nice day, O-Fi'," he said. "Velly fine day!"

"It's a swell day," I said, "but you've got your dates mixed. It isn't laundry day."

"No laundly," he said, grinning, and passed me the basket. It was full of leaf lettuce and carrots and string beans and green peas, with two bunches of white icicle radishes sticking up in it like bouquets.

After that he came three times a week, regular as sunrise, with vegetables that were the envy of every gardener in town. And when Mother tried to pay him for them he beamed and bobbed and shook his head. I remember her saying finally, in a kind of despair, that she wouldn't take his baskets free any more, but he always came, and we always took them. It would have hurt his feelings if we hadn't.

It was Mother who suggested that I give the Chinese the suckers I caught in the river. We never ate them, because suckers are full of little needle-bones and don't taste very good. I just fished for the fun of it. So one afternoon I went down to the potato field in the river bottom, near the flume, with four big suckers on a willow crotch. Mah Li was moving down the field with a hoe, loosening the ground around the vines. When I gave him the fish he looked surprised, beamed, nodded, trotted down to the riverbank and packed them in grass, and rolled them up in a big handkerchief.

"Nice, O-Fi'," he said. I guess that was the way he said thanks.

That afternoon I hung around and helped him a little in the field, and went over with him to see his own garden. I remember him stooping among his tomato vines feeling the fruit till he found a big, red, firm one, and rubbing it off on his blouse and handing it to me. And I remember how heavy and sun-warmed that tomato was, and how I had to jump backward and stick out my face because the juice spurted and ran down my chin when I bit into it. We stood in the plant-smelling garden, under the yellow summer hills, with the sun heavy and hot on our heads, and laughed at each other, and I think that's where I first found out that Mah Li was human.

After that I was around the field a good deal. Whenever I didn't have anything else to do I'd go down and help him, or sit on the riverbank and fish while he worked. Just to watch him in a garden made you know he loved it. I used to watch him to see how long he'd swing the hoe without taking a rest, and sometimes I'd fish for two hours before he'd pause. Then he'd sit down on his heels, the way I've seen Chinese squat on the rails when they work on a section gang, and stay perfectly still for about ten minutes. He was so quiet then that bumblebees would blunder into him and crawl around and fly away again, and butterflies would light on his face. He let them sit there with their wings breathing in and out, and never made so much as the flicker of an eyelash that would disturb them. When he was ready to go to work again his hand would come up slowly, to pick them off so gently that they never knew he touched them.

His yellow hands were very gentle with everything they touched, even with the potato bugs we picked into tin cans and burned. Many afternoons in August I worked down the rows with him while he went bent-kneed along, his face placid and contented and his eyes sharp for bugs. He could do it three times as fast as I could, and cleaner too. We'd meet at the ends of rows every now and again, and dump the striped bugs out into piles, and Mah Li would pour kerosene over them and touch a match to it. Then we'd go down the rows again while the stinking smudge went up behind.

And then there was the magpie that I ran across in the brush one day when I was coming up from fishing. It was a young one, with a hurt wing so that it couldn't fly, but it ran like a pheasant with that one wing trailing, and I had a chase before I caught it. It was still pecking at my fingers and flapping to get away when I brought it up to show Mah Li.

The Chink's face looked as if a lamp had gone on behind it. He chirped with his lips, quietly, and put out a dry hand to stroke the feathers on the bird's head. After a minute he lifted it out of my hands and held its body cradled in his palm, stroking its head, chirping at it. And

it lay in his hand quietly as if it were on a nest; it made no
attempt to peck him or to get away.

"He likes you," I said.

Mah Li's shaved head nodded very slowly, his lips
going in a singsong lullaby and his finger moving gently
on the magpie's head.

"Think his wing is broken?"

He nodded again; his pigtail crawled up his back with
the bend of his head, and then crawled down.

"You better keep him," I said. "Maybe you can fix his
wing."

Mah Li fixed his narrow black eyes on me. I was always
being surprised by his eyes, because just talking to him,
working with him, I thought of him as another person,
like anybody else. Then every once in a while I'd see
those eyes, flat on his face, with scarcely any sockets for
them to sink back into, and so narrow that it looked as if
the skin had grown over and almost covered them.

"Slicee tongue," Mah Li said. "Talkee."

That night he carried the magpie home. A month
later, when I saw it perched on the back of a chair in
Mah Jim's kitchen, glossy and full of life, it opened its
mouth and made squawking noises that sounded almost
like words. By the middle of October he had it so tame
that it rode around on his shoulder, balancing with its tail
and squawking if he moved too fast and disturbed its foot-
ing, and whenever he chirped at it it squawked and jabbered. I laughed like anything when I heard what it said.
It said "O-Fi'! O-Fi'! Nice, O-Fi'!"

So that's the way we were, friends — very good friends,
in a way — even though Mah Li touched my life only on
one of its outside edges. He was like a book I went back
to read when there was nothing else doing. And I sup-

pose it was that quality of unreality about our friendship, the strange and foreign things about him — pigtail and singsong and slant eyes — that made me think of him always in a special way, and forced me into the wrong loyalty that night at the end of October in 1918.

I came downtown that night about eight o'clock to join the gang and pull off some Hallowe'en tricks. You were everybody's enemy on Hallowe'en. You hauled your own father's buggy up on somebody's barn, and pushed over your own outhouse along with everybody else's. I say that to explain, in a way, how I came to be lined up against the Chinks that night. Things like that were automatic on Hallowe'en.

We had planned to meet at Mah Jim's, but I found the crowd gathered a block up the street. They were all sore. I didn't understand very clearly then, but I gathered that they'd been fooling in the restaurant and Tad McGovern had hooked a handful of bars from the candy counter. Mah Jim saw him, and raised a fuss, but Tad wouldn't give them back. He challenged Mah Jim to wrestle for them. The Chink got excited, and jabbered, and the kids all ragged him, and finally Mah Jim got really mad. I never saw him that way, but he must have been, because he jumped on Tad and took the bars away from him, and when three or four other kids took hold of him to put him down he shook them off and grabbed up the poker from the stove and ran the whole crowd out. So now they were just on the verge of getting even. They were going to tip over the Chinks' privy first, and then put the hospital sign on their front door, and then pour water down their chimney and put their fire out, and some other things.

I joined in and we went sneaking back through the alley toward Mah Jim's. It was a cold night, with a light snow that didn't quite cover the ground. In the dark it was just possible to see the pale patches where the snow lay. We crept up behind the laundry, just a couple of rods from the outhouse. Mah Jim must have closed up his restaurant after the ruckus with the gang, because there wasn't a light. The privy was just a vague blob of shadow in the dark.

We gathered behind Tad, waiting for the signal. Sometimes people stood guard on their privies, and we had developed a raiding technique that didn't give them a chance to do anything. When Tad whistled we rushed out pell-mell, about a dozen of us. Our hands found the front of the privy and we heaved hard, all in one hard running push. There was a startled yelp from inside, a yelp almost like a dog's, as the privy lifted and tottered and went over with a crash.

Tad let out a whoop. "Gee, the Chink's in there!"

"Let's lock him in!" somebody said, and a half-dozen boys dived for the door to hold it down. Someone found a nail, and they hammered it in with a rock.

I stood back, because I didn't quite like the idea of the Chink's being locked in there in the cold, and because I was a little scared at the silence from inside. After that one yelp there hadn't been a sound. Even when Tad put his face down close to the boards and said, "Hey there, you Chink Mah Jim!" there was no answer. Tad laughed right out loud. "Gee, he's so mad he can't speak," he said. He put his face down again. "When you get tired you can come out the hole," he said.

Then one of the scouts stationed at the back of the laundry jiggered us and we scattered. I ducked behind a shed in the back lot and listened. Someone was calling from the side of the restaurant. "Boys!" he said. "Boys, come out. I want to talk to you."

In the dark somebody made a spluttering noise with

his mouth. "Try and catch us," he said. But the voice went right on. I recognized it as belonging to Mr. Menefee, the principal of the school. "I don't want to catch you. I want to talk to you."

"What do you want to talk about?" I yelled, and felt big and brave for coming right back at Mr. Menefee that way. But Tad McGovern, over behind the hardware store, shouted at me: "Shut up! It's a trick."

"No, it isn't a trick," Mr. Menefee said. "Word of honor, boys. I just want to speak to you a minute."

There was such an anxious, worried tone in his voice that I stepped out from behind the shed and into the open. I could hear others coming too, cautiously, ready to break and run, but Mr. Menefee didn't make a move, and soon we were all around him where he stood in the faint light from the street with his overcoat up around his ears and his hands in his pockets.

"I just wanted to tell you," he said, "that it wouldn't be quite decent to pull any pranks tonight. Three people are down sick and Doctor Carroll says it's the flu."

His voice was so solemn, and the thought of the flu was so awful, that we stood there shuffling our feet without being able to say anything. We'd heard plenty about the flu. It killed you off in twenty-four hours, and you died in delirium, and after you were dead you turned black and shriveled. I felt it then like a great shadowy Fear in the dark all around me, while Mr. Menefee stood and looked at us and waited for his words to sink in.

"We're all going to have to help," he said finally. "I hate to take you away from your fun. You're entitled to it on Hallowe'en. But this is a time when everybody has to pitch in. Are you willing to help?"

That gave us our tongues, like a chorus of dogs after a porcupine. "Sure," we said. "Sure, Mr. Menefee!"

He lined it up for us. We were to go to the drugstore

and get bundles of flu masks and bottles of eucalyptus oil, which we were to distribute to every house in town, warning people not to come out without their masks, and not to come out at all except when they had to. The town was going to be quarantined and nobody could leave it.

It was like being Paul Revere, and in the excitement of hearing all that I forgot for a minute about Mah Jim locked in the overturned privy. Then I caught myself listening, and all at once I remembered what I was listening for. I was expecting the Chink to hammer on the door and yell to get out. But there wasn't a sound from out in back.

Mr. Menefee snapped to attention the way he did when we were having fire drill in school. "All right, men! What are we standing around for?"

The crowd shuffled their feet, and I knew most of them were thinking, just as I was, of the privy out behind with the Chink in it.

"Mr. Menefee," I said, and stopped.

"What?" I could see him bend over and stare around at us sharply. "You haven't started anything already, have you?" he said.

The silence came down again. Every one of us was ashamed of what we'd just done, I imagine, except Tad McGovern. But none of us dared admit we'd done anything. It would have been a kind of treason. We were soldiers in the army, helping protect the town against the plague. We couldn't just stand there and admit we'd done something pretty raw, something we shouldn't have dared do to a white man. It made us look small and mean and vicious, and we wanted to look heroic.

Tad McGovern was right at my elbow. "Naw," he said. "We were just getting ready to start."

Mr. Menefee snapped to attention again. "Good!" he

said. "All right, on the jump now. Divide up into squads, half of you into each end of town. And remember to put on your own masks and keep them on."

Some of the boys jumped and ran, and in a second we were all running for the drugstore. All the time I wanted to turn around and go back and say, "Mr. Menefee, we pushed over the Chinks' privy and Mah Jim's in there." But I kept on running, and got my bundle of masks in the drugstore, and my package of eucalyptus oil bottles, and opened one and soused a mask with it and put it on, and gathered with the others outside, where we split.

The eucalyptus oil smelled so bad, and came so strong into my mouth and nose through the mask, that I almost gagged, and that made me think about myself for a while. But while we were running from door to door up in the Poverty Lane end of town I got thinking more and more about how the Chinks didn't ever wear very heavy clothes, and how Mah Jim might be freezing out there, catching the flu, and how he'd be too big to crawl out through the hole. I mentioned it to the boy I was with, but he said he was sure a grown man could kick that nail loose with one kick. The Chink was already out, he said. He'd be sitting by his fire right now, cussing us in Chinese.

Still I wasn't satisfied. Suppose he was hurt? Everything had been dark when we pushed the privy over. That meant that if Mah Li had gone to bed in his laundry room he wouldn't know Mah Jim was still out. And if Mah Jim was hurt he'd lie there all night.

It gnawed at me until, after we had raised Orullian's house, I was ready to quit the army and go back to see if the Chink was all right. The excitement had worn off completely. I was cold, my nose was running into my mask, the stink of the oil made my stomach roll every time I took a breath. And so the first chance I got I stuck the remaining masks and bottles into my mackinaw pocket and cut out across the irrigation ditch toward town.

Everything was quiet when I slipped into the black back yard. Probably everything's all right, I thought. Probably he did kick the door out and get loose. But when I felt for the door and tried to open it, it was still nailed down.

"Mah Jim!" I said. I knocked on the boards and listened. Not a sound. I could feel sweat start out all over me, and my hands shook as I groped around in the dark for a stone. What if he was dead? What if we'd killed him?

With the rock I hammered and pulped the edge of the board where the nail was, until I could spring the door past. And when I scratched a match and looked down inside, into the overturned privy that looked like a big coffin, I saw not Mah Jim, but Mah Li, and he was sprawled back against the downward wall with his legs across the seat, absolutely quiet, and his pigtail hanging across the bend of his arm.

It took me five minutes to rouse Mah Jim. I could hear him moving inside, and I yelled and cried that Mah Li was hurt, but he didn't open the door for a long time, and then only a crack. I suppose he thought it was another trick. My flu mask had slipped down over my chin, and I was crying. "Help me get him out," I said. "He's back here. He's hurt. Come on."

Finally he came, and we got Mah Li out and carried him into the kitchen. He lay perfectly still, his face like a mask, every line smoothed out of it and his eyes shut. His breathing sounded too loud in the bare room. I couldn't take my eyes off his face, and while Mah Jim was squatting and feeling over his body I thought of the butterflies that used to crawl on Mah Li's face when he was resting. This was a different kind of stillness, and it scared me.

For five minutes Mah Jim squatted there, his pigtail hanging, and didn't say a word. I could feel the silence in the kitchen swell up around me; the only audible sound was the slow loud breathing of Mah Li, each breath coming with a hard finality, as if it were the last one he'd ever breathe. My nose kept running, and I'd lost my handkerchief, so that I had to sniffle every minute or so. I hated it, because it sounded as if I were crying, and I didn't want to seem to cry.

I kept thinking how I could have done something when the privy went over and I heard the yell from inside, how I'd had the chance to tell Mr. Menefee and get Mah Li out, but hadn't taken it. And I stood there thinking, What if I'd hauled off and socked Tad McGovern when he first jumped on that door to hold it down? I had just come up, not knowing anything about the privy-tipping, and I said loudly, What's going on here? and then I hit Tad and he fell down and I felt the jar in my wrist from the blow, and then three or four others jumped me, and I tossed them off and punched them in the nose until they all stood around me in an amazed ring, and I stood there with my fists up and said, "Come on, you cowards! You're so brave, picking on a poor harmless old Chink. Come on and get a taste of knuckles, any three of you at a time!"

But all the time while I was doing that in my mind I heard that rough slow breathing, and saw Mah Jim in the lamplight squatting by Mah Li's body, and I was sick with shame, and sniffled, and hated the smell of eucalyptus hanging under my nose.

"Is he hurt bad?" I said. "Can you tell what's the matter?"

I almost whispered it, afraid to talk right out loud. Mah Jim rose, and his eyes glittered. His face, like a slotted mask the color of dry lemon peel, made me swallow. I

began to remember all the stories I'd heard about Chinks
— how if they ever got it in for you, or if you did them an
injustice, they'd slice your eyeballs and cut off your ears
and split your nostrils and pierce your eardrums and pull
out your toenails by the roots. Staring into his glittering
slit eyes, I thought sure he was going for me, and my
knees went weak. A kind of black fog came up in front of
me; I lost Mah Jim's face, the room rocked, I could feel
myself falling. Then the fog cleared again, and I was still
on my feet, Mah Jim was staring at me, Mah Li was unconscious on the floor.

My shame was greater than my fear, and I didn't run,
but I couldn't meet Mah Jim's eyes. I looked away to
where the magpie was sitting on a chair back, with his
white wing feathers almost hidden and his eyes as black
and glittering as Mah Jim's.

"I better get the doctor," I said, and swallowed. The
moment I said it I wondered why I hadn't done it already.
I was starting for the door, full of relief at being able to do
something, glad to get away, when I took a last look at
Mah Jim, hoping he'd look kinder, hoping perhaps that
he'd give me a word that would make me feel better
about my own shame. And I stood there, half turned,
staring at him. He hadn't moved, hadn't raised a hand,
hadn't spoken, but I knew exactly what he meant. He
meant no. He didn't want the doctor, even to save Mah
Li's life. He didn't want any white man around, didn't
want anything to do with us any more. There was bitterness, and anger, and a strange unreachable patience in
his look that stopped me cold in the doorway.

And after a minute, in the face of Mah Jim's bitter
dignity, I mumbled that I hoped Mah Li would be all
right, that I'd come to see him tomorrow, and sneaked
out. As I shut the door and stood shivering on the step I

heard the magpie croaking and jawing inside. "Nice!" it
said. "Nice, O-Fi'!"

Later, when I lay in bed at home with my head under
the covers, shivering between the cold sheets and breathing hard with my mouth open to warm the bed, I resolved
that next morning I would take the doctor down, Mah Jim
or no Mah Jim. "You can't just lock the doors when somebody's sick or hurt," I'd tell him. "You have to have help,
and I'm the one that's going to see you get it."

But I never did wake up to do what I planned. My
sleep was haunted by wild dreams, flashes, streamers of
insane color that went like northern lights across my
nightmares. Once I woke up and discovered that I had
been vomiting in my bed, but before I could do more than
gag and gasp for somebody to come I was out again. I
remember a hand on my head, and a face over me, and
once a feeling of floating. I opened my eyes then, to see
the stair rails writhing by me like snakes, and I shut my
eyes again to keep from dying. When I woke up it was a
week later; I was in bed with my mother in the sixth-
grade room of the schoolhouse, and my nose was
bleeding.

They kept us in the schoolhouse ten more days. After
I was home, lying in bed in the dining room where it was
warm, I felt good, full of the tired quietness that comes
after sickness, and sleepy all the time, and pleased that I
was getting well. Once or twice a day I got up in a bath-
robe and tottered a few steps on crazy knees so that everybody laughed at me as if I were a child just taking his
first steps.

On the fourth morning at home I felt perfectly well.
When I woke up the sun was shining in the dining-room
windows, and outside I could see the clean snow and the

tracked path that led up past Shawn's house. Then I realized that something had awakened me, and listened.
There was a mild, light tapping on the kitchen door. For
a minute I forgot I was still weak, and jumped out of bed
so fast that I sprawled on hands and knees, but laughing
at myself, still feeling well and full of life. I got up and
found my slippers and tottered into the kitchen, hanging
to walls and doorjambs. On the back step Mah Jim was
standing, with a basket on his arm.

"Nice day, O-Fi," he said, just the way Mah Li used to
say it when he brought the vegetables. All in a rush the
memory of that Hallowe'en night came back to me. I'd
forgotten it completely during my sickness. I pulled Mah
Jim inside and shut the door. "How's Mah Li?" I said.

His face perfectly blank, Mah Jim passed me the basket,
covered with a clean dish towel. I lifted the cover and
there was the magpie, looking ruffled and mad. I didn't
understand. "You mean he's giving me the magpie?" I
said.

Mah Jim nodded.

"Is he all right now?"

Like a wooden man, full of ancient and inscrutable patience, Mah Jim stood with his hands in the sleeves of his
blouse. "All lightee now," he said.

The magpie shook its feathers, snapped its long tail,
opened its beak, and its harsh squawk cut in. "O-Fi'!
O-Fi'! Nice, O-Fi'!" I put out a finger to stroke its head
the way Mah Li did, and it pecked me a sharp dig on the
hand. I was so relieved about Mah Li, and so bursting
with the feeling of being well, that I laughed out loud.

"That's swell," I said. "Tell him thanks very much. Tell
him I sure appreciate having it, Mah Jim. And tell him
I'm glad he's well again."

He stood silently, and I began to remember how sinister he'd looked in the kitchen that night, and how he'd scared me then. To keep the silence from getting too thick I kept on talking. "I've been sick myself," I said. "I got sick that same night, or I'd have been over to see him." The sunlight flashed on the windshield of a car turning around in the road, and the light was so bright and gay that I wanted to yell for just feeling good. I bragged. "They thought I was going to die. I had a fever of a hundred and five, and was unconscious for a week, and my nose bled like anything."

I stopped. Mah Jim had not moved; his face was yellow parchment with the slit eyes bright and still in it. "So you tell Mah Li I'll be down to see him soon as I get on my feet," I said.

Something in the way he looked stopped me. Why did Mah Li send him with the magpie? I wondered. Why didn't he come himself? Mah Jim took his hands out of his sleeves and made a short, stiff little bow.

"Mah Li dead," he said. "We go back China. Bye, O-Fi'. Nice day."

He opened the door and shuffled out, and I sat still in the kitchen chair too shocked to feel anything really, except just the things around me. I felt the cold draft on my bare ankles, and I felt the sun warm on my arm and shoulder, but I couldn't feel anything about Mah Li. I didn't really feel anything yet when I started to cry. The tears just came up slowly the way a spring fills, and hung, and brimmed over, and the first ones ran down my face and splashed warm on the back of my hand.

Chip Off the Old Block

SITTING ALONE looking at the red eyes of the parlor heater, Chet thought how fast things happened. One day the flu hit. Two days after that his father left for Montana to get a load of whiskey to sell for medicine. The next night he got back in the midst of a blizzard with his hands and feet frozen, bringing a sick homesteader he had picked up on the road; and now this morning all of them, the homesteader, his father, his mother, his brother Bruce, were loaded in a sled and hauled to the schoolhouse-hospital. It was scary how fast they all got it, even his father, who seldom got anything and was tougher than boiled owl. Everybody, he thought with some pride, but him. His mother's words as she left were a solemn burden on his mind. "You'll have to hold the fort, Chet. You'll have to be the man of the house." And his father, sweat on his face even in the cold, his frozen hands held tenderly in

246

his lap, saying, "Better let the whiskey alone. Put it away somewhere till we get back."

So he was holding the fort. He accepted the duty soberly. In the two hours since his family had left he had swept the floors, milked old Red and thrown down hay for her, brought in scuttles of lignite. And sitting now in the parlor he knew he was scared. He heard the walls tick and the floors creak. Every thirty seconds he looked up from his book, and finally he yawned, stretched, laid the book down, and took a stroll through the whole house, cellar to upstairs, as if for exercise. But his eyes were sharp, and he stepped back a little as he threw open the doors of bedrooms and closets. He whistled a little between his teeth and looked at the calendar in the hall to see what day it was. November 4, 1918.

A knock on the back door sent him running. It was the young man named Vickers who had taken his family away. He was after beds and blankets for the schoolhouse. Chet helped him knock the beds down and load them on the sled. He would sleep on the couch in the parlor; it was warmer there, anyway; no cold floors to worry about.

In the kitchen, making a list of things he had taken, Vickers saw the keg, the sacked cases of bottles, the pile of whiskey-soaked straw sheaths from the bottles that had been broken on the trip. "Your dad doesn't want to sell any of that, does he?" he said.

Chet thought briefly of his father's injunction to put the stuff away. But gee, the old man had frozen his hands and feet and caught the flu getting it, and now when people came around asking . . . "Sure," he said. "That's what he bought it for, flu medicine."

"What've you got?"

"Rye and bourbon," Chet said. "There's some Irish, but

I think he brought that special for somebody." He rummaged among the sacks. "Four dollars a bottle, I think it is," he said, and looked at Vickers to see if that was too much. Vickers didn't blink. "Or is it four-fifty?" Chet said.

Vickers's face was expressionless. "Sure it isn't five? I wouldn't want to cheat you." He took out his wallet, and under his eyes Chet retreated. "I'll go look," he said. "I think there's a list."

He stood in the front hall for a minute or two before he came back. "Four-fifty," he said casually. "I thought probably it was."

Vickers counted out twenty-seven dollars. "Give me six rye," he said. With the sack in his hand he stood in the back door and looked at Chet and laughed. "What are you going to do with that extra three dollars?"

Chet felt his heart stop while he might have counted ten. His face began to burn. "What three dollars?"

"Never mind," Vickers said. "I was just ragging you. Got all you need to eat here?"

"I got crocks of milk," Chet said. He grinned at Vickers in relief, and Vickers grinned back. "There's bread Ma baked the other day, and spuds. If I need any meat I can go shoot a rabbit."

"Oh." Vickers's eyebrows went up. "You're a hunter, eh?"

"I shot rabbits all last fall for Mrs. Rieger," Chet said. "She's 'nemic and has to eat rabbits and prairie chickens and stuff. She lent me the shotgun and bought the shells."

"Mmm," Vickers said. "I guess you can take care of yourself. How old are you?"

"Twelve."

"That's old enough," said Vickers. "That's pretty old, in fact. Well, Mervin, if you need anything you call the school and I'll see that you get it."

"My name isn't Mervin," Chet said. "It's Chet."

"Okay," Vickers said. "Don't get careless with the fires."

"What do you think I am?" Chet said in scorn. He raised his hand stiffly as Vickers went out. A little tongue of triumph licked up in him. That three bucks would look all right, all right. Next time he'd know better than to change the price, too. He took the bills out of his pocket and counted them. Twenty-seven dollars was a lot of dough. He'd show Ma and Pa whether he could hold the fort or not.

But holding the fort was tiresome. By two o'clock he was bored stiff, and the floors were creaking again in the silence. Then he remembered suddenly that he was the boss of the place. He could go or come as he pleased, as long as the cow was milked and the house kept warm. He thought of the two traps he had set in muskrat holes under the river bank. The blizzard and the flu had made him forget to see to them. And he might take Pa's gun and do a little hunting.

"Well," he said in the middle of the parlor rug, "I guess I will."

For an hour and a half he prowled the river brush. Over on the path toward Heathcliff's he shot a snowshoe rabbit, and the second of his traps yielded a stiffly frozen muskrat. The weight of his game was a solid satisfaction as he came up the dugway swinging the rabbit by its feet, the muskrat by its plated tail.

Coming up past the barn, he looked over towards Van Dam's, then the other way, toward Chapman's, half hoping that someone might be out, and see him. He whistled loudly, sang a little into the cold afternoon air, but the desertion of the whole street, the unbroken fields of snow where ordinarily there would have been dozens of sled tracks and fox-and-goose paths, let a chill in upon his pride. He came up the back steps soberly and opened the door.

The muskrat's slippery tail slid out of his mitten and the frozen body thumped on the floor. Chet opened his mouth, shut it again, speechless with surprise and shock. Two men were in the kitchen. His eyes jumped from the one by the whiskey keg to the other, sitting at the table drinking whiskey from a cup. The one drinking he didn't know. The other was Louis Treat, a halfbreed who hung out down at the stable and sometimes worked a little for the Half-Diamond Bar. All Chet knew about him was that he could braid horsehair ropes and sing a lot of dirty songs.

"Aha!" said Louis Treat. He smiled at Chet and made a rubbing motion with his hands. "We 'ave to stop to get warm. You 'ave been hunting?"

"Yuh," Chet said automatically. He stood where he was, his eyes swinging between the two men. The man at the table raised his eyebrows at Louis Treat.

"Ees nice rabbit there," Louis said. His bright black button eyes went over the boy. Chet lifted the rabbit and looked at the frozen beads of blood on the white fur. "Yuh," he said. He was thinking about what his father always said. You could trust an Indian, if he was your friend, and you could trust a white man sometimes, if money wasn't involved, and you could trust a Chink more than either, but you couldn't trust a halfbreed.

Louis' voice went on, caressingly. "You 'ave mushrat too, eh? You lak me to 'elp you peel thees mushrat?" His hand, dipping under the sheepskin and into his pants pocket, produced a long-bladed knife that jumped open with the pressure of his thumb on a button.

Chet dropped the rabbit and took off his mitts. "No thanks," he said. "I can peel him."

Shrugging, Louis put the knife away. He turned to thump the bung hard into the keg, and nodded at the other man, who rose. "Ees tam we go," Louis said. "We 'ave been told to breeng thees wiskey to the 'ospital."

"Who told you?" Chet's insides grew tight, and his mind was setting like plaster of Paris. If Pa was here he'd scatter these thieves all the way to Chapman's. But Pa wasn't here. He watched Louis Treat. You could never trust a halfbreed.

"The doctor, O'Malley," Louis said. Keeping his eye on Chet, he jerked his head at the other man. " 'Ere, you tak' the other end."

His companion, pulling up his sheepskin collar, stooped and took hold of the keg. Chet, with no blood in his face and no breath in his lungs, hesitated a split second and then jumped. Around the table, in the dining room door, he was out of their reach, and the shotgun was pointed straight at their chests. With his thumb he cocked both barrels, click, click.

Louis Treat swore. "Put down that gun!"

"No, sir!" Chet said. "I won't put it down till you drop that keg and get out of here!"

The two men looked at each other. Louis set his end gently back on the chair, and the other did the same. "We 'ave been sent," Louis said. "You do not understan' w'at I mean."

"I understand all right," Chet said. "If Doctor O'Malley had wanted that, he'd've sent Mr. Vickers for it this morning."

The second man ran his tongue over his teeth and spat on the floor. "Think he knows how to shoot that thing?"

Chet's chest expanded. The gun trembled so that he braced it against the frame of the door. "I shot that rabbit, didn't I?" he said.

The halfbreed's teeth were bared in a bitter grin. "You are a fool," he said.

"And you're a thief!" Chet said. He covered the two carefully as they backed out, and when they were down the steps he slammed and bolted the door. Then he raced for the front hall, made sure that door was locked, and peeked out the front window. The two were walking side by side up the irrigation ditch toward town, pulling an empty box sled. Louis was talking furiously with his hands.

Slowly and carefully Chet uncocked the gun. Ordinarily he would have unloaded, but not now, not with thieves like those around. He put the gun above the mantel, looked in the door of the stove, threw in a half-scuttle of lignite, went to the window again to see if he could still see the two men. Then he looked at his hands. They were shaking. So were his knees. He sat down suddenly on the couch, unable to stand.

For days the only people he saw were those who came to buy whiskey. They generally sat a while in the kitchen and talked about the flu and the war, but they weren't much company. Once Miss Landis, his schoolteacher, came apologetically and furtively with a two-quart fruit jar under her coat, and he charged her four dollars a quart for bulk rye out of the keg. His secret hoard of money mounted to eighty-five dollars, to a hundred and eight.

When there was none of that business (he had even forgotten by now that his father had told him not to meddle with it), he moped around the house, milked the cow, telephoned to the hospital to see how his folks were. One day his dad was pretty sick. Two days later he was better, but his mother had had a relapse because they were so short of beds they had had to put Brucie in with her. The milk crocks piled up in the cellarway, staying miraculously sweet, until he told the schoolhouse nurse over the phone about all the milk he had, and then Doctor O'Malley sent down old Gundar Moe to pick it up for the sick people.

Sometimes he stood on the porch on sunny, cold mornings and watched Lars Poulsen's sled go out along the road on the way to the graveyard, and the thought that maybe Mom or Bruce or Pa might die and be buried out there on the knoll by the sandhills made him swallow and go back inside where he couldn't see how deserted the street looked, and where he couldn't see the sled and the streaming gray horses move out toward the south bend of the river. He resolved to be a son his parents could be proud of, and sat down at the piano determined to learn a piece letter-perfect. But the dry silence of the house weighed on him; before long he would be lying with his forehead on the keyboard, his finger picking on one monotonous note. That way he could concentrate on how different it sounded with his head down, and forget to be afraid.

And at night, when he lay on the couch and stared into the sleepy red eyes of the heater, he heard noises that walked the house, and there were crosses in the lamp chimneys when he lighted them, and he knew that someone would die.

On the fifth day he sat down at the dining-room table determined to write a book. In an old atlas he hunted up a promising locale. He found a tributary of the Amazon called the Tapajos, and firmly, his lips together in concentration, he wrote his title across the top of a school tablet: "The Curse of the Tapajos." All that afternoon he wrote enthusiastically. He created a tall, handsome young explorer and a halfbreed guide very like Louis Treat. He plowed through steaming jungles, he wrestled

pythons and other giant serpents which he spelled boy
constructors. All this time he was looking for the Lost
City of Gold. And when the snakes got too thick even for
his taste, and when he was beginning to wonder himself
why the explorer didn't shoot the guide, who was constantly trying to poison the flour or stab his employer in
his tent at midnight, he let the party come out on a broad
pampa and see in the distance, crowning a golden hill,
the lost city for which they searched. And then suddenly
the explorer reeled and fell, mysteriously stricken, and the
halfbreed guide, smiling with sinister satisfaction, disappeared quietly into the jungle. The curse of the Tapajos,
which struck everyone who found that lost city, had struck
again. But the young hero was not dead. . . .

Chet gnawed his pencil and stared across the room. It
was going to be hard to figure out how his hero escaped.
Maybe he was just stunned, not killed. Maybe a girl
could find him there, and nurse him back to health. . . .

He rose, thinking, and wandered over to the window. A
sled came across the irrigation ditch and pulled on over
to Chance's house. Out of it got Mr. Chance and Mrs.
Chance and Ed and Harvey Chance. They were well,
then. People were starting to come home cured. He
rushed to the telephone and called the hospital. No, the
nurse said, his family weren't well yet; they wouldn't be
home for three or four days at least. But they were all
better. How was he doing? Did he need anything?

No, Chet said, he didn't need anything.

But at least he wasn't the only person on the street any
more. That night after milking he took a syrup pail of
milk to the Chances. They were all weak, all smiling. Mrs.
Chance cried every time she spoke, and they were awfully
grateful for the milk. He promised them, over their protests, that he would bring them some every day, and chop
wood and haul water for them until they got really strong.

Mr. Chance, who had the nickname of Dictionary because
he strung off such jaw-breaking words, told him he was a
benefactor and a Samaritan, and called upon his own sons
to witness this neighborly kindness and be edified and
enlarged. Chet went home in the dark, wondering if it
might not be a good idea, later in his book somewhere,
to have his explorer find a bunch of people, or maybe just
a beautiful and ragged girl, kept in durance vile by some
tribe of pigmies or spider men or something, and have
him rescue them and confound their captors.

On the afternoon of the eighth day Chet sat in the
kitchen at Chance's. His own house had got heavier and
heavier to bear, and there wasn't much to eat there but
milk and potatoes, and both stores were closed because of
the flu. So he went a good deal to Chance's, doing their
chores and talking about the hospital, and listening to Mr.
Chance tell about the Death Ward where they put people
who weren't going to get well. The Death Ward was the
eighth-grade room, his own room, and he and Ed Chance
speculated on what it would be like to go back to that
room where so many people had died — Mrs. Rieger, and
old Gypsy Davy from Poverty Flat, and John Chapman,
and a lot of people. Mrs. Chance sat by the stove and
when anyone looked at her or spoke to her she shook her
head and smiled and the tears ran down. She didn't seem
unhappy about anything; she just couldn't help crying.

Mr. Chance said over and over that there were certainly going to be a multitude of familiar faces missing
after this thing was over. The town would never be the
same. He wouldn't be surprised if the destitute and
friendless were found in every home in town, adopted and
cared for by friends. They might have to build an institution to house the derelict and the bereaved.

He pulled his sagging cheeks and said to Chet, "Mark

my words, son, you are one of the fortunate. In that hospital I said to myself a dozen times, 'Those poor Mason
boys are going to lose their father.' I lay there — myself
in pain, mind you — and the first thing I'd hear some old
and valued friend would be moved into the Death Ward.
I thought your father was a goner when they moved him
in."

Chet's throat was suddenly dry as dust. "Pa isn't in
there!"

"Ira," said Mrs. Chance, and shook her head and smiled
and wiped the tears away. "Now you've got the child all
worked up."

"He isn't in there now," said Mr. Chance. "By the grace
of the Almighty" — he bent his head and his lips moved —
"he came out again. He's a hard man to kill. Hands and
feet frozen, double pneumonia, and still he came out."

"Is he all right now?" Chet said.

"Convalescing," Mr. Chance said. "Convalescing beau-
tifully." He raised a finger under Chet's nose. "Some
people are just hard to kill. But on the other hand, you
take a person like that George Valet. I hesitate to say
before the young what went on in that ward. Shameful,
even though the man was sick." His tongue ticked against
his teeth, and his eyebrows raised at Chet. "They cleaned
his bed six times a day," he said, and pressed his lips together. "It makes a man wonder about God's wisdom," he
said. "A man like that, his morals are as loose as his
bowels."

"Ira!" Mrs. Chance said.

"I would offer you a wager," Mr. Chance said. "I wager
that a man as loose and discombobulated as that doesn't
live through this epidemic."

"I wouldn't bet on a person's life that way," she said.

"Ma," Harvey called from the next room, where he was
lying down. "What's all the noise about?"

They stopped talking and listened. The church bell was ringing madly. In a minute the bell in the firehouse joined it. The heavy bellow of a shotgun, both barrels, rolled over the snowflats between their street and the main part of town. A six-shooter went off, bang-bang-bang-bang-bang-bang, and there was the sound of distant yelling.

"Fire?" Mr. Chance said, stooping to the window.

"Here comes somebody," Ed said. The figure of a boy was streaking across the flat. Mr. Chance opened the door and shouted at him. The boy ran closer, yelling something unintelligible. It was Spot Orullian.

"What?" Mr. Chance yelled.

Spot cupped his hands to his mouth, standing in the road in front of Chet's as if unwilling to waste a moment's time. "War's over!" he shouted, and wheeled and was gone up the street toward Van Dam's.

Mr. Chance closed the door slowly. Mrs. Chance looked at him, and her lips jutted and trembled, her weak eyes ran over with tears, and she fell into his arms. The three boys, not quite sure how one acted when a war ended, but knowing it called for celebration, stood around uneasily. They shot furtive grins at one another, looked with furrowed brows at Mrs. Chance's shaking back.

"Now Uncle Joe can come home," Ed said. "That's what she's bawling about."

Chet bolted out the door, raced over to his own house, pulled the loaded shotgun from the mantel, and burst out into the yard again. He blew the lid off the silence in their end of town, and followed the shooting with a wild yell. Ed and Harvey, leaning out their windows, answered him, and the heavy boom-boom of a shotgun came from the downtown district.

Carrying the gun, Chet went back to Chance's. He felt grown-up, a householder. The end of the war had to be

celebrated; neighbors had to get together and raise cain.
He watched Mrs. Chance, still incoherent, rush to the calendar and put a circle around the date, November 11. "I
don't ever want to forget what day it happened on," she
said.

"Everyone in the world will remember this day," said
Mr. Chance, solemnly, like a preacher. Chet looked at
him, his mind clicking.

"Mr. Chance," he said, "would you like a drink, to celebrate?"

Mr. Chance looked startled. "What?"

"Pa's got some whiskey. He'd throw a big party if he
was home."

"I don't think we should," said Mrs. Chance dubiously.
"Your father might . . ."

"Oh, Mama," Mr. Chance said, and laid his arm across
her back like a log. "One bumper to honor the day. One
leetle stirrup-cup to those boys of the Allies. Chester here
is carrying on his father's tradition like a man." He bowed
and shook Chet's hand formally. "We'd be delighted,
Sir," he said, and they all laughed.

Somehow, nobody knew just how, the party achieved
proportions. Mr. Chance suggested, after one drink, that
it would be pleasant to have a neighbor or two, snatched
from the terrors of the plague, come and join in the
thanksgiving; and Chet, full of hospitality, said sure, that
would be a keen idea. So Mr. Chance called Jewel King,
and when Jewel came he brought Chubby Klein with
him, and a few minutes later three more came, knocked,
looked in to see the gathering with cups in their hands,
and came in with alacrity when Chet held the door wide.
Within an hour there were eight men, three women, and
the two Chance boys, besides Chet. Mr. Chance wouldn't

let the boys have any whiskey, but Chet, playing bartender, sneaked a cup into the dining room and all sipped
it and smacked their lips.

"Hey, look, I'm drunk," Harvey said. He staggered,
hiccoughed, caught himself, bowed low and apologized,
staggered again. "Hic," he said. "I had a drop too much."
The three laughed together secretly while loud voices
went up in the kitchen.

"Gentlemen," Mr. Chance was saying, "I give you those
heroic laddies in khaki who looked undaunted into the
eyes of death and saved this ga-lorious empire from the
rapacious Huns."

"Yay!" the others said, banging cups on the table.
"Give her the other barrel, Dictionary."

"I crave your indulgence for a moment," Mr. Chance
said. "For one leetle moment, while I imbibe a few
swallows of this delectable amber fluid."

The noise went up and up. Chet went among them
stiff with pride at having done all this, at being accepted
here as host, at having men pat him on the back and
shake his hand and tell him, 'You're all right, kid, you're
a chip off the old block. What's the word from the folks?"
He guggled liquor out of the sloshing cask into a milk
crock, and the men dipped largely and frequently. About
four o'clock, two more families arrived and were wel-
comed with roars. People bulged the big kitchen; their
laughter rattled the window frames. Occasionally Dictionary Chance rose to propose a toast to "those gems of
purest ray serene, those unfailing companions on life's
bitter pilgrimage, the ladies, God bless 'em!" Every so
often he suggested that it might be an idea worth serious
consideration that some liquid refreshments be decanted
from the aperture in the receptacle.

The more liquid refreshments Chet decanted from the

aperture in the receptacle, the louder and more eloquent
Mr. Chance became. He dominated the kitchen like an
evangelist. He swung and swayed and stamped, he led a
rendition of "God Save the King," he thundered denunci-
ations on the Beast of Berlin, he thrust a large fist into the
lapels of new arrivals and demanded detailed news of
the war's end. Nobody knew more than that it was over.

But Dictionary didn't forget to be grateful, either. At
least five times during the afternoon he caught Chet up in
a long arm and publicly blessed him. Once he rose and
cleared his throat for silence. Chubby Klein and Jewel
King booed and hissed, but he bore their insults with
dignity. "Siddown!" they said. "Speech!" said others. Mr.
Chance waved his hands abroad, begging for quiet.
Finally they gave it to him, snickering.

"Ladies and gen'lemen," he said, "we have come together on this auspicious occasion . . ."

"What's suspicious about it?" Jewel King said.

" . . . on this auspicious occasion, to do honor to our
boys in Flander's field, to celebrate the passing of the
dread incubus of Spanish Influenza . . ."

"Siddown!" said Chubby Klein.

" . . . and last, but not least, we are gathered here to
honor our friendship with the owners of this good and
hospitable house, Bo Mason and Sis, may their lives be
long and strewn with flowers, and this noble scion of a
noble stock, this tender youth who kept the home fires
burning through shock and shell and who opened his
house and his keg to us as his father would have done.
Ladies and gen'lemen, the Right Honorable Chester
Mason, may he live to bung many a barrel."

Embarrassed and squirming and unsure of what to do
with so many faces laughing at him, so many mouths
cheering him, Chet crowded into the dining-room door
and tried to act casual, tried to pretend he didn't feel

proud and excited and a man among men. And while he stood there with the noise beating at him in raucous approbation, the back door opened and the utterly flabbergasted face of his father looked in.

There was a moment of complete silence. Voices dropped away to nothing, cups hung at lips. Then in a concerted rush they were helping Bo Mason in. He limped heavily on bandaged and slippered feet, his hands wrapped in gauze, his face drawn and hollow-eyed and noticeably thinner than it had been ten days ago. After him came Chet's mother, half carrying Bruce, and staggering under his weight. Hands took Bruce away from her, sat him on the open oven door, and led her to a chair. All three of them, hospital-pale, rested and looked around the room. And Chet's father did not look pleased.

"What the devil is this?" he said.

From his station in the doorway Chet squeaked, "The war's over!"

"I know the war's over, but what's this?" He jerked a bandaged hand at the uncomfortable ring of people. Chet swallowed and looked at Dictionary Chance.

Dictionary's suspended talents came back to him. He strode to lay a friendly hand on his host's back; he swung and shook his hostess' hand; he twinkled at the white-faced, big-eyed Bruce on the oven door.

"This, Sir," he boomed, "is a welcoming committee of your friends and neighbors, met here to rejoice over your escape from the dread sickness which has swept to untimely death so many of our good friends, God rest their souls! On the invitation of your manly young son here we have been celebrating not only that emancipation, but the emancipation of the entire world from the dread plague of war." With the cup in his hand he bent and twinkled at Bo Mason. "How's it feel to get back, old hoss?"

Bo grunted. He looked across at his wife and laughed

a short, choppy laugh. The way his eyes came around and rested on Chet made Chet stop breathing. But his father's voice was hearty enough when it came. "You got a snootful," he said. "Looks like you've all got a snootful."

"Sir," said Dictionary Chance, "I haven't had such a delightful snootful since the misguided government of this province suspended the God-given right of its free people to purchase and imbibe and ingest intoxicating beverages."

He drained his cup and set it on the table. "And now," he said, "it is clear that our hosts are not completely recovered in their strength. I suggest that we do whatever small tasks our ingenuity and gratitude can suggest, and silently steal away."

"Yeah," the others said. "Sure. Sure thing." They brought in the one bed from the sled and set it up, swooped together blankets and mattresses and turned them over to the women. Before the beds were made people began to leave. Dictionary Chance, voluble to the last, stopped to praise the excellent medicinal waters he had imbibed, and to say a word for Chet, before Mrs. Chance, with a quick pleading smile, led him away. The door had not even closed before Chet felt his father's cold eye on him.

"All right," his father said. "Will you please tell me why in the name of Christ you invited that God-damned windbag and all the rest of those sponges over here to drink up my whiskey?"

Chet stood sullenly in the door, boiling with sulky resentment. He had held the fort, milked the cow, kept the house, sold all that whiskey for all it was worth, run Louis Treat and the other man out with a gun. Everybody else praised him, but you could depend on Pa to think more of that whiskey the neighbors had drunk than of anything else. He wasn't going to explain or defend himself. If the old man was going to be that stingy, he could take a flying leap in the river.

"The war was over," he said. "I asked them over to celebrate."

His father's head wagged. He looked incredulous and at his wits' end. "You asked them over!" he said. "You said, 'Come right on over and drink up all the whiskey my dad almost killed himself bringing in.'" He stuck his bandaged hands out. "Do you think I got these and damned near died in that hospital just to let a bunch of blotters . . . Why, God damn you," he said. "Leave the house for ten days, tell you exactly what to do, and by Jesus everything goes wrong. How long have they been here?"

"Since about two."

"How much did they drink?"

"I don't know. Three crocks full, I guess."

His father's head weaved back and forth, he looked at his wife and then at the ceiling . . . "Three crocks. At least a gallon, twelve dollars' worth. Oh Jesus Christ, if you had the sense of a pissant . . ."

Laboriously, swearing with the pain, he hobbled to the keg. When he put his hand down to shake it, his whole body stiffened.

"It's half empty!" he said. He swung on Chet, and Chet met his furious look. Now! his mind said. Now let him say I didn't hold the fort.

"I sold some," he said, and held his father's eyes for a minute before he marched out stiff-backed into the living room, dug the wad of bills from the vase on the mantel, and came back. He laid the money in his father's hand. "I sold a hundred and twenty-four dollars' worth," he said.

The muscles in his father's jaw moved. He glanced at Chet's mother, let the breath out hard through his nose. "So you've been selling whiskey," he said. "I thought I told you to leave that alone?"

"People wanted it for medicine," Chet said. "Should I've let them die with the flu? They came here wanting to buy it and I sold it. I thought that was what it was for."

The triumph that had been growing in him ever since he went for the money was hot in his blood now. He saw the uncertainty in his father's face, and he almost beat down his father's eyes.

"I suppose," his father said finally, "you sold it for a dollar a bottle, or something."

"I sold it for plenty," Chet said. "Four-fifty for bottles and four for quarts out of the keg. That's more than you were going to get, because I heard you tell Ma."

His father sat down on the chair and fingered the bills, looking at him. "You didn't have any business selling anything," he said. "And then you overcharge people."

"Yeah!" Chet said, defying him now. "If it hadn't been for me there wouldn't't've been any to sell. Louis Treat and another man came and tried to steal that whole keg, and I run 'em out with a shotgun."

"What?" his mother said.

"I did!" Chet said. "I made 'em put it down and get out."

Standing in the doorway still facing his father, he felt the tears hot in his eyes and was furious at himself for crying. He hoped his father would try thrashing him. He just hoped he would. He wouldn't make a sound; he'd grit his teeth and show him whether he was man enough to stand it. . . . He looked at his father's gray expressionless face and shouted, "I wish I'd let them take it! I just wish I had!"

And suddenly his father was laughing. He reared back

in the chair and threw back his head and roared, his bandaged hands held tenderly before him like helpless paws. He stopped, caught his breath, looked at Chet again, and shook with a deep internal rumbling. "Okay," he said. "Okay, kid. You're a man. I wouldn't take it away from you."

"Well, there's no need to laugh," Chet said. "I don't see anything to laugh about."

He watched his father twist in his chair and look at his mother. "Look at him," his father said. "By God, he'd eat me if I made a pass at him."

"Well, don't laugh!" Chet said. He turned and went into the living room, where he sat on the couch and looked at his hands the way he had when Louis Treat and the other man were walking up the ditch. His hands were trembling, the same way. But there was no need to laugh, any more than there was need to get sore over a little whiskey given to the neighbors.

His mother came in and sat down beside him, laid a hand on his head. "Don't be mad at Pa," she said. "He didn't understand. He's proud of you. We all are."

"Yeah?" said Chet. "Why doesn't *he* come and tell me that?"

His mother's smile was gentle and a little amused. "Because he's ashamed of himself for losing his temper, I suppose," she said. "He never did know how to admit he was wrong."

Chet set his jaw and looked at the shotgun above the mantel. He guessed he had looked pretty tough himself when he had the drop on Louis Treat and his thieving friend. He stiffened his shoulders under his mother's arm. "Just let him start anything," he said. "Just let him try to get hard."

His mother's smile broadened, but he glowered at her. "And there's no need to laugh!" he said.

❦ ❦ ❦

The Sweetness
of the Twisted Apples

FOR A WHILE the road was graded, with the marks of a scraper blade gouged into the banks on both sides. Then the graded road swung right, and a painted sign on a stake said "Harrow." Harrow was where they had come from. But straight ahead a barely traveled road led on between high banks like hedgerows. From the brief clearing at the fork they saw the wild wooded side of South Maid Hill, the maples stained with autumn, and far up, one scarlet tree like an incredible flower.

Ross slowed down — his foot on the clutch. "Which?"

"Oh, straight on!" Margaret said. "That other one circles right back to the highway."

"Chance of getting stuck."

"There are tracks."

"Not many."

"Enough to show it's passable."

"You're crazy," he said. "Vermont-autumn crazy."

He eased the car into the trail, and Margaret leaned back in the open car and watched the sky pour over her in one blue rounding cascade, carrying with it branches of trees and little cream-puff clouds.

She said, "Who wouldn't be? Days like these. There's such a wonderful resigned tranquillity about everything."

She got a sour-fragrant whiff of his pipe and rolled her head back against the seat to look at him — a shaggy man with a kind face, a painter, inexplicably her husband. It was so fine for him to be there, smoking, his square hairy hands on the wheel, and so wonderful that the day was such a day as it was, that she shivered with an almost unbearable sense of life and well-being.

In the quick sun-and-shadow of the woods, white trunks of birches flashed. The car wallowed through a low spot where a spring muddied the road, and she got the scent of mint, clean and cold. On the other side of the swale they met a stone wall that within a few feet bent off to the right and was swallowed in impenetrable brush.

Margaret turned and stared back, but the wall did not appear again. It was lost in the woods, still carefully enclosing some obliterated and overgrown meadow, and all the labor that had built it was gone for the greater comfort of woodchucks and foxes. "It doesn't seem as if anything in America could be this old," she said.

The trail climbed steeply, rocky as the bed of a brook, and gravel chattered under the tires. Someone had chopped away limbs that overhung the road. At one place a log had been laid across the ruts and half buried, to act as a dam against washouts. Then, at the top of the rise, a fence of split cedar rails jutted out of the trees, and a weathered house with staggering sheds and a sag-backed barn. A foxhound charged out, heavy-voiced, and a man working in one of the sheds straightened up and stared silently. When they were almost past, Margaret saw a woman in the doorway of the house.

The bay of meadow slipped behind; the woods came close again, beeches and maples leaning inward, black spruces edging into the narrow way. A dead-windowed house stared at them suddenly from a clearing; across the road a barn had collapsed in a spiral of timbers and twisted roof.

They nosed on across the almost-wiped-out opening and into more woods, where hazel scrub scraped the sides of the car and poplars made yellow intervals like sunlight. The road went steadily up, gullied by rains. It bore only wagon tracks now; the automobile tracks had stopped with the first barn they had passed.

On the left a barbed-wire fence came out of the brush and paralleled the road. Through the thinning woods something glittered in the direct sun, and as they pulled out into another farmyard Margaret saw that there were tin patches on the barn's roof like bright metal teeth in a mouth, and that the gray side of the barn was streaked with new yellow boards. The slanting gable window of the house was stuffed with burlap bags, but there were signs of busyness around the yard: a homemade saw rig with an old car hooked on for power, and under the loft window of the barn a new homemade hay wagon with automobile wheels and two flat tires.

Ross stopped. A woman and a child were already on their way out to the road. The woman wore burst and run-over shoes, and her hair needed combing, but she had a rather sweet, serene face. The child was wizened, sharp-featured; she hugged her skinny elbows as she walked along beside her mother.

For an instant Margaret had an almost shamefaced image of how she and Ross must appear to these isolated farm people — the expensive glitter and shine of the car, the hand-blocked yellow scarf around her own hair, the silver watch band on Ross's wrist.

"Hello," she said, and smiled.

The woman smiled back. "Guess you folks are lost."

"Not exactly," Margaret said. "We were driving around and found this road and decided to see where it went."

"*Used* to go on over to Island Pond."

"Doesn't it any more?"

"Runs smack into the woods and stops!" the child said.

The words came in a burst and ended in a startled hiccup of laughter. Looking closer, Margaret saw that the girl was not a child at all. She couldn't have been five feet tall or weighed more than eighty pounds, but her face, when you looked at all closely, was not a child's face. It would have been impossible to say how old she was. But the thing that burned behind the pinched features and the shy eyes was no child's spirit. It was sharp and tart, medicinal as woods' herbs.

"What's happened on this road?" Ross said. "People all move away?"

The woman bent forward, her arms folded conversationally, "Seem's if they did. We ain't been here but three years ourselves. We lost our other place, over by Willoughby — it was three years, wa'n't it, Sary? Your last year in high school, and while you was goin' out. Yes, three years. Seem's if we hardly moved in. The road was closed long before we come. Used to be a carriage road run from the four corners, where you folks turned off, clean into Island Pond. We're the only folks on it on this side any more. Us and Will Canby's boy, back down a piece."

"How far on can we get?" Margaret asked.

"Maybe a half-mile. Up to the schoolhouse anyway."

"Past that," the girl said. "Up to the orchard."

"You sure, Sary? In a car?"

An expression that was almost disdain crossed Sary's face. "I *know*, Mumma. We used to go up there when I was goin' out."

"That was a year," her mother said doubtfully.

" 'Tisn't changed," Sary said.

The mother regarded her daughter briefly with an expression that seemed to Margaret at once anxious and complacent. "Sary had a disappointment," she said mildly. "For over a year she was a-goin' out . . ."

"Oh, *Mumma!*" Sary said, and swung half around. There was a pause.

"I'm sorry my mister's not home to meet you folks," the woman said. "He went in to see if he could get some kind of a gear for his car. He's had it all over the shed for two weeks — ain't been able to get together all the parts."

"Maybe we'll have another chance," Margaret said. "We're staying through the winter. My husband's a painter, and we'll be driving all over after pictures."

"Well, now," the woman said.

She stepped back as Ross shifted gears, and she and her daughter stood together looking after the car. Margaret waved, and they both lifted their hands. Then a lane of ancient maples, lopsided and burly and with leaves that stained the sun into puddles of red and gold, cut them off.

"I gather we're going on to the head of navigation," Ross said.

"Just to see," she said. "Doesn't it give you a funny feeling to think that twenty or thirty years ago this was a carriage road with farms all along it, and now it's just a dead-end ghost road in the wilderness?"

"Ghosts are only interesting up to a point," Ross said. "I'd rather paint people than ghosts."

"Even funny little people like those women?"

He gave her a straight, surprised look. "What was funny about them?"

"I don't know," she said, feeling obscurely rebuked. "Maybe they weren't."

In the dooryard of another abandoned farm, just above the boarded-up shell of a one-room school, a tall elm had split and blocked the road. Below the house they looked down a gentle slope through gnarled apple trees to a multiple fold of the hills.

Against the crawling edge of woods and the eyeless emptiness of the farmhouse, against the whole irrational patternlessness of decay, the orchard kept its design. Though the tops were unpruned and overgrown, the trunks marched where a farmer's hands had set them to march, and among the thinning leaves hung an unbelievably heavy crop of runty apples, reddening for no harvest.

Ross sat still a moment, looking, and then with a grunt reached into the back seat for the easel and water colors.

While he painted she took a walk up past the split elm, up the road which had once been the street of a little village of a half-dozen houses. There was a church, as blind-windowed as the schoolhouse down the road, one corner of its steeple collapsed so that the squat spire tilted drunkenly forward. There were four houses scattered up the road for a quarter of a mile, all of them gutted, their shingles overgrown with moss, their sheds sagging open. In an old sugarhouse she found, stacked carefully on a landing above the rusty pan and arch, several dozen old-fashioned wooden sap buckets, handmade, hooped with twisted pliable wood rather than with iron. They seemed

as ancient as artifacts out of a buried city; she took a
pair of them along for flowerpots.

At the head of the village she came through a broken
rail fence into the burying ground. A half-dozen graves
had pretentious monuments above them; most had only
rounded headboards of stone or wood. There were dates
as early as 1778, but the latest date she found was on the
grave of a child who had died in 1914.

In the open sunlight she sat on a gravestone and
thought how it might have been to be the last family left
on such a road, and to bury your child among the dead
who had been gathering for a hundred and fifty years, and
then to move away and leave the road empty behind you.
She imagined how it might have seemed to some old
grandmother who had lived in the village for eighty
years, watching the hill farms go dead like lights going
out, watching the decay spread inward from the remote
farms to the near ones, to the place next door.

There would have been attempts to bring farms back;
the banks would have found renters. But after a while
the renters would be gone too. There would be auctions
and then empty barns, empty houses. There would be
a day when you would come to your door and see nothing
alive, hear no human sound, in your whole village.

She stood up uneasily. A hawk was methodically
coursing the meadow beyond the graveyard. It was very
still. She felt oppressed by the wide silent sky and afraid
of the somehow threatening edge where meadow met
woods, where not a leaf stirred but where something
watched. The thought of Ross painting down in the
orchard, abstracted, his pipe in his teeth, was like the
thought of home on a cold night. She went back down
the blighted road carrying her archaic sap buckets. On
every house and building she passed, failure and death
were posted like contagion warnings.

The moment she got where she could see him at his easel down in the orchard everything was safe again. She turned off and came through the old trees, running her fingers over the welted scars of prunings, picking a runty apple and rubbing it on the sleeve of her flannel shirt. It took a lovely waxy shine, for all its warped shape, and she experimentally bit into it, half expecting the woody bitter pucker of a wild apple.

Instead, the flesh of the apple cracked firmly, and juice spurted out onto her chin — sweet, golden, with a strange wild tang.

"Ross," she called. "For heaven's sake, you know what?"

She gathered some of the apples and took them over to him, talking as she came, eating her apple and waving it. The whole performance was a gabble.

Ross laughed at her. "Somewhere I've read about this," he said. "An excited woman with an apple."

"But just taste one!" she said. "They're *wonderful!*"

"That's what the other woman said."

"Oh, get excited for once," she said, and threw an apple at him. He made a gagging face and bit into it.

"Isn't that delicious?" she said.

His munching paused, and he leered. "Suddenly," he said, "I perceive that you are naked. Go find a fig tree."

"Oh, hush! You know what I *am* going to do? I'm going to fill the whole back end of the car with these, and we're going to take them down and have Robidoux make them into cider."

Ross threw the gnawed core away and wiped his fingers on his jeans. "Okay. Make that your project for the afternoon."

"You're about as sensitive as an oak burl," she said. "Who ever told you you should be an artist?"

"It was my father's dying wish," he said.

She took her two sap buckets and went to picking,

staggering the full buckets up to dump them into the turtleback and then going into the orchard for more. The sun was mellow through the gnarled trees, the air was winy with apples. She entirely forgot her ominous sense of being watched, and in the orchard's ripe warmth she did not remember that she was still on the road of failure and decay — not until she looked up from pouring a bucketful of apples into the car and saw with a jarring shock the thin girl from down the road. In the moment of irritation that followed the shock it seemed to her that the girl had a face like a jackal — something that sniffed around dead campfires and rocked-over graves.

"Look's if you was takin' home some apples," the girl said.

"I hope nobody minds. We took it for granted nobody picked them any more."

"Nobody minds," the girl said. "They just fall off and rot, mostly."

Margaret picked up her buckets and started back. The girl came along. They started picking from a tree behind Ross, and the girl looked curiously at the picture growing on the easel. With her starved collarbones and peaked face, she herself was part of the general decay, and Margaret asked a question that might have been unfortunate.

"How do you like living up here? Isn't it sort of haunted, living near a dead village?"

The girl's eyes flashed up, quick and shy. " 'Tisn't haunted. I used to come up here considerable with my young man when I was goin' out."

"Really? You mean you had dates up here, in this place?"

"Went out for near a year," the girl said, and her look touched Margaret again, an odd look of importance or pride — the look a little girl might wear when showing off her dolls. "He was real interested. Mumma says she never saw a young man more interested."

Down at the easel Ross turned half around to listen. For some reason Margaret felt that she should move slowly and speak quietly, as she would around a nervous horse. "Don't you go out with him any more?"

The girl's thin lips closed down; her eyes were on Margaret's face as if watching the effect of her words.

"I had a disappointment," she said flatly.

"Oh, I'm sorry," Margaret said.

The girl went on busily gathering apples. "Went and got married."

"He did? To someone else?"

"That's what."

"Where has he gone to now?"

"Hasn't gone nowhere. Lives right down below us there."

"And he's still your only neighbor?" Margaret said. "That must be terribly hard."

The girl's glance was direct, a little puzzled. "We still neighbor," she said. "Won't for long, though. He's aimin' to get another place."

"And then you'll be the only family on the road."

"E-yeah," the girl said.

Margaret went on picking, watching the girl sidelong. Like a little brown bird hopping in a garden after all the other birds have gone south, she went around under the gnarled trees — reaching, stretching, tiptoeing for apples free from worms — and for a moment she seemed the saddest thing on the whole sad road.

The leaf-stained sunlight tranced Margaret's eyes, and she saw the orchard and the old buildings on a summer night, a chilly Vermont summer night after chores — the dim flare of northern lights in the sky and the blackboard darkness at the edge of the woods scratched with chalk lines of light by the fireflies.

She saw this girl and her young man under the old orchard trees, the only young things in a place of age and death. Especially, and with pitiless clarity, she saw this girl, too frail for love, too childish or too prematurely old, too skimped and bony-chested, lying in his arms with her peaked face upturned for kisses and her scrawny little body quiet under the farm boy's big hard hands.

The single chance that her lifetime would offer her, the one moment when pollen might blow from stamen to pistil, when the accident of fertility might cheat a sterile heritage. And something had gone wrong. She wondered what. Any trivial thing might have done it. Probably the girl herself didn't know. Perhaps it was only that she herself wasn't adequate, that skin and bones and an eagerness for love were not enough.

Ross's picture was finished, and as he stepped back Margaret saw that he had moved the house down into the orchard for dramatic contrast, to get the sagging corner, the broken window, the gaunt decay of the entrance, into the same composition with the fruited orchard retreating in perfect order to the edge of the folded hills. The girl came close to look.

"It's real like," she said. "A body'd know it in a minute."

With difficulty Margaret shook herself out of the mood.

"I wonder how long," she said, "how many years an orchard like this will go on living and bearing?"

"Years and years," the girl said. "It's wonderful how apple trees hang on sometimes."

Wiping a brush, Ross turned his easy warm smile on her. "How is it in the spring? Pretty?"

It was surprising how responsive her wry little face was.

"Oh, land, just like a posy bed! It don't have very big apples any more, but it's a sight in the spring."

She stood with folded arms, as her mother had stood by the side of the car in the farmyard. Margaret, for all her watching, could find no trace of bitterness or frustration or anger in the girl. Starved as it was, the gnomish face was serene.

"Springtime, we used to come up here most every night, when I was goin' out," she said.

THE END